SHAKESPEARE'S SONNETS AND A LOVER'S COMPLAINT

BY

WILLIAM SHAKESPEARE

KALPAZ

ISBN: 978-93-5128-438-3(PB)

First Published in 1609
Indian Reprint in 2017

Published by

Kalpaz Publications
C-30, Satyawati Nagar,
Delhi – 110052
E-mail: kalpaz@hotmail.com
Website: kalpazpublications.com
Ph.: +91-9212142040

SHAKESPEARE'S SONNETS AND A LOVER'S COMPLAINT

The Globe Theater

CONTENTS

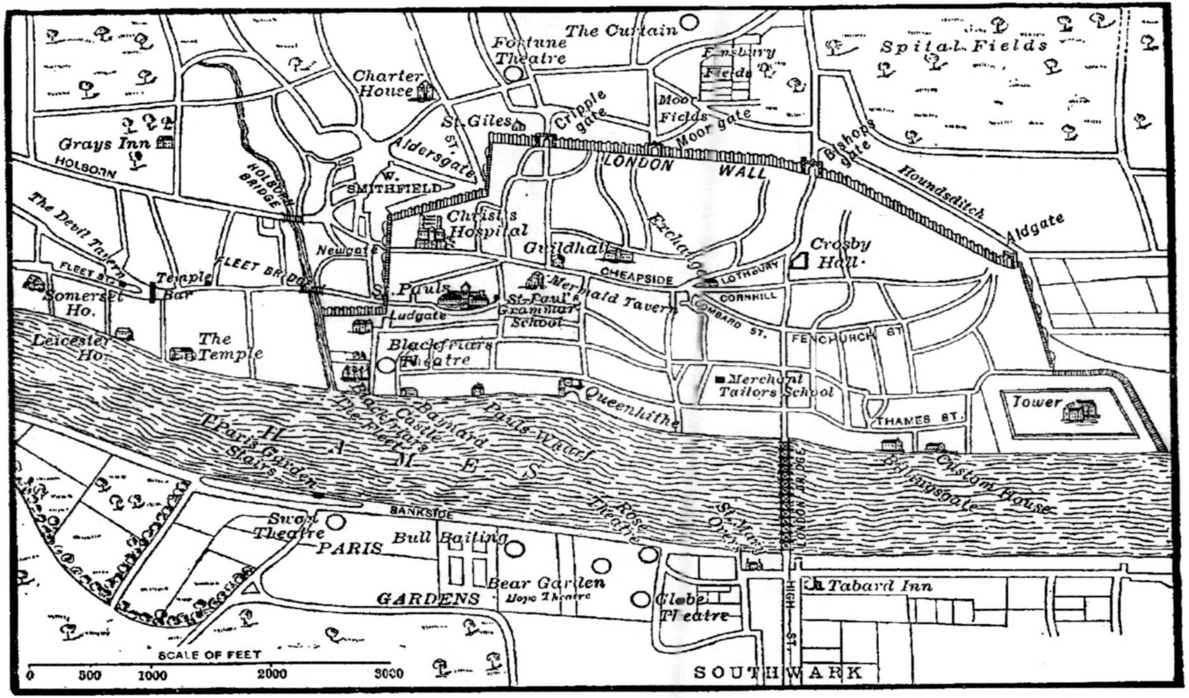

Map of Elizabethan London

INTRODUCTION

I

SHAKESPEARE'S LIFE AND WORKS

William Shakespeare was baptized at Stratford-on-Avon on April 26, 1564, so that the date of his birth is probably April 22 or 23. He was the son of John Shakespeare, who had left his father's farm at Snitterfield about thirteen years before, and had come to Stratford, where he engaged in business (especially in the sale of agricultural produce), and became one of the prominent citizens of the town, holding office in the borough more than once. He married, in 1557, Mary Arden, the daughter of a wealthy farmer of excellent family, whose home was at Wilmcote, near Stratford. The dramatist, accordingly, came of good English stock.

Shakespeare grew up in the little town of Stratford, in one of the most beautiful districts of England. He received his education in the Stratford grammar school, where he got the "small Latin and less Greek" with which Ben Jonson credited him. But his training, at least in Latin, was doubtless pretty thorough, and Jonson's statement must be interpreted in the light of his own very unusual scholarship. Shakespeare, nevertheless, was not primarily a scholar; his immense knowledge of men and things was gained in other ways.

In 1582, when he was a mere boy of less than nineteen years, Shakespeare married Anne Hathaway, a woman of twenty-seven, the daughter of a neighboring farmer in the little village of Shottery. The marriage does not seem to have been a very happy one; and three years later, in 1585, Shakespeare left Stratford, without his family (three children had been born to him), and went up to London. The tradition that he abandoned Stratford on account of difficulties into which he had fallen through poaching on the estate of Sir Thomas Lucy may have at least an element of truth in it, but there is no certainty regarding the details.

The London to which Shakespeare went in 1585 or 1586 must not be thought of as the vast metropolis we know to-day. It was a city of between one and two hundred thousand inhabitants only. But it was the center of the stirring life of a period more keenly alive, perhaps, than any other in English history, and it afforded a stimulating environment for the development of a genius like Shakespeare's. It was a time when horizons had been almost immeasurably widened. The discovery of the New World, with the possibilities which it was still thought to hold of realizing the dreams of centuries, had quickened men's imaginations to a degree which it is difficult for us to grasp. The Reformation had brought with it a new freedom of thought; the Revival of Learning had opened up another new world, and from Italy especially—"that great limbec of working brains," as one of Shakespeare's contemporaries called it—young Englishmen were eagerly bringing back new literary forms. The war with Spain, that culminated in the defeat of the Armada, was awakening a new national consciousness. In a word, when Shakespeare came up to London, he found a community intensely alive at every point,—a community surpassingly adapted to call out just such powers as he possessed, and no less ready to respond to what it thus called out.

Particularly was this true in connection with the drama. Plays founded (for the most part) on the Bible had been popular all over England for centuries. Then, as the Latin comedies and tragedies—especially those of Plautus and Seneca—were more and more studied in the schools, and as the influence of the Renaissance in Italy and France had spread to England, the field had widened. And just at the time when Shakespeare arrived in London a group of young university men were giving the drama a fresh impetus and enlarging still further its scope. Plays of all sorts were being written, in response to the varying popular demand; delicate court comedies, like John Lyly's; plays that experimented in many fields, like those of Peele and Greene; crude but powerful tragedies, like Kyd's; dramas like Marlowe's, that expressed, in the new medium of blank verse, the boundless aspirations of the time; plays that dealt with history, mythology, fairy-lore, adventure, crime—everything was grist that came to the playwrights' mill, and the demand for more plays was steadily growing.

And with the demand for more plays went hand in

hand the demand for more theaters. When Shakespeare came to London there were only two. Before *Hamlet* was written six new ones had been established. With one exception they were without the city walls, since theaters were forbidden within the civic jurisdiction, and the most popular of them, including the Globe, were just across the river, on what was known as the Bankside. Here, then, either across London Bridge or in little boats, came of an afternoon (for the plays were always given by daylight) the throngs of Londoners—tradesmen, gallants, staid citizens, soldiers, sailors—who formed the audience at the Rose, the Swan, the Globe, and (later) the Hope. Their destination, however, was very different from the theaters we know. The buildings were round or hexagonal, and for the most part open to the sky, except for a sort of hood that in some cases projected over the stage. The larger part of the audience stood in the pit (see note on III, ii, 12), where the admission price was low; there were, however, galleries as well, and seats were also provided on the stage. And the stage itself was utterly unlike ours. It projected straight out into the body of the theater—in one case, we know (for the plans have been preserved), practically half the distance to the outer wall—so that it was surrounded by spectators on three of its four sides, and actually had spectators seated on it too. An Elizabethan play, in other words, stood in the most intimate relation to its audience; the stage was a little island in a sea of upturned faces, and the sea encroached upon the island even then. There were no long waits for shifts of scenery; the plays proceeded with few pauses, and with a continuity of action unknown to the modern stage. What Shakespeare found, then, was a community that eagerly demanded plays, a keen and active competition to supply that demand, and stage conditions which permitted the swiftest and most intimate response between actors and audience.

What Shakespeare *did* was first of all to become an actor, and an actor he seems to have remained until towards the close of his career. But he must very soon have begun to serve his apprenticeship as a playwright too—collaborating (as the custom was) with more experienced dramatists in the writing of new plays, in revamping older plays, in combining two plays into one—doing, in a word, the sort of hack-work that regularly belonged to the initial stages of his craft. Within half a dozen years, however, his own plays began to appear, and for the next two decades—from about 1591 to about 1611—one followed another, with steadily growing power. Nor was he only actor and playwright. In 1599 he became a shareholder in the Globe Theater, and he later acquired an interest in the Blackfriars—a private theater within the city walls.[1] As actor, as playwright, and as manager, then, Shakespeare knew his profession to the minutest details. Thorough and practical knowledge of his craft joined with his genius to make him what he was.

[1] The Blackfriars, unlike the public theaters, was roofed over, artificially lighted, and it charged higher admission. Although it was within the city walls, it was on ground not within the civic jurisdiction.

The general order and character of his plays is indicated in Professor Pierce's bibliography that follows this Introduction. One thing may be emphasized here. Shakespeare's plays show a development which is the result not only of growing powers, but also of conscious effort to improve upon what he had already done. Again and again it happens that a situation, a type of character, a dramatic device of some sort, a method of handling a plot, which has left, in its execution in an earlier play, something to be desired, is taken up again in a later play, and done surpassingly and once for all. Nothing is farther removed from fact than the rather stupid catchword, "Shakespeare never repeats." He was constantly repeating, because, for one reason, he was constantly trying to do better something that he had done not so well before. The common idea that genius is independent of a hard-earned mastery of technique and of an artistic conscience which demands that one proceed "from well to better, daily self-surpast"—this fallacy never had a better refutation than Shakespeare's development affords.

Something of this care which Shakespeare (contrary to the widespread popular idea) exercised in his work may be seen by comparing the Second Quarto of *Hamlet* with the First. To do this with any degree of thoroughness lies beyond the purpose of a school study of the play. But one brief passage will serve at least to illustrate Shakespeare's methods in revision. The reading of the First Quarto for I, i, 150-52 is as follows:

> The Cock that is the trumpet to the *morne,*
> Doth with his earley and shrill *crowing* throate
> Awake the god of day, and at his *sound,* etc.

These lines have become, in the Second Quarto, the following:

> The cock that is the trumpet to the *morne,*
> Doth with his lofty and shrill *sounding* throat
> Awake the God of day, and at his *warning,* etc.

It is clear at a glance that the change from "shrill *crowing*" to "shrill *sounding*" has made it necessary to substitute another word for *sound* in the next line. But the word actually substituted (*warning*) introduces at once a rime with *morning* two lines before. The further change from *morning* to *morne* of course grows out of the necessity of avoiding such a rime. The interest of comparisons like these is endless. For us, however, in our study, its chief value lies in the light it throws on one reason for Shakespeare's success—his capacity, that is, for taking pains, which is one ingredient even of genius such as his.

His career, moreover, was successful, even when judged by other than literary standards. For his creative power was not inconsistent with a keen and practical business sense. His income as an actor, as a shareholder in two remunerative theaters, and as the most popular playwright of his day was a large and growing one. In 1597, only eleven years after he came up to London, he bought the largest house in Stratford, known as New Place, and during the following years improved it, making at intervals other investments in and about the town. In 1611, at the height of his fame, he returned to Stratford, twenty-six years after he had left it, and lived there, on his own estate, until his death at the age of fifty-two, April 23, 1616.

After his death his friend and greatest rival, Ben Jonson, wrote of him: "I loved the man and do honor his memory, on this side idolatry, as well as any. He was, indeed, honest and of an open and free nature." It is useless to try to piece out the facts of his biography from his plays; but the more thoroughly one studies them, the profounder is one's conviction of the soundness and wholesomeness of character, and of the deepening moral insight, of the man who wrote them.

II

HAMLET

THE first question about a Shakespearean play has to do with its text—with the form and manner, that is, in which the play has come down to us. Shakespeare's plays were published in two different forms. Sixteen of them appeared in small volumes called quartos, each containing a single play. And all of them, except *Pericles,* were published (the remaining twenty for the first time) in 1623, in a large volume known as the First Folio. For a number of the sixteen plays referred to there are two or more quartos (in two cases as many as six); and three folios (dated 1632, 1663, and 1685) followed the first. The play of *Hamlet* exists in three forms: one, known as the First Quarto, published in 1603; another, known as the Second Quarto, published in 1604; the third is the text that is found in the First Folio of 1623.

These three forms of the play differ from one another in many ways. The First Quarto is little more than half as long as the Second, and the text is evidently imperfect, and in many passages incorrect. In the Second Quarto the arrangement of the scenes is different, and in addition to the fact that the play is "enlarged to almost as much againe as it was" (as the title-page states), the characterization and the treatment in general are vastly improved. The text of the First Folio is essentially that of the Second Quarto, but a number of passages that occur in the Second Quarto are omitted in the Folio, and the Folio contains a few passages that do not appear in the Quartos. The text of the play as it is found in modern editions is made up by combining the texts of the Second Quarto and First Folio, with some aid, here and there, from the First Quarto.

The relations of the two Quartos to each other, and of the Folio to both, have been much disputed. But it seems fairly clear that the First Quarto represents a pirated edition of the first form of Shakespeare's play, probably taken down hastily and surreptitiously in shorthand by some agent of the publishers, and possibly pieced out to a slight degree from actors' copies; that the Second Quarto represents an authorized (but not very well printed) edition of the play as Shakespeare had meantime thoroughly revised it; and that the differences between the First Folio and the Second Quarto are in the main to be accounted for by supposing that the omissions—now in the one, now in the other—represent cuts for acting purposes, due to the great length of the play. Even to-day the ordinary stage performance of *Hamlet* never includes the full text.

But after we know how the play has reached us, we have still to ask how the story that it tells reached Shakespeare. For the great dramatists, whose supreme originality lies in giving new form and meaning to what is already known, rarely, if ever, invent their own plots, and *Hamlet* offers no exception. The story of the play is very old. It appears first about the beginning of the thirteenth century, in the *History of the Danes* by Saxo Grammaticus.[1] The story, as it is there told, is very different from the one we know, four hundred years later, in Shakespeare. It is a rude and brutal tale, with elements in it that go back to a still more primitive stage of civilization. But certain essential facts of the play are present in the history. The fratricide on which the drama is based; the marriage between the murderer and Hamlet's mother; Hamlet's feigned madness in order to accomplish his revenge; the device (in a very different form, however, from that of the play) of using his love for a woman in order to lead him to betray himself; the killing of an eavesdropper (who has hidden under the rushes

[1] Translated (in part) from the Latin in *The First Nine Books of the Danish History of Saxo Grammaticus,* by Oliver Elton (Folk Lore Society, 1893), pp. 106-130.

on the floor); the dispatch of Hamlet to England with two companions; the altering of the letter, and Hamlet's return (not, however, through the aid of the pirates),—all these details are present in the older story. But there is no ghost, and Hamlet's savage revenge is wholly different, while he himself lives to become king, and is later killed through the treachery of his second wife. Saxo's story was retold in French in 1570, in Belleforest's *Histoires Tragiques,*[1] which was not translated into English until five years after the First Quarto was published. Shakespeare may possibly have known Belleforest; he almost certainly did not know Saxo. The story seems to have reached him in another way.

At least fifteen of Shakespeare's thirty-seven plays—including the *Merchant of Venice, King John, Henry V, Romeo and Juliet, Julius Cæsar,* and *King Lear*—are more or less directly based upon earlier plays, and no clearer insight into Shakespeare's genius and originality can be gained than that which comes from a study of what he has done with the crude materials at his hand. In the case of *Hamlet* we know, from a number of interesting contemporary allusions, that there was an earlier play, although, unfortunately, it has not come down to us. But its author was very probably Thomas Kyd, and from an extremely popular play of Kyd's that is extant—*The Spanish Tragedy*—we can guess something of the character of the older *Hamlet.* For both plays—the *Spanish Tragedy* and the earlier *Hamlet,* which Shake-

[1] Translation in Hazlitt's *Shakespeare's Library,* Part I, Vol. II, pp. 211-279.

speare almost certainly used—very evidently appealed strongly to one of the marked tastes of an Elizabethan audience—its fondness for what is often called the Tragedy of Blood. And if we consider the mere framework of Shakespeare's *Hamlet,* in connection with what we know of the *Spanish Tragedy,* it is not difficult to form some idea of the older play. A ghost, insanity, real or assumed, revenge, adultery, suicide, poisoning, stabbing—all the elements of sheer melodrama are present. And the amazing thing that Shakespeare has done is to take this old story of blood and lust and revenge, and make it the vehicle of his own profoundest thought and his supremest artistry, so that it stands as one of the two or three greatest tragedies in the world. The mere inventing of a plot is little; it is what the dramatist does with what he finds that counts.

What he has to do first and foremost is to make a *play.* The Ghost, Hamlet's assumed madness, the killing of Polonius, Ophelia's suicide, the exchange of the letters—all these are but the raw materials of a drama. They must be bound together into a single *action,* and that action must have a definite *movement.* And such a movement, in a tragedy, involves a conflict between two opposing forces. In *Hamlet* this conflict takes the form (we shall see another side of it in a moment) of a contest between Hamlet and the King. The play starts out with relative equilibrium; the contest has not yet begun. The real movement is initiated when the disclosure of the Ghost (the Exciting Force) stirs Hamlet to revenge. From that point up to the success of the play within the play the action rises; Hamlet is the aggressor, and the King is on the defensive. But with Hamlet's refusal to kill the King while he is praying, comes the turning-point, and the so-called Falling (or Return) Action begins; the King is the aggressor, and Hamlet is steadily forced to the wall, until, with the success of the King's and Laertes's plot against him, the catastrophe ensues. One may even indicate by a diagram the typical movement of a tragedy:

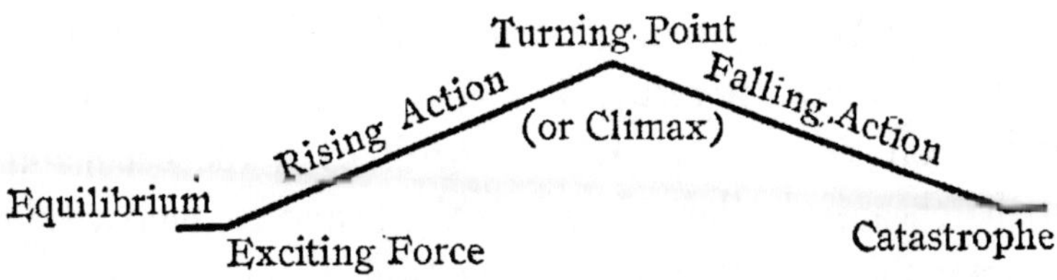

The details of the movement in *Hamlet* are elaborated in the introductory notes to the different scenes, and the interest of the story is not diminished but enhanced by observing the dramatic structure of the play.

But there is another conflict involved beside the contest between the two protagonists. One sometimes hears a tragedy spoken of as if it were merely a play with an unhappy ending. But the thing that really makes a tragedy is—to use a German poet's phrase—the human spirit in conflict with itself or with the course of the world. In *Romeo and Juliet,* the first of Shakespeare's great tragedies, the conflict is of the latter type. It is Fate, as embodied in the family and the state, against which Romeo and Juliet—like the heroes of Greek tragedy—contend in vain. But in the later Shakespearean tragedies, the emphasis is on the conflict of the hero with himself—or rather, perhaps, the conflict within him of opposing passions or tendencies—that leads to his undoing. The great heroes of tragedy—Hamlet, Macbeth, Othello, Lear, Œdipus, Faust—are exceptional persons, to be sure; but they are the battleground of contending forces that are universal in their application and in their appeal And the great tragedies hold their lasting power *because* the tragic struggle is thus universal, as well as because it finds embodiment in actions of compelling, sometimes of enthralling, interest. The mere story of *Hamlet*—of his contest with the King—thrills even the occupants of the cheapest gallery; but it is the tragic conflict within Hamlet himself that challenges and holds our deeper interest.

And the problem of Hamlet himself is one of the most baffling—and fascinating, too—in all literature. He is so real a person that men talk and write about him as they do about Cæsar or Napoleon or any of the great complex figures that have really lived. And no attempt to pluck out the heart of his mystery will ever be wholly successful, just because he is so absolutely real a *person*. But two or three of the most famous attempts to explain him may be given, as bringing out, at all events, certain phases of his complexity. That of Goethe is perhaps the best known of all:[1]

To me it is clear that Shakespeare meant, in the present case, to represent the effects of a great action laid upon a soul unfit

[1] *Wilhelm Meister's Lehrjahre,* Book IV, Chapter XIII (Carlyle's translation). This view is admirably criticised in one

Richard III.

King John.
Three historical dramas, each dealing with the struggles and downfall of an English king.

II. THE PERIOD OF GREAT HISTORIES AND COMEDIES

The Merchant of Venice.
The story of two young lovers who are brought together by the devotion of a faithful friend, and who in turn save this friend from the revenge of Shylock the Jew.

The Taming of the Shrew.
An ingenious farcical comedy, in which a shrewish wife is tamed into gentleness.

King Henry IV, Parts I and II.
Stately pictures of English civil wars, interspersed with the delightful comedy of Falstaff and his companions.

King Henry V.
A picture of the English conquests in France, centering around Henry V as a national hero.

Merry Wives of Windsor.
A laughable series of practical jokes played on Falstaff.

Much Ado About Nothing.

As You Like It.

Twelfth Night.
Three romantic comedies of the highest rank. *Much Ado* combines the delightful wit-combats of Beatrice and Benedict with the touching story of a lady unjustly accused but finally cleared. *As You Like It* is a picture of pastoral life far from the world's uproar in the forest of Arden. *Twelfth Night* traces the fortunes of a shipwrecked heroine who by unselfish devotion wins a noble lover.

All's Well That Ends Well.

Troilus and Cressida.

Measure for Measure.
Three bitter, sarcastic comedies, revealing the baser aspects of human nature.

III. THE PERIOD OF GREAT TRAGEDIES

Julius Cæsar.

A picture of the national upheaval connected with the death of Cæsar. Its central figure is the noble but misguided patriot Brutus.

Hamlet.

One of the most thoughtful and poetical of dramas, centering around the story of a son called to avenge a murdered father.

Othello.

The tragedy of a noble but passionate man who becomes the dupe of a villain, and through mistaken jealousy murders his innocent bride.

King Lear.

The tragedy of ingratitude. King Lear gives all his lands to his two eldest daughters, but their cruelty leads to his death and that of his one faithful child Cordelia.

Macbeth.

A terrible picture of the retribution which follows ambition and murder. Macbeth assassinates his predecessor to become king, but is overthrown and dies miserably in the hour of defeat.

Antony and Cleopatra.

The tragedy of a great soldier who sacrifices an empire for love of a fascinating but wicked woman.

Timon of Athens.

The tragedy of a noble Athenian who ruins himself by unwise generosity.

Coriolanus.

The tragedy of a noble Roman whose brave but unreasonably haughty spirit makes him the enemy and desolator of his country.

IV. ROMANTIC TALES OF SHAKESPEARE'S LATER YEARS

Pericles.

The adventures of a family who are long separated and finally united.

Cymbeline.

A Winter's Tale.

Two stories of mistaken jealousy, with frequent threats of disaster but with a happy ending. *Cymbeline* is a story of ancient Britain; the scene of the *Winter's Tale* is laid in Sicily and Bohemia.

The Tempest.

The story of an exiled duke on an enchanted island. Here he brings his enemies within his power and is restored to his dukedom.

King Henry VIII.

A series of picturesque events in the life of King Henry and Cardinal Wolsey.

Shakespeare's non-dramatic works include:

Venus and Adonis (1593).

The Rape of Lucrece (1594).

Sonnets (1609).

The Passionate Pilgrim (1599).

A collection of short poems, containing a few by Shakespeare.

Interior of Fortune Theater

The Tragedy of Hamlet,
Prince of Denmark

DRAMATIS PERSONÆ

CLAUDIUS, *king of Denmark.*
HAMLET, *son to the late, and nephew to the present king.*
POLONIUS, *lord chamberlain.*
HORATIO, *friend to Hamlet.*
LAERTES, *son to Polonius.*
VOLTIMAND, CORNELIUS, ROSENCRANTZ, GUILDENSTERN, OSRIC, A Gentleman, } *courtiers.*
A Priest.
MARCELLUS, BERNARDO, } *officers.*
FRANCISCO, *a soldier.*
REYNALDO, *a servant to Polonius.*
Players.
Two clowns, grave-diggers.
FORTINBRAS, *prince of Norway.*
A Captain.
English Ambassadors.

GERTRUDE, *queen of Denmark, and mother to Hamlet.*
OPHELIA, *daughter to Polonius.*

Lords, Ladies, Officers, Soldiers, Sailors, Messengers, and other Attendants.

Ghost of Hamlet's Father.

SCENE: *Denmark.*

The Tragedy of Hamlet, Prince of Denmark

ACT FIRST

Scene I

Elsinore. A platform before the castle.

Francisco *at his post. Enter to him* Bernardo.

Ber. Who's there?
Fran. Nay, answer me: stand, and unfold yourself.
Ber. Long live the king!
Fran. Bernardo?
Ber. He.
Fran. You come most carefully upon your hour.
Ber. 'Tis now struck twelve; get thee to bed, Francisco.
Fran. For this relief much thanks: 'tis bitter cold,
And I am sick at heart.
Ber. Have you had quiet guard?
Fran. Not a mouse stirring.
Ber. Well, good night.
If you do meet Horatio and Marcellus,
The rivals of my watch, bid them make haste.
Fran. I think I hear them. Stand, ho! Who's there?

Enter HORATIO *and* MARCELLUS.

Hor. Friends to this ground.
Mar. And liegemen to the Dane.
Fran. Give you good night.
Mar. O, farewell, honest soldier:
Who hath relieved you?
Fran. Bernardo hath my place.
Give you good night. [*Exit.*
Mar. Holla! Bernardo!
Ber. Say,
What, is Horatio there?
Hor. A piece of him.
Ber. Welcome, Horatio; welcome, good Marcellus.
Mar. What, has this thing appear'd again to-night?
Ber. I have seen nothing.
Mar. Horatio says 'tis but our fantasy,
And will not let belief take hold of him
Touching this dreaded sight, twice seen of us:
Therefore I have entreated him along
With us to watch the minutes of this night,
That if again this apparition come,
He may approve our eyes and speak to it.
Hor. Tush, tush, 'twill not appear.
Ber. Sit down a while;
And let us once again assail your ears,
That are so fortified against our story,
What we have two nights seen.
Hor. Well, sit we down,
And let us hear Bernardo speak of this.

Ber. Last night of all,
When yond same star that's westward from the pole
Had made his course to illume that part of heaven
Where now it burns, Marcellus and myself,
The bell then beating one,—

Enter GHOST.

Mar. Peace, break thee off; look, where it comes again!
Ber. In the same figure, like the king that's dead.
Mar. Thou art a scholar; speak to it, Horatio.
Ber. Looks it not like the king? mark it, Horatio.
Hor. Most like: it harrows me with fear and wonder.
Ber. It would be spoke to.
Mar. Question it, Horatio.
Hor. What art thou, that usurp'st this time of night,
Together with that fair and warlike form
In which the majesty of buried Denmark
Did sometimes march? by heaven I charge thee, speak!
Mar. It is offended.
Ber. See, it stalks away!
Hor. Stay! speak, speak! I charge thee, speak!
[*Exit Ghost.*
Mar. 'Tis gone, and will not answer.
Ber. How now, Horatio! you tremble and look pale:
Is not this something more than fantasy?
What think you on't?
Hor. Before my God, I might not this believe
Without the sensible and true avouch
Of mine own eyes.

Mar. Is it not like the king?
Hor. As thou art to thyself:
Such was the very armor he had on
When he the ambitious Norway combated;
So frown'd he once, when, in an angry parle,
He smote the sledded Polacks on the ice.
'Tis strange.
Mar. Thus twice before, and jump at this dead hour,
With martial stalk hath he gone by our watch.
Hor. In what particular thought to work I know not;
But, in the gross and scope of my opinion,
This bodes some strange eruption to our state.
Mar. Good now, sit down, and tell me, he that knows,
Why this same strict and most observant watch
So nightly toils the subject of the land,
And why such daily cast of brazen cannon,
And foreign mart for implements of war;
Why such impress of shipwrights, whose sore task
Does not divide the Sunday from the week;
What might be toward, that this sweaty haste
Doth make the night joint-laborer with the day:
Who is't that can inform me?
Hor. That can I;
At least the whisper goes so. Our last king,
Whose image even but now appear'd to us,
Was, as you know, by Fortinbras of Norway,
Thereto prick'd on by a most emulate pride,
Dared to the combat; in which our valiant Hamlet—
For so this side of our known world esteem'd him—

Did slay this Fortinbras; who by a seal'd compact,
Well ratified by law and heraldry,
Did forfeit, with his life, all those his lands
Which he stood seized of, to the conqueror:
Against the which, a moiety competent
Was gaged by our king; which had return'd
To the inheritance of Fortinbras,
Had he been vanquisher; as, by the same covenant,
And carriage of the article design'd,
His fell to Hamlet. Now, sir, young Fortinbras,
Of unimproved mettle hot and full,
Hath in the skirts of Norway here and there
Shark'd up a list of lawless resolutes,
For food and diet, to some enterprise
That hath a stomach in't: which is no other—
As it doth well appear unto our state—
But to recover of us, by strong hand
And terms compulsatory, those foresaid lands
So by his father lost: and this, I take it,
Is the main motive of our preparations,
The source of this our watch and the chief head
Of this post-haste and romage in the land.

Ber. I think it be no other but e'en so:
Well may it sort that this portentous figure
Comes armed through our watch, so like the king
That was and is the question of these wars.

Hor. A mote it is to trouble the mind's eye.
In the most high and palmy state of Rome,
A little ere the mightiest Julius fell,

The graves stood tenantless, and the sheeted dead
Did squeak and gibber in the Roman streets:
. . . .
As stars with trains of fire and dews of blood,
Disasters in the sun; and the moist star,
Upon whose influence Neptune's empire stands,
Was sick almost to doomsday with eclipse:
And even the like precurse of fierce events,
As harbingers preceding still the fates
And prologue to the omen coming on,
Have heaven and earth together demonstrated
Unto our climatures and countrymen.

Re-enter Ghost.

But soft, behold! lo, where it comes again!
I'll cross it, though it blast me. Stay, illusion!
If thou hast any sound, or use of voice,
Speak to me:
If there be any good thing to be done,
That may to thee do ease and grace to me,
Speak to me:
If thou art privy to thy country's fate,
Which, happily, foreknowing may avoid,
O, speak!
Or if thou hast uphoarded in thy life
Extorted treasure in the womb of earth,
For which, they say, you spirits oft walk in death,
Speak of it: stay, and speak! [*The cock crows.*]
Stop it, Marcellus.

Mar. Shall I strike at it with my partisan?

Hor. Do, if it will not stand.
Ber. 'Tis here!
Hor. 'Tis here!
Mar. 'Tis gone! [*Exit Ghost.*
We do it wrong, being so majestical,
To offer it the show of violence;
For it is, as the air, invulnerable,
And our vain blows malicious mockery.
Ber. It was about to speak, when the cock crew.
Hor. And then it started like a guilty thing
Upon a fearful summons. I have heard,
The cock, that is the trumpet to the morn,
Doth with his lofty and shrill-sounding throat
Awake the god of day; and, at his warning,
Whether in sea or fire, in earth or air,
The extravagant and erring spirit hies
To his confine: and of the truth herein
This present object made probation.
Mar. It faded on the crowing of the cock.
Some say that ever 'gainst that season comes
Wherein our Saviour's birth is celebrated,
The bird of dawning singeth all night long:
And then, they say, no spirit dare stir abroad,
The nights are wholesome; then no planets strike,
No fairy takes, nor witch hath power to charm,
So hallow'd and so gracious is the time.
Hor. So have I heard and do in part believe it.
But look, the morn, in russet mantle clad,
Walks o'er the dew of yon high eastward hill:
Break we our watch up; and by my advice,

Let us impart what we have seen to-night
Unto young Hamlet; for, upon my life,
This spirit, dumb to us, will speak to him:
Do you consent we shall acquaint him with it,
As needful in our loves, fitting our duty?

Mar. Let's do't, I pray; and I this morning know
Where we shall find him most conveniently.
[*Exeunt.*

Scene II

A room of state in the castle.

Flourish. Enter the King, Queen, Hamlet, Polonius, Laertes, Voltimand, Cornelius, Lords, *and* Attendants.

King. Though yet of Hamlet our dear brother's death
The memory be green, and that it us befitted
To bear our hearts in grief and our whole kingdom
To be contracted in one brow of woe,
Yet so far hath discretion fought with nature
That we with wisest sorrow think on him,
Together with remembrance of ourselves.
Therefore our sometime sister, now our queen,
The imperial jointress to this warlike state,
Have we, as 'twere with a defeated joy,—
With an auspicious and a dropping eye,
With mirth in funeral and with dirge in marriage,
In equal scale weighing delight and dole,—
Taken to wife: nor have we herein barr'd

Your better wisdoms, which have freely gone
With this affair along. For all, our thanks.
Now follows, that you know, young Fortinbras,
Holding a weak supposal of our worth,
Or thinking by our late dear brother's death
Our state to be disjoint and out of frame,
Colleagued with the dream of his advantage,
He hath not fail'd to pester us with message,
Importing the surrender of those lands
Lost by his father, with all bonds of law,
To our most valiant brother. So much for him.
Now for ourself and for this time of meeting:
Thus much the business is: we have here writ
To Norway, uncle of young Fortinbras,—
Who, impotent and bed-rid, scarcely hears
Of this his nephew's purpose,—to suppress
His further gait herein; in that the levies,
The lists and full proportions, are all made
Out of his subject: and we here dispatch
You, good Cornelius, and you, Voltimand,
For bearers of this greeting to old Norway;
Giving to you no further personal power
To business with the king, more than the scope
Of these delated articles allow.
Farewell, and let your haste commend your duty.

Cor. / *Vol.* In that and all things will we show our duty.

King. We doubt it nothing: heartily farewell.
[*Exeunt Voltimand and Cornelius.*
And now, Laertes, what's the news with you?

You told us of some suit; what is't, Laertes?
You cannot speak of reason to the Dane,
And lose your voice: what wouldst thou beg, Laertes,
That shall not be my offer, not thy asking?
The head is not more native to the heart,
The hand more instrumental to the mouth,
Than is the throne of Denmark to thy father.
What wouldst thou have, Laertes?

Laer. My dread lord,
Your leave and favor to return to France;
From whence though willingly I came to Denmark,
To show my duty in your coronation,
Yet now, I must confess, that duty done,
My thoughts and wishes bend again toward France
And bow them to your gracious leave and pardon.

King. Have you your father's leave? What says Polonius?

Pol. He hath, my lord, wrung from me my slow leave
By laborsome petition, and at last
Upon his will I seal'd my hard consent:
I do beseech you, give him leave to go.

King. Take thy fair hour, Laertes; time be thine,
And thy best graces spend it at thy will!
But now, my cousin Hamlet, and my son,—

Ham. [*Aside*] A little more than kin, and less than kind.

King. How is it that the clouds still hang on you?

Ham. Not so, my lord; I am too much i' the sun.

Queen. Good Hamlet, cast thy nighted color off,
And let thine eye look like a friend on Denmark.
Do not for ever with thy vailed lids
Seek for thy noble father in the dust:

Thou know'st 'tis common; all that lives must die,
Passing through nature to eternity.

Ham. Ay, madam, it is common.

Queen. If it be,
Why seems it so particular with thee?

Ham. Seems, madam! nay, it is; I know not 'seems.'
'Tis not alone my inky cloak, good mother,
Nor customary suits of solemn black,
Nor windy suspiration of forced breath,
No, nor the fruitful river in the eye,
Nor the dejected havior of the visage,
Together with all forms, moods, shapes of grief,
That can denote me truly: these indeed seem,
For they are actions that a man might play:
But I have that within which passeth show;
These but the trappings and the suits of woe.

King. 'Tis sweet and commendable in your nature, Hamlet,
To give these mourning duties to your father:
But, you must know, your father lost a father;
That father lost, lost his, and the survivor bound
In filial obligation for some term
To do obsequious sorrow: but to persevere
In obstinate condolement is a course
Of impious stubbornness; 'tis unmanly grief;
It shows a will most incorrect to heaven,
A heart unfortified, a mind impatient,
An understanding simple and unschool'd:
For what we know must be and is as common
As any the most vulgar thing to sense,

Why should we in our peevish opposition
Take it to heart? Fie! 'tis a fault to heaven,
A fault against the dead, a fault to nature,
To reason most absurd, whose common theme
Is death of fathers, and who still hath cried,
From the first corse till he that died to-day,
'This must be so.' We pray you, throw to earth
This unprevailing woe, and think of us
As of a father: for let the world take note,
You are the most immediate to our throne,
And with no less nobility of love
Than that which dearest father bears his son,
Do I impart toward you. For your intent
In going back to school in Wittenberg,
It is most retrograde to our desire:
And we beseech you, bend you to remain
Here in the cheer and comfort of our eye,
Our chiefest courtier, cousin and our son.

Queen. Let not thy mother lose her prayers, Hamlet:
I pray thee, stay with us; go not to Wittenberg.

Ham. I shall in all my best obey you, madam.

King. Why, 'tis a loving and a fair reply:
Be as ourself in Denmark. Madam, come;
This gentle and unforced accord of Hamlet
Sits smiling to my heart: in grace whereof,
No jocund health that Denmark drinks to-day,
But the great cannon to the clouds shall tell,
And the king's rouse the heaven shall bruit again,
Re-speaking earthly thunder. Come away.

[*Flourish. Exeunt all but Hamlet.*

Ham. O, that this too too solid flesh would melt,
Thaw and resolve itself into a dew!
Or that the Everlasting had not fix'd
His canon 'gainst self-slaughter! O God! God!
How weary, stale, flat and unprofitable,
Seem to me all the uses of this world!
Fie on't! ah fie! 'tis an unweeded garden,
That grows to seed; things rank and gross in nature
Possess it merely. That it should come to this!
But two months dead! nay, not so much, not two:
So excellent a king; that was, to this,
Hyperion to a satyr; so loving to my mother
That he might not beteem the winds of heaven
Visit her face too roughly. Heaven and earth!
Must I remember? why, she would hang on him,
As if increase of appetite had grown
By what it fed on: and yet, within a month—
Let me not think on't—Frailty, thy name is woman!—
A little month, or ere those shoes were old
With which she follow'd my poor father's body,
Like Niobe, all tears:—why she, even she,—
O God! a beast, that wants discourse of reason,
Would have mourn'd longer,—married with my uncle,
My father's brother, but no more like my father
Than I to Hercules: within a month,
Ere yet the salt of most unrighteous tears
Had left the flushing in her galled eyes,
She married. O, most wicked speed, to post

With such dexterity to incestuous sheets!
It is not, nor it cannot come to good:
But break, my heart, for I must hold my tongue!

Enter Horatio, Marcellus, *and* Bernardo.

Hor. Hail to your lordship!
Ham. I am glad to see you well:
Horatio,—or I do forget myself.
Hor. The same, my lord, and your poor servant ever.
Ham. Sir, my good friend; I'll change that name with you:
And what make you from Wittenberg, Horatio?
Marcellus?
Mar. My good lord—
Ham. I am very glad to see you. [*To Ber.*] Good even, sir.
But what, in faith, make you from Wittenberg?
Hor. A truant disposition, good my lord.
Ham. I would not hear your enemy say so,
Nor shall you do my ear that violence,
To make it truster of your own report
Against yourself: I know you are no truant.
But what is your affair in Elsinore?
We'll teach you to drink deep ere you depart.
Hor. My lord, I came to see your father's funeral.
Ham. I pray thee, do not mock me, fellow-student;
I think it was to see my mother's wedding.
Hor. Indeed, my lord, it follow'd hard upon.
Ham. Thrift, thrift, Horatio! the funeral baked-meats
Did coldly furnish forth the marriage tables.

Would I had met my dearest foe in heaven
Or ever I had seen that day, Horatio!
My father!—methinks I see my father.
Hor. O where, my lord?
Ham. In my mind's eye, Horatio.
Hor. I saw him once; he was a goodly king.
Ham. He was a man, take him for all in all,
I shall not look upon his like again.
Hor. My lord, I think I saw him yesternight.
Ham. Saw? who?
Hor. My lord, the king your father.
Ham. The king my father!
Hor. Season your admiration for a while,
With an attent ear, till I may deliver,
Upon the witness of these gentlemen,
This marvel to you.
Ham. For God's love, let me hear.
Hor. Two nights together had these gentlemen,
Marcellus and Bernardo, on their watch,
In the dead vast and middle of the night,
Been thus encounter'd. A figure like your father,
Armed at point exactly, cap-a-pe,
Appears before them, and with solemn march
Goes slow and stately by them: thrice he walk'd
By their oppress'd and fear-surprised eyes,
Within his truncheon's length; whilst they, distill'd
Almost to jelly with the act of fear,
Stand dumb, and speak not to him. This to me
In dreadful secrecy impart they did;
And I with them the third night kept the watch:

Where, as they had deliver'd, both in time,
Form of the thing, each word made true and good,
The apparition comes: I knew your father;
These hands are not more like.

Ham. But where was this?

Mar. My lord, upon the platform where we watch'd.

Ham. Did you not speak to it?

Hor. My lord, I did,
But answer made it none: yet once methought
It lifted up it head and did address
Itself to motion, like as it would speak:
But even then the morning cock crew loud,
And at the sound it shrunk in haste away
And vanish'd from our sight.

Ham. 'Tis very strange.

Hor. As I do live, my honor'd lord, 'tis true,
And we did think it writ down in our duty
To let you know of it.

Ham. Indeed, indeed, sirs, but this troubles me.
Hold you the watch to-night?

Mar., *Ber.* We do, my lord.

Ham. Arm'd, say you?

Mar., *Ber.* Arm'd, my lord.

Ham. From top to toe?

Mar., *Ber.* My lord, from head to foot.

Ham. Then saw you not his face?

Hor. O, yes, my lord; he wore his beaver up.

Ham. What, look'd he frowningly?

Hor. A countenance more in sorrow than in anger.

Ham. Pale or red?

Hor. Nay, very pale.

Ham. And fix'd his eyes upon you?

Hor. Most constantly.

Ham. I would I had been there.

Hor. It would have much amazed you.

Ham. Very like, very like. Stay'd it long?

Hor. While one with moderate haste might tell a hundred.

Mar., *Ber.* Longer, longer.

Hor. Not when I saw't.

Ham. His beard was grizzled,—no?

Hor. It was, as I have seen it in his life,
A sable silver'd.

Ham. I will watch to-night;
Perchance 'twill walk again.

Hor. I warrant it will.

Ham. If it assume my noble father's person,
I'll speak to it, though hell itself should gape
And bid me hold my peace. I pray you all,
If you have hitherto conceal'd this sight,
Let it be tenable in your silence still;
And whatsoever else shall hap to-night,
Give it an understanding, but no tongue:
I will requite your loves. So fare you well:
Upon the platform, 'twixt eleven and twelve,
I'll visit you.

All. Our duty to your honor.

Ham. Your loves, as mine to you: farewell.
[*Exeunt all but Hamlet.*
My father's spirit in arms! all is not well;
I doubt some foul play: would the night were come!
Till then sit still, my soul: foul deeds will rise,
Though all the earth o'erwhelm them, to men's eyes.
[*Exit.*

Scene III

A room in Polonius's house.

Enter Laertes *and* Ophelia.

Laer. My necessaries are embark'd: farewell:
And, sister, as the winds give benefit
And convoy is assistant, do not sleep,
But let me hear from you.
Oph. Do you doubt that?
Laer. For Hamlet and the trifling of his favor,
Hold it a fashion and a toy in blood,
A violet in the youth of primy nature,
Forward, not permanent, sweet, not lasting,
The perfume and suppliance of a minute;
No more.
Oph. No more but so?
Laer. Think it no more:
For nature crescent does not grow alone
In thews and bulk, but, as this temple waxes,
The inward service of the mind and soul
Grows wide withal. Perhaps he loves you now,

And now no soil nor cautel doth besmirch
The virtue of his will: but you must fear,
His greatness weigh'd, his will is not his own;
For he himself is subject to his birth:
He may not, as unvalued persons do,
Carve for himself, for on his choice depends
The safety and health of this whole state;
And therefore must his choice be circumscribed
Unto the voice and yielding of that body
Whereof he is the head. Then if he says he loves you,
It fits your wisdom so far to believe it
As he in his particular act and place
May give his saying deed; which is no further
Than the main voice of Denmark goes withal.
Then weigh what loss your honor may sustain,
If with too credent ear you list his songs,
Or lose your heart, or your chaste treasure open
To his unmaster'd importunity.
Fear it, Ophelia, fear it, my dear sister,
And keep you in the rear of your affection,
Out of the shot and danger of desire.
The chariest maid is prodigal enough,
If she unmask her beauty to the moon:
Virtue itself 'scapes not calumnious strokes:
The canker galls the infants of the spring
Too oft before their buttons be disclosed,
And in the morn and liquid dew of youth
Contagious blastments are most imminent.
Be wary then; best safety lies in fear:
Youth to itself rebels, though none else near.

Oph. I shall the effect of this good lesson keep,
As watchman to my heart. But, good my brother,
Do not, as some ungracious pastors do,
Show me the steep and thorny way to heaven,
Whiles, like a puff'd and reckless libertine,
Himself the primrose path of dalliance treads,
And recks not his own rede.

Laer. O, fear me not.
I stay too long: but here my father comes.

Enter POLONIUS.

A double blessing is a double grace;
Occasion smiles upon a second leave.

Pol. Yet here, Laertes! Aboard, aboard, for shame!
The wind sits in the shoulder of your sail,
And you are stay'd for. There; my blessing with thee!
And these few precepts in thy memory
See thou character. Give thy thoughts no tongue,
Nor any unproportion'd thought his act.
Be thou familiar, but by no means vulgar.
Those friends thou hast, and their adoption tried,
Grapple them to thy soul with hoops of steel;
But do not dull thy palm with entertainment
Of each new-hatch'd, unfledged comrade. Beware
Of entrance to a quarrel; but being in,
Bear't that the opposed may beware of thee.
Give every man thy ear, but few thy voice;
Take each man's censure, but reserve thy judgment.

Costly thy habit as thy purse can buy,
But not express'd in fancy; rich, not gaudy;
For the apparel oft proclaims the man,
And they in France of the best rank and station
Are of a most select and generous chief in that.
Neither a borrower nor a lender be:
For loan oft loses both itself and friend,
And borrowing dulls the edge of husbandry.
This above all: to thine own self be true,
And it must follow, as the night the day,
Thou canst not then be false to any man.
Farewell: my blessing season this in thee!

Laer. Most humbly do I take my leave, my lord.

Pol. The time invites you; go, your servants tend.

Laer. Farewell, Ophelia, and remember well
What I have said to you.

Oph. 'Tis in my memory lock'd,
And you yourself shall keep the key of it.

Laer. Farewell. [*Exit.*

Pol. What is't, Ophelia, he hath said to you?

Oph. So please you, something touching the Lord Hamlet.

Pol. Marry, well bethought:
'Tis told me, he hath very oft of late
Given private time to you, and you yourself
Have of your audience been most free and bounteous:
If it be so—as so 'tis put on me,
And that in way of caution—I must tell you,
You do not understand yourself so clearly
As it behoves my daughter and your honor.
What is between you? give me up the truth.

Oph. He hath, my lord, of late made many tenders
Of his affection to me.
Pol. Affection! pooh! you speak like a green girl,
Unsifted in such perilous circumstance.
Do you believe his tenders, as you call them?
Oph. I do not know, my lord, what I should think.
Pol. Marry, I'll teach you: think yourself a baby,
That you have ta'en these tenders for true pay,
Which are not sterling. Tender yourself more dearly;
Or—not to crack the wind of the poor phrase,
Running it thus—you'll tender me a fool.
Oph. My lord, he hath importuned me with love
In honorable fashion.
Pol. Ay, fashion you may call it; go to, go to.
Oph. And hath given countenance to his speech, my lord,
With almost all the holy vows of heaven.
Pol. Ay, springes to catch woodcocks. I do know,
When the blood burns, how prodigal the soul
Lends the tongue vows: these blazes, daughter,
Giving more light than heat, extinct in both,
Even in their promise, as it is a-making,
You must not take for fire. From this time
Be somewhat scanter of your maiden presence;
Set your entreatments at a higher rate
Than a command to parley. For Lord Hamlet,
Believe so much in him, that he is young,
And with a larger tether may he walk
Than may be given you: in few, Ophelia,
Do not believe his vows; for they are brokers,
Not of that dye which their investments show,

But mere implorators of unholy suits,
Breathing like sanctified and pious bawds,
The better to beguile. This is for all:
I would not, in plain terms, from this time forth,
Have you so slander any moment leisure,
As to give words or talk with the Lord Hamlet.
Look to't, I charge you: come your ways.
Oph. I shall obey, my lord. [*Exeunt.*

SCENE IV

The platform.

Enter HAMLET, HORATIO, *and* MARCELLUS.

Ham. The air bites shrewdly; it is very cold.
Hor. It is a nipping and an eager air.
Ham. What hour now?
Hor. I think it lacks of twelve.
Mar. No, it is struck.
Hor. Indeed? I heard it not: then it draws near the season
Wherein the spirit held his wont to walk.
[*A flourish of trumpets, and ordnance shot off within.*
What doth this mean, my lord?
Ham. The king doth wake to-night and takes his rouse,
Keeps wassail, and the swaggering up-spring reels;
And, as he drains his draughts of Rhenish down,
The kettle-drum and trumpet thus bray out
The triumph of his pledge.
Hor. Is it a custom?

Ham. Ay, marry, is't:
But to my mind, though I am native here
And to the manner born, it is a custom
More honor'd in the breach than the observance.
This heavy-headed revel east and west
Makes us traduc'd and tax'd of other nations:
They clepe us drunkards, and with swinish phrase
Soil our addition; and indeed it takes
From our achievements, though perform'd at height,
The pith and marrow of our attribute.
So, oft it chances in particular men,
That for some vicious mole of nature in them,
As, in their birth,—wherein they are not guilty,
Since nature cannot choose his origin,—
By the o'ergrowth of some complexion,
Oft breaking down the pales and forts of reason,
Or by some habit that too much o'er-leavens
The form of plausive manners, that these men,
Carrying, I say, the stamp of one defect,
Being nature's livery, or fortune's star,—
Their virtues else—be they as pure as grace,
As infinite as man may undergo—
Shall in the general censure take corruption
From that particular fault: the dram of eale
Doth all the noble substance of a doubt
To his own scandal.

Enter Ghost.

Hor. Look, my lord, it comes!
Ham. Angels and ministers of grace defend us!

Be thou a spirit of health or goblin damn'd,
Bring with thee airs from heaven or blasts from hell,
Be thy intents wicked or charitable,
Thou comest in such a questionable shape
That I will speak to thee: I'll call thee Hamlet,
King, father, royal Dane: O, answer me!
Let me not burst in ignorance; but tell
Why thy canonized bones, hearsed in death,
Have burst their cerements; why the sepulcher,
Wherein we saw thee quietly inurn'd,
Hath oped his ponderous and marble jaws,
To cast thee up again. What may this mean,
That thou, dead corse, again in complete steel,
Revisit'st thus the glimpses of the moon,
Making night hideous; and we fools of nature
So horridly to shake our disposition
With thoughts beyond the reaches of our souls?
Say, why is this? wherefore? what should we do?
[*Ghost beckons Hamlet.*

Hor. It beckons you to go away with it,
As if it some impartment did desire
To you alone.

Mar. Look, with what courteous action
It waves you to a more removed ground:
But do not go with it.

Hor. No, by no means.

Ham. It will not speak; then I will follow it.

Hor. Do not, my lord.

Ham. Why, what should be the fear?

I do not set my life at a pin's fee;
And for my soul, what can it do to that,
Being a thing immortal as itself?
It waves me forth again: I'll follow it.

Hor. What if it tempt you toward the flood, my lord,
Or to the dreadful summit of the cliff
That beetles o'er his base into the sea,
And there assume some other horrible form,
Which might deprive your sovereignty of reason
And draw you into madness? think of it:
The very place puts toys of desperation,
Without more motive, into every brain
That looks so many fathoms to the sea
And hears it roar beneath.

Ham. It waves me still.
Go on; I'll follow thee.

Mar. You shall not go, my lord.

Ham. Hold off your hands.

Hor. Be ruled; you shall not go.

Ham. My fate cries out,
And makes each petty artery in this body
As hardy as the Nemean lion's nerve.
Still am I call'd. Unhand me, gentlemen.
By heaven, I'll make a ghost of him that lets me!
I say, away! Go on; I'll follow thee.

[*Exeunt Ghost and Hamlet.*

Hor. He waxes desperate with imagination.

Mar. Let's follow; 'tis not fit thus to obey him.

Hor. Have after. To what issue will this come?

Mar. Something is rotten in the state of Denmark.

Hor. Heaven will direct it.
Mar. Nay, let's follow him.
[*Exeunt.*

SCENE V

Another part of the platform.

Enter GHOST *and* HAMLET.

Ham. Whither wilt thou lead me? speak; I'll go no further.
Ghost. Mark me.
Ham. I will.
Ghost. My hour is almost come,
When I to sulphurous and tormenting flames
Must render up myself.
Ham. Alas, poor ghost!
Ghost. Pity me not, but lend thy serious hearing
To what I shall unfold.
Ham. Speak; I am bound to hear.
Ghost. So art thou to revenge, when thou shalt hear.
Ham. What?
Ghost. I am thy father's spirit,
Doom'd for a certain term to walk the night,
And for the day confined to fast in fires,
Till the foul crimes done in my days of nature
Are burnt and purged away. But that I am forbid
To tell the secrets of my prison-house,
I could a tale unfold whose lightest word
Would harrow up thy soul, freeze thy young blood,
Make thy two eyes, like stars, start from their spheres,

Thy knotted and combined locks to part
And each particular hair to stand an end,
Like quills upon the fretful porpentine:
But this eternal blazon must not be
To ears of flesh and blood. List, list, O, list!
If thou didst ever thy dear father love—

Ham. O God!

Ghost. Revenge his foul and most unnatural murder.

Ham. Murder!

Ghost. Murder most foul, as in the best it is,
But this most foul, strange, and unnatural.

Ham. Haste me to know't, that I, with wings as swift
As meditation or the thoughts of love,
May sweep to my revenge.

Ghost. I find thee apt;
And duller shouldst thou be than the fat weed
That roots itself in ease on Lethe wharf,
Wouldst thou not stir in this. Now, Hamlet, hear:
'Tis given out that, sleeping in my orchard,
A serpent stung me; so the whole ear of Denmark
Is by a forged process of my death
Rankly abused: but know, thou noble youth,
The serpent that did sting thy father's life
Now wears his crown.

Ham. O my prophetic soul!
My uncle!

Ghost. Ay, that incestuous, that adulterate beast,
With witchcraft of his wit, with traitorous gifts,—
O wicked wit and gifts, that have the power
So to seduce!—won to his shameful lust

The will of my most seeming-virtuous queen:
O Hamlet, what a falling-off was there!
From me, whose love was of that dignity
That it went hand in hand even with the vow
I made to her in marriage, and to decline
Upon a wretch, whose natural gifts were poor
To those of mine!
But virtue, as it never will be moved,
Though lewdness court it in a shape of heaven,
So lust, though to a radiant angel link'd,
Will sate itself in a celestial bed
And prey on garbage.
But, soft! methinks I scent the morning air;
Brief let me be. Sleeping within my orchard,
My custom always of the afternoon,
Upon my secure hour thy uncle stole,
With juice of cursed hebenon in a vial,
And in the porches of my ears did pour
The leperous distilment; whose effect
Holds such an enmity with blood of man
That swift as quicksilver it courses through
The natural gates and alleys of the body,
And with a sudden vigor it doth posset
And curd, like eager droppings into milk,
The thin and wholesome blood: so did it mine;
And a most instant tetter bark'd about,
Most lazar-like, with vile and loathsome crust,
All my smooth body.
Thus was I, sleeping, by a brother's hand
Of life, of crown, of queen, at once dispatch'd:

Cut off even in the blossoms of my sin,
Unhousel'd, disappointed, unaneled,
No reckoning made, but sent to my account
With all my imperfections on my head:
O, horrible! O, horrible! most horrible!
If thou hast nature in thee, bear it not;
Let not the royal bed of Denmark be
A couch for luxury and damned incest.
But, howsoever thou pursuest this act,
Taint not thy mind, nor let thy soul contrive
Against thy mother aught: leave her to heaven
And to those thorns that in her bosom lodge,
To prick and sting her. Fare thee well at once!
The glow-worm shows the matin to be near,
And 'gins to pale his uneffectual fire:
Adieu, adieu! Hamlet, remember me. [*Exit.*

Ham. O all you host of heaven! O earth! what else?
And shall I couple hell? O, fie! Hold, hold, my heart;
And you, my sinews, grow not instant old,
But bear me stiffly up. Remember thee!
Ay, thou poor ghost, while memory holds a seat
In this distracted globe. Remember thee!
Yea, from the table of my memory
I'll wipe away all trivial fond records,
All saws of books, all forms, all pressures past,
That youth and observation copied there;
And thy commandment all alone shall live
Within the book and volume of my brain,
Unmix'd with baser matter: yes, by heaven!
O most pernicious woman!

O villain, villain, smiling, damned villain!
My tables,—meet it is I set it down,
That one may smile, and smile, and be a villain;
At least I'm sure it may be so in Denmark.
[*Writing.*
So, uncle, there you are. Now to my word;
It is 'Adieu, adieu! remember me.'
I have sworn't.

Hor.
Mar. [*Within*] My lord, my lord!

Mar. [*Within*] Lord Hamlet!

Hor. [*Within*] Heaven secure him!

Ham. So be it!

Mar. [*Within*] Illo, ho, ho, my lord!

Ham. Hillo, ho, ho, boy! come, bird, come.

Enter HORATIO *and* MARCELLUS.

Mar. How is't, my noble lord?

Hor. What news, my lord?

Ham. O, wonderful!

Hor. Good my lord, tell it.

Ham. No; you'll reveal it.

Hor. Not I, my lord, by heaven.

Mar. Nor I, my lord.

Ham. How say you, then; would heart of man once think it?
But you'll be secret?

Hor.
Mar. Ay, by heaven, my lord.

Ham. There's ne'er a villain dwelling in all Denmark
But he's an arrant knave.
Hor. There needs no ghost, my lord, come from the grave
To tell us this.
Ham. Why, right; you are i' the right;
And so, without more circumstance at all,
I hold it fit that we shake hands and part:
You, as your business and desire shall point you;
For every man hath business and desire,
Such as it is; and for my own poor part,
Look you, I'll go pray.
Hor. These are but wild and whirling words, my lord.
Ham. I'm sorry they offend you, heartily;
Yes, faith, heartily.
Hor. There's no offence, my lord.
Ham. Yes, by Saint Patrick, but there is, Horatio,
And much offence too. Touching this vision here,
It is an honest ghost, that let me tell you:
For your desire to know what is between us,
O'ermaster't as you may. And now, good friends,
As you are friends, scholars and soldiers,
Give me one poor request.
Hor. What is't, my lord? we will.
Ham. Never make known what you have seen to-night.
Hor., *Mar.* My lord, we will not.
Ham. Nay, but swear't.
Hor. In faith,
My lord, not I.
Mar. Nor I, my lord, in faith.

Ham. Upon my sword.

Mar. We have sworn, my lord, already.

Ham. Indeed, upon my sword, indeed.

Ghost. [*Beneath*] Swear.

Ham. Ah, ha, boy! say'st thou so? art thou there, truepenny?
Come on: you hear this fellow in the cellarage:
Consent to swear.

Hor. Propose the oath, my lord.

Ham. Never to speak of this that you have seen,
Swear by my sword.

Ghost. [*Beneath*] Swear.

Ham. Hic et ubique? then we'll shift our ground.
Come hither, gentlemen,
And lay your hands again upon my sword:
Never to speak of this that you have heard,
Swear by my sword.

Ghost. [*Beneath*] Swear.

Ham. Well said, old mole! canst work i' the earth so fast?
A worthy pioner! Once more remove, good friends.

Hor. O day and night, but this is wondrous strange!

Ham. And therefore as a stranger give it welcome.
There are more things in heaven and earth, Horatio,
Than are dreamt of in your philosophy.
But come;
Here, as before, never, so help you mercy,
How strange or odd soe'er I bear myself,
As I perchance hereafter shall think meet
To put an antic disposition on,

That you, at such times seeing me, never shall,
With arms encumber'd thus, or this head-shake,
Or by pronouncing of some doubtful phrase,
As 'Well, well, we know,' or 'We could, an if we would,'
Or 'If we list to speak,' or 'There be, an if they might,'
Or such ambiguous giving out, to note
That you know aught of me: this not to do,
So grace and mercy at your most need help you,
Swear.

Ghost. [*Beneath*] Swear.

Ham. Rest, rest, perturbed spirit! [*They swear.*] So, gentlemen,
With all my love I do commend me to you:
And what so poor a man as Hamlet is
May do, to express his love and friending to you,
God willing, shall not lack. Let us go in together;
And still your fingers on your lips, I pray.
The time is out of joint: O cursed spite,
That ever I was born to set it right!
Nay, come, let's go together. [*Exeunt.*

ACT SECOND

SCENE I

A room in Polonius's house.

Enter POLONIUS *and* REYNALDO.

Pol. Give him this money and these notes, Reynaldo.
Rey. I will, my lord.
Pol. You shall do marvelous wisely, good Reynaldo,
Before you visit him, to make inquire
Of his behavior.
Rey. My lord, I did intend it.
Pol. Marry, well said, very well said. Look you, sir,
Inquire me first what Danskers are in Paris,
And how, and who, what means, and where they keep,
What company, at what expense; and finding
By this encompassment and drift of question
That they do know my son, come you more nearer
Than your particular demands will touch it:
Take you, as 'twere, some distant knowledge of him,
As thus, 'I know his father and his friends,
And in part him': do you mark this, Reynaldo?
Rey. Ay, very well, my lord.
Pol. 'And in part him; but,' you may say, 'not well:
But if't be he I mean, he's very wild,
Addicted so and so'; and there put on him
What forgeries you please; marry, none so rank

As may dishonor him; take heed of that;
But, sir, such wanton, wild and usual slips
As are companions noted and most known
To youth and liberty.

Rey. As gaming, my lord.

Pol. Ay, or drinking, fencing, swearing, quarreling,
Drabbing: you may go so far.

Rey. My lord, that would dishonor him.

Pol. Faith, no; as you may season it in the charge.
You must not put another scandal on him,
That he is open to incontinency;
That's not my meaning: but breathe his faults so quaintly
That they may seem the taints of liberty,
The flash and outbreak of a fiery mind,
A savageness in unreclaimed blood,
Of general assault.

Rey. But, my good lord,—

Pol. Wherefore should you do this?

Rey. Ay, my lord,
I would know that.

Pol. Marry, sir, here's my drift,
And, I believe, it is a fetch of warrant:
You laying these slight sullies on my son,
As 'twere a thing a little soil'd i' the working,
Mark you,
Your party in converse, him you would sound,
Having ever seen in the prenominate crimes
The youth you breathe of guilty, be assured
He closes with you in this consequence;

'Good sir,' or so, or 'friend,' or 'gentleman,'
According to the phrase or the addition
Of man and country.

Rey. Very good, my lord.

Pol. And then, sir, does he this—he does—what was I about to say? By the mass, I was about to say something: where did I leave?

Rey. At 'closes in the consequence,' at 'friend or so,' and 'gentleman.'

Pol. At 'closes in the consequence,' ay, marry;
He closes with you thus: 'I know the gentleman;
I saw him yesterday, or t'other day,
Or then, or then, with such, or such; and, as you say,
There was a' gaming; there o'ertook in's rouse;
There falling out at tennis': or perchance,
'I saw him enter such a house of sale'
Videlicet, a brothel, or so forth.
See you now;
Your bait of falsehood takes this carp of truth:
And thus do we of wisdom and of reach,
With windlasses and with assays of bias,
By indirections find directions out:
So by my former lecture and advice,
Shall you my son. You have me, have you not?

Rey. My lord, I have.

Pol. God be wi' you; fare you well.

Rey. Good my lord!

Pol. Observe his inclination in yourself.

Rey. I shall, my lord.

Pol. And let him ply his music.

Rey. Well, my lord.
Pol. Farewell! [*Exit Reynaldo.*

Enter Ophelia.

How now, Ophelia! what's the matter?
Oph. O, my lord, my lord, I have been so affrighted!
Pol. With what, i' the name of God?
Oph. My lord, as I was sewing in my closet,
Lord Hamlet, with his doublet all unbraced,
No hat upon his head, his stockings foul'd,
Ungarter'd and down-gyved to his ancle;
Pale as his shirt, his knees knocking each other,
And with a look so piteous in purport
As if he had been loosed out of hell
To speak of horrors,—he comes before me.
Pol. Mad for thy love?
Oph. My lord, I do not know,
But truly I do fear it.
Pol. What said he?
Oph. He took me by the wrist and held me hard;
Then goes he to the length of all his arm,
And, with his other hand thus o'er his brow,
He falls to such perusal of my face
As he would draw it. Long stay'd he so;
At last, a little shaking of mine arm,
And thrice his head thus waving up and down,
He raised a sigh so piteous and profound
As it did seem to shatter all his bulk
And end his being: that done, he lets me go:
And, with his head over his shoulder turn'd,

He seem'd to find his way without his eyes;
For out o' doors he went without their helps,
And, to the last, bended their light on me.

Pol. Come, go with me: I will go seek the king.
This is the very ecstasy of love,
Whose violent property fordoes itself
And leads the will to desperate undertakings
As oft as any passion under heaven
That does afflict our natures. I am sorry.
What, have you given him any hard words of late?

Oph. No, my good lord, but, as you did command,
I did repel his letters and denied
His access to me.

Pol. That hath made him mad.
I am sorry that with better heed and judgment
I had not quoted him: I fear'd he did but trifle
And meant to wreck thee; but beshrew my jealousy!
By heaven, it is as proper to our age
To cast beyond ourselves in our opinions
As it is common for the younger sort
To lack discretion. Come, go we to the king:
This must be known; which, being kept close, might move
More grief to hide than hate to utter love.
Come. [*Exeunt.*

SCENE II

A room in the castle.

Flourish. Enter KING, QUEEN, ROSENCRANTZ, GUILDENSTERN, *and* ATTENDANTS.

King. Welcome, dear Rosencrantz and Guildenstern!
Moreover that we much did long to see you,
The need we have to use you did provoke
Our hasty sending. Something have you heard
Of Hamlet's transformation; so call it,
Sith nor the exterior nor the inward man
Resembles that it was. What it should be,
More than his father's death, that thus hath put him
So much from the understanding of himself,
I cannot dream of: I entreat you both,
That, being of so young days brought up with him
And sith so neighbor'd to his youth and havior,
That you vouchsafe your rest here in our court
Some little time: so by your companies
To draw him on to pleasures, and to gather
So much as from occasion you may glean,
Whether aught, to us unknown, afflicts him thus,
That, open'd, lies within our remedy.
Queen. Good gentlemen, he hath much talk'd of you;
And sure I am two men there are not living
To whom he more adheres. If it will please you
To show us so much gentry and good will
As to expend your time with us a while

For the supply and profit of our hope,
Your visitation shall receive such thanks
As fits a king's remembrance.

Ros. Both your majesties
Might, by the sovereign power you have of us,
Put your dread pleasures more into command
Than to entreaty.

Guil. But we both obey,
And here give up ourselves, in the full bent
To lay our service freely at your feet,
To be commanded.

King. Thanks, Rosencrantz and gentle Guildenstern.

Queen. Thanks, Guildenstern and gentle Rosencrantz:
And I beseech you instantly to visit
My too much changed son. Go, some of you,
And bring these gentlemen where Hamlet is.

Guil. Heavens make our presence and our practices
Pleasant and helpful to him!

Queen. Ay, amen!

[*Exeunt Rosencrantz, Guildenstern, and some Attendants.*

Enter POLONIUS.

Pol. The ambassadors from Norway, my good lord,
Are joyfully return'd.

King. Thou still hast been the father of good news.

Pol. Have I, my lord? I assure my good liege,
I hold my duty as I hold my soul,
Both to my God and to my gracious king:
And I do think, or else this brain of mine
Hunts not the trail of policy so sure

As it hath used to do, that I have found
The very cause of Hamlet's lunacy.

King. O, speak of that; that do I long to hear.

Pol. Give first admittance to the ambassadors;
My news shall be the fruit to that great feast.

King. Thyself do grace to them, and bring them in.
[*Exit Polonius.*

He tells me, my dear Gertrude, he hath found
The head and source of all your son's distemper.

Queen. I doubt it is no other but the main;
His father's death and our o'erhasty marriage.

King. Well, we shall sift him.

Re-enter POLONIUS, *with* VOLTIMAND *and* CORNELIUS.

Welcome, my good friends!
Say, Voltimand, what from our brother Norway?

Volt. Most fair return of greetings and desires.
Upon our first, he sent out to suppress
His nephew's levies, which to him appear'd
To be a preparation 'gainst the Polack,
But better look'd into, he truly found
It was against your highness: whereat grieved,
That so his sickness, age and impotence
Was falsely borne in hand, sends out arrests
On Fortinbras; which he, in brief, obeys,
Receives rebuke from Norway, and in fine
Makes vow before his uncle never more
To give the assay of arms against your majesty.
Whereon old Norway, overcome with joy,
Gives him three thousand crowns in annual fee,

And his commission to employ those soldiers,
So levied as before, against the Polack:
With an entreaty, herein further shown,
[*Giving a paper.*
That it might please you to give quiet pass
Through your dominions for this enterprise,
On such regards of safety and allowance
As therein are set down.

King. It likes us well;
And at our more consider'd time we'll read,
Answer, and think upon this business.
Meantime we thank you for your well-took labor:
Go to your rest; at night we'll feast together:
Most welcome home!
[*Exeunt Voltimand and Cornelius.*

Pol. This business is well ended.
My liege, and madam, to expostulate
What majesty should be, what duty is,
Why day is day, night night, and time is time,
Were nothing but to waste night, day and time.
Therefore, since brevity is the soul of wit
And tediousness the limbs and outward flourishes,
I will be brief. Your noble son is mad:
Mad call I it; for, to define true madness,
What is't but to be nothing else but mad?
But let that go.

Queen. More matter, with less art.

Pol. Madam, I swear I use no art at all.
That he is mad, 'tis true: 'tis true 'tis pity,
And pity 'tis 'tis true: a foolish figure;

But farewell it, for I will use no art.
Mad let us grant him then: and now remains
That we find out the cause of this effect,
Or rather say, the cause of this defect,
For this effect defective comes by cause:
Thus it remains and the remainder thus.
Perpend.
I have a daughter,—have while she is mine,—
Who, in her duty and obedience, mark,
Hath given me this: now gather, and surmise.
[*Reads.*

'To the celestial and my soul's idol, the most beautified Ophelia,'—

That's an ill phrase, a vile phrase; 'beautified' is a vile phrase; but you shall hear. Thus:
[*Reads.*

'In her excellent white bosom, these,' &c.

Queen. Came this from Hamlet to her?

Pol. Good madam, stay awhile; I will be faithful.
[*Reads.*

'Doubt thou the stars are fire;
Doubt that the sun doth move;
Doubt truth to be a liar;
But never doubt I love.

'O dear Ophelia, I am ill at these numbers; I have not art to reckon my groans: but that I love thee best, O most best, believe it. Adieu.

'Thine evermore, most dear lady, whilst this machine is to him, Hamlet.'

This in obedience hath my daughter shown me;

And more above, hath his solicitings,
As they fell out by time, by means and place,
All given to mine ear.

King. But how hath she
Received his love?

Pol. What do you think of me?

King. As of a man faithful and honorable.

Pol. I would fain prove so. But what might you think,
When I had seen this hot love on the wing,—
As I perceived it, I must tell you that,
Before my daughter told me,—what might you,
Or my dear majesty your queen here, think,
If I had play'd the desk or table-book,
Or given my heart a winking, mute and dumb,
Or look'd upon this love with idle sight;
What might you think? No, I went round to work,
And my young mistress thus I did bespeak:
'Lord Hamlet is a prince, out of thy star;
This must not be': and then I prescripts gave her,
That she should lock herself from his resort,
Admit no messengers, receive no tokens.
Which done, she took the fruits of my advice;
And he repulsed—a short tale to make—
Fell into a sadness, then into a fast,
Thence to a watch, thence into a weakness,
Thence to a lightness, and by this declension
Into the madness wherein now he raves
And all we mourn for.

King. Do you think 'tis this?

Queen. It may be, very likely.

Pol. Hath there been such a time—I'd fain know that—
That I have positively said ''Tis so,'
When it proved otherwise?

King. Not that I know.

Pol. [*Pointing to his head and shoulder*] Take this from this, if this be otherwise:
If circumstances lead me, I will find
Where truth is hid, though it were hid indeed
Within the center.

King. How may we try it further?

Pol. You know, sometimes he walks four hours together
Here in the lobby.

Queen. So he does indeed. 161

Pol. At such a time I'll loose my daughter to him:
Be you and I behind an arras then;
Mark the encounter: if he love her not
And be not from his reason fall'n thereon,
Let me be no assistant for a state,
But keep a farm and carters.

King. We will try it.

Queen. But look where sadly the poor wretch comes reading.

Pol. Away, I do beseech you, both away:
I'll board him presently. 169

[*Exeunt King, Queen, and Attendants.*

Enter HAMLET, *reading.*

O, give me leave:
How does my good Lord Hamlet?

Ham. Well, God-a-mercy.

Pol. Do you know me, my lord?

Ham. Excellent well; you are a fishmonger.

Pol. Not I, my lord.

Ham. Then I would you were so honest a man.

Pol. Honest, my lord!

Ham. Ay, sir; to be honest, as this world goes, is to be one man picked out of ten thousand.

Pol. That's very true, my lord.

Ham. For if the sun breed maggots in a dead dog, being a god kissing carrion,—Have you a daughter?

Pol. I have, my lord.

Ham. Let her not walk i' the sun: conception is a blessing; but not as your daughter may conceive. Friend, look to't.

Pol. [*Aside*] How say you by that? Still harping on my daughter: yet he knew me not at first; he said I was a fishmonger: he is far gone, far gone: and truly in my youth I suffered much extremity for love; very near this. I'll speak to him again.—What do you read, my lord?

Ham. Words, words, words.

Pol. What is the matter, my lord?

Ham. Between who?

Pol. I mean, the matter that you read, my lord.

Ham. Slanders, sir: for the satirical rogue says here that old men have grey beards, that their faces are wrinkled, their eyes purging thick amber and plum-tree gum, and that they have a plentiful lack of wit, together with most weak hams:

all which, sir, though I most powerfully and potently believe, yet I hold it not honesty to have it thus set down; for yourself, sir, should be old as I am, if like a crab you could go backward.

Pol. [*Aside*] Though this be madness, yet there is method in't.—Will you walk out of the air, my lord?

Ham. Into my grave.

Pol. Indeed, that is out of the air. [*Aside*] How pregnant sometimes his replies are! a happiness that often madness hits on, which reason and sanity could not so prosperously be delivered of. I will leave him, and suddenly contrive the means of meeting between him and my daughter.—My honorable lord, I will most humbly take my leave of you.

Ham. You cannot, sir, take from me any thing that I will more willingly part withal: except my life, except my life, except my life.

Pol. Fare you well, my lord.

Ham. These tedious old fools!

Re-enter Rosencrantz *and* Guildenstern.

Pol. You go to seek the Lord Hamlet; there he is.

Ros. [*To Polonius*] God save you, sir! [*Exit Polonius.*

Guil. My honored lord!

Ros. My most dear lord!

Ham. My excellent good friends! How dost thou, Guildenstern? Ah, Rosencrantz! Good lads, how do you both?

Ros. As the indifferent children of the earth.

Guil. Happy, in that we are not over-happy;
On Fortune's cap we are not the very button.

Ham. Nor the soles of her shoe?

Ros. Neither, my lord.

Ham. Then you live about her waist, or in the middle of her favors? What's the news?

Ros. None, my lord, but that the world's grown honest.

Ham. Then is doomsday near: but your news is not true. Let me question more in particular: what have you, my good friends, deserved at the hands of Fortune, that she sends you to prison hither?

Guil. Prison, my lord!

Ham. Denmark's a prison.

Ros. Then is the world one.

Ham. A goodly one; in which there are many confines, wards and dungeons, Denmark being one o' the worst.

Ros. We think not so, my lord.

Ham. Why, then, 'tis none to you; for there is nothing either good or bad, but thinking makes it so: to me it is a prison.

Ros. Why, then, your ambition makes it one; 'tis too narrow for your mind.

Ham. O God, I could be bounded in a nut-shell and count myself a king of infinite space, were it not that I have bad dreams.

Guil. Which dreams indeed are ambition; for the

very substance of the ambitious is merely the shadow of a dream.

Ham. A dream itself is but a shadow.

Ros. Truly, and I hold ambition of so airy and light a quality that it is but a shadow's shadow.

Ham. Then are our beggars bodies, and our monarchs and outstretched heroes the beggars' shadows. Shall we to the court? for, by my fay, I cannot reason.

Ros.
Guil. } We'll wait upon you.

Ham. No such matter: I will not sort you with the rest of my servants, for, to speak to you like an honest man, I am most dreadfully attended. But, in the beaten way of friendship, what make you at Elsinore?

Ros. To visit you, my lord; no other occasion.

Ham. Beggar that I am, I am even poor in thanks; but I thank you: and sure, dear friends, my thanks are too dear a halfpenny. Were you not sent for? Is it your own inclining? Is it a free visitation? Come, deal justly with me: come, come; nay, speak.

Guil. What should we say, my lord?

Ham. Why, anything, but to the purpose. You were sent for; and there is a kind of confession in your looks which your modesties have not craft enough to color: I know the good king and queen have sent for you.

Ros. To what end, my lord?

Ham. That you must teach me. But let me conjure you, by the rights of our fellowship, by the consonancy of our youth, by the obligation of our ever-preserved love, and by what more dear a better proposer could charge you withal, be even and direct with me, whether you were sent for, or no?

Ros. [*Aside to Guil.*] What say you?

Ham. [*Aside*] Nay, then, I have an eye of you.— If you love me, hold not off.

Guil. My lord, we were sent for.

Ham. I will tell you why; so shall my anticipation prevent your discovery, and your secrecy to the king and queen moult no feather. I have of late —but wherefore I know not—lost all my mirth, forgone all custom of exercises; and indeed it goes so heavily with my disposition that this goodly frame, the earth, seems to me a sterile promontory; this most excellent canopy, the air, look you, this brave o'erhanging firmament, this majestical roof fretted with golden fire, why, it appears no other thing to me than a foul and pestilent congregation of vapors. What a piece of work is a man! how noble in reason! how infinite in faculty! in form and moving how express and admirable! in action how like an angel! in apprehension how like a god! the beauty of the world! the paragon of animals! And yet, to me, what is this quintessence of dust?

man delights not me; no, nor woman neither, though by your smiling you seem to say so.

Ros. My lord, there was no such stuff in my thoughts.

Ham. Why did you laugh then, when I said 'man delights not me'?

Ros. To think, my lord, if you delight not in man, what lenten entertainment the players shall receive from you: we coted them on the way; and hither are they coming, to offer you service.

Ham. He that plays the king shall be welcome; his majesty shall have tribute of me; the adventurous knight shall use his foil and target; the lover shall not sigh gratis; the humorous man shall end his part in peace; the clown shall make those laugh whose lungs are tickle o' the sere; and the lady shall say her mind freely, or the blank verse shall halt for't. What players are they?

Ros. Even those you were wont to take such delight in, the tragedians of the city.

Ham. How chances it they travel? their residence, both in reputation and profit, was better both ways.

Ros. I think their inhibition comes by the means of the late innovation.

Ham. Do they hold the same estimation they did when I was in the city? are they so followed?

Ros. No, indeed, are they not.

Ham. How comes it? do they grow rusty?

Ros. Nay, their endeavor keeps in the wonted pace: but there is, sir, an aery of children, little eyases, that cry out on the top of question, and are most tyrannically clapped for't: these are now the fashion, and so berattle the common stages—so they call them—that many wearing rapiers are afraid of goose-quills and dare scarce come thither.

Ham. What, are they children? who maintains 'em? how are they escoted? Will they pursue the quality no longer than they can sing? will they not say afterwards, if they should grow themselves to common players,—as it is most like, if their means are no better,—their writers do them wrong, to make them exclaim against their own succession?

Ros. Faith, there has been much to do on both sides, and the nation holds it no sin to tarre them to controversy: there was for a while no money bid for argument unless the poet and the player went to cuffs in the question.

Ham. Is't possible?

Guil. O, there has been much throwing about of brains.

Ham. Do the boys carry it away?

Ros. Ay, that they do, my lord; Hercules and his load too.

Ham. It is not very strange; for my uncle is king of Denmark, and those that would maks mows at him while my father lived, give twenty, forty, fifty, an hundred ducats a-piece for his picture in little. 'Sblood, there is something in this more than natural, if philosophy could find it out.

[*Flourish of trumpets within.*

Guil. There are the players.

Ham. Gentlemen, you are welcome to Elsinore. Your hands, come then: the appurtenance of welcome is fashion and ceremony: let me comply with you in this garb, lest my extent to the players, which, I tell you, must show fairly outward, should more appear like entertainment than yours. You are welcome: but my uncle-father and aunt-mother are deceived.

Guil. In what, my dear lord?

Ham. I am but mad north-north-west: when the wind is southerly I know a hawk from a handsaw.

Re-enter POLONIUS.

Pol. Well be with you, gentlemen!

Ham. Hark you, Guildenstern; and you too: at each ear a hearer: that great baby you see there is not yet out of his swaddling-clouts.

Ros. Happily he's the second time come to them; for they say an old man is twice a child.

Ham. I will prophesy he comes to tell me of the players; mark it. You say right, sir: o' Monday morning; 'twas so, indeed.

Pol. My lord, I have news to tell you.

Ham. My lord, I have news to tell you. When Roscius was an actor in Rome,—

Pol. The actors are come hither, my lord.

Ham. Buz, buz!

Pol. Upon mine honor,—

Ham. Then came each actor on his ass,—

Pol. The best actors in the world, either for tragedy, comedy, history, pastoral, pastoral-comical, historical-pastoral, tragical-historical, tragical-comical-historical-pastoral, scene individable, or poem unlimited: Seneca cannot be too heavy, nor Plautus too light. For the law of writ and the liberty, these are the only men.

Ham. O Jephthah, judge of Israel, what a treasure hadst thou!

Pol. What a treasure had he, my lord?

Ham. Why,

'One fair daughter, and no more,
The which he loved passing well.'

Pol. [*Aside*] Still on my daughter.

Ham. Am I not i' the right, old Jephthah?

Pol. If you call me Jephthah, my lord, I have a daughter that I love passing well.

Ham. Nay, that follows not.

Pol. What follows, then, my lord?

Ham. Why,

'As by lot, God wot,'

and then, you know,

'It came to pass, as most like it was,'—

the first row of the pious chanson will show you more; for look, where my abridgment comes.

Enter four or five PLAYERS.

You are welcome, masters; welcome, all. I am glad to see thee well. Welcome, good friends. O, my old friend! Thy face is valanced since I saw thee last; comest thou to beard me in Denmark? What, my young lady and mistress! By'r lady, your ladyship is nearer to heaven than when I saw you last, by the altitude of a chopine. Pray God, your voice, like a piece of uncurrent gold, be not cracked within the ring. Masters, you are all welcome. We'll e'en to't like French falconers, fly at any thing we see: we'll have a speech straight: come, give us a taste of your quality; come, a passionate speech.

First Play. What speech, my lord?

Ham. I heard thee speak me a speech once, but it was never acted; or, if it was, not above once; for the play, I remember, pleased not the million; 'twas caviare to the general: but it was —as I received it, and others, whose judgments in such matters cried in the top of mine— an excellent play, well digested in the scenes, set down with as much modesty as cunning. I remember, one said there were no sallets in the lines to make the matter savory, nor no matter in the phrase that might indict the author of affectation; but called it an honest method, as wholesome as sweet, and by very much more handsome than fine. One speech in it I chiefly loved: 'twas Æneas' tale to Dido; and thereabout of it especially, where he speaks of Priam's slaughter: if it live in your memory, begin at this line; let me see, let me see;

'The rugged Pyrrhus, like the Hyrcanian beast,'—
It is not so:—it begins with 'Pyrrhus':—
'The rugged Pyrrhus, he whose sable arms,
Black as his purpose, did the night resemble
When he lay couched in the ominous horse,
Hath now this dread and black complexion smear'd
With heraldry more dismal: head to foot
Now is he total gules; horridly trick'd
With blood of fathers, mothers, daughters, sons,
Baked and impasted with the parching streets,
That lend a tyrannous and damned light
To their lord's murder: roasted in wrath and fire,
And thus o'er-sized with coagulate gore,
With eyes like carbuncles, the hellish Pyrrhus
Old grandsire Priam seeks.'
So, proceed you.

Pol. 'Fore God, my lord, well spoken, with good accent and good discretion.

First Play. 'Anon he finds him
Striking too short at Greeks; his antique sword,
Rebellious to his arm, lies where it falls,
Repugnant to command: unequal match'd,
Pyrrhus at Priam drives; in rage strikes wide;

But with the whiff and wind of his fell sword
The unnerved father falls. Then senseless Ilium,
Seeming to feel this blow, with flaming top
Stoops to his base, and with a hideous crash
Takes prisoner Pyrrhus' ear: for, lo! his sword,
Which was declining on the milky head
Of reverend Priam, seem'd i' the air to stick:
So, as a painted tyrant, Pyrrhus stood,
And like a neutral to his will and matter,
Did nothing.
But, as we often see, against some storm,
A silence in the heavens, the rack stand still,
The bold winds speechless and the orb below
As hush as death, anon the dreadful thunder
Doth rend the region, so, after Pyrrhus' pause,
Aroused vengeance sets him new a-work;
And never did the Cyclops' hammers fall
On Mars's armor forged for proof eterne
With less remorse than Pyrrhus' bleeding sword
Now falls on Priam.
Out, out, thou strumpet, Fortune! All you gods,
In general synod take away her power;
Break all the spokes and fellies from her wheel,
And bowl the round nave down the hill of heaven
As low as to the fiends!'

Pol. This is too long.

Ham. It shall to the barber's, with your beard.
Prithee, say on: he's for a jig or a tale of bawdry, or he sleeps: say on: come to Hecuba.

First Play. 'But who, O, who had seen the mobled queen—'

Ham. 'The mobled queen'?

Pol. That's good; 'mobled queen' is good.

First Play. 'Run barefoot up and down, threatening the flames
With bisson rheum; a clout upon that head
Where late the diadem stood, and for a robe,
About her lank and all o'er-teemed loins,
A blanket, in the alarm of fear caught up:
Who this had seen, with tongue in venom steep'd,
'Gainst Fortune's state would treason have pronounced:
But if the gods themselves did see her then,
When she saw Pyrrhus make malicious sport
In mincing with his sword her husband's limbs,
The instant burst of clamor that she made,
Unless things mortal move them not at all,
Would have made milch the burning eyes of heaven,
And passion in the gods.'

Pol. Look, whether he has not turned his color and has tears in's eyes. Prithee, no more.

Ham. 'Tis well; I'll have thee speak out the rest of this soon. Good my lord, will you see the players well bestowed? Do you hear, let them be well used, for they are the abstract and brief chronicles of the time: after your death you were better have a bad epitaph than their ill report while you live.

Pol. My lord, I will use them according to their desert.

Ham. God's bodykins, man, much better: use every man after his desert, and who shall 'scape whipping? Use them after your own honor and dignity: the less they deserve, the more merit is in your bounty. Take them in.

Pol. Come, sirs.

Ham. Follow him, friends: we'll hear a play to-morrow. [*Exit Polonius with all the Players but the First.*] Dost thou hear me, old friend; can you play the Murder of Gonzago?

First Play. Ay, my lord.

Ham. We'll ha't to-morrow night. You could, for a need, study a speech of some dozen or sixteen lines, which I would set down and insert in't, could you not?

First Play. Ay, my lord.

Ham. Very well. Follow that lord; and look you mock him not. [*Exit First Player.*] My good friends, I'll leave you till night: you are welcome to Elsinore.

Ros. Good my lord!

Ham. Ay, so, God be wi' ye! [*Exeunt Rosencrantz and Guildenstern.*] Now I am alone.
O, what a rogue and peasant slave am I!
Is it not monstrous that this player here,
But in a fiction, in a dream of passion,
Could force his soul so to his own conceit
That from her working all his visage wann'd;

Tears in his eyes, distraction in's aspect,
A broken voice, and his whole function suiting
With forms to his conceit? and all for nothing!
For Hecuba!
What's Hecuba to him, or he to Hecuba,
That he should weep for her? What would he do,
Had he the motive and the cue for passion
That I have? He would drown the stage with tears
And cleave the general ear with horrid speech,
Make mad the guilty and appall the free,
Confound the ignorant, and amaze indeed
The very faculties of eyes and ears.
Yet I,
A dull and muddy-mettled rascal, peak,
Like John-a-dreams, unpregnant of my cause,
And can say nothing; no, not for a king,
Upon whose property and most dear life
A damn'd defeat was made. Am I a coward?
Who calls me villain? breaks my pate across?
Plucks off my beard, and blows it in my face?
Tweaks me by the nose? gives me the lie i' the throat,
As deep as to the lungs? who does me this?
Ha!
'Swounds, I should take it: for it cannot be
But I am pigeon-liver'd and lack gall
To make oppression bitter, or ere this
I should have fatted all the region kites
With this slave's offal: bloody, bawdy villain!
Remorseless, treacherous, lecherous, kindless villain!

O, vengeance!
Why, what an ass am I! This is most brave,
That I, the son of a dear father murder'd,
Prompted to my revenge by heaven and hell,
Must, like a whore, unpack my heart with words,
And fall a-cursing, like a very drab,
A scullion!
Fie upon't! foh! About, my brain! I have heard
That guilty creatures sitting at a play,
Have by the very cunning of the scene
Been struck so to the soul that presently
They have proclaim'd their malefactions;
For murder, though it have no tongue, will speak
With most miraculous organ. I'll have these players
Play something like the murder of my father
Before mine uncle: I'll observe his looks;
I'll tent him to the quick: if he but blench,
I know my course. The spirit that I have seen
May be the devil; and the devil hath power
To assume a pleasing shape; yea, and perhaps
Out of my weakness and my melancholy,
As he is very potent with such spirits,
Abuses me to damn me. I'll have grounds
More relative than this. The play's the thing
Wherein I'll catch the conscience of the king.

[*Exit.*

ACT THIRD

SCENE I

A room in the castle.

Enter KING, QUEEN, POLONIUS, OPHELIA, ROSENCRANTZ, *and* GUILDENSTERN.

King. And can you, by no drift of circumstance,
Get from him why he puts on this confusion,
Grating so harshly all his days of quiet
With turbulent and dangerous lunacy?
Ros. He does confess he feels himself distracted;
But from what cause he will by no means speak.
Guil. Nor do we find him forward to be sounded,
But, with a crafty madness, keeps aloof,
When we would bring him on to some confession
Of his true state.
Queen. Did he receive you well?
Ros. Most like a gentleman.
Guil. But with much forcing of his disposition.
Ros. Niggard of question; but, of our demands,
Most free in his reply.
Queen. Did you assay him
To any pastime?
Ros. Madam, it so fell out, that certain players
We o'er-raught on the way: of these we told him,
And there did seem in him a kind of joy
To hear of it: they are about the court,

And, as I think, they have already order
This night to play before him.

Pol. 'Tis most true:
And he beseech'd me to entreat your majesties
To hear and see the matter.

King. With all my heart; and it doth much content me
To hear him so inclined.
Good gentlemen, give him a further edge,
And drive his purpose on to these delights.

Ros. We shall, my lord.

[*Exeunt Rosencrantz and Guildenstern.*

King. Sweet Gertrude, leave us too;
For we have closely sent for Hamlet hither,
That he, as 'twere by accident, may here
Affront Ophelia:
Her father and myself, lawful espials,
Will so bestow ourselves that, seeing unseen,
We may of their encounter frankly judge,
And gather by him, as he is behaved,
If't be the affliction of his love or no
That thus he suffers for.

Queen. I shall obey you.
And for your part, Ophelia, I do wish
That your good beauties be the happy cause
Of Hamlet's wildness: so shall I hope your virtues
Will bring him to his wonted way again,
To both your honors.

Oph. Madam, I wish it may. [*Exit Queen.*

Pol. Ophelia, walk you here. Gracious, so please you,

We will bestow ourselves. [*To Ophelia.*] Read on this book;
That show of such an exercise may color
Your loneliness. We are oft to blame in this,—
'Tis too much proved—that with devotion's visage
And pious action we do sugar o'er
The devil himself.

King. [*Aside*] O, 'tis too true!
How smart a lash that speech doth give my conscience!
The harlot's cheek, beautied with plastering art,
Is not more ugly to the thing that helps it
Than is my deed to my most painted word:
O heavy burthen!

Pol. I hear him coming: let's withdraw, my lord.

[*Exeunt King and Polonius.*

Enter HAMLET.

Ham. To be, or not to be: that is the question:
Whether 'tis nobler in the mind to suffer
The slings and arrows of outrageous fortune,
Or to take arms against a sea of troubles,
And by opposing end them. To die: to sleep;
No more; and by a sleep to say we end
The heart-ache and the thousand natural shocks
That flesh is heir to, 'tis a consummation
Devoutly to be wish'd. To die, to sleep;
To sleep: perchance to dream: ay, there's the rub;
For in that sleep of death what dreams may come,
When we have shuffled off this mortal coil,

Must give us pause: there's the respect
That makes calamity of so long life;
For who would bear the whips and scorns of time,
The oppressor's wrong, the proud man's contumely,
The pangs of despised love, the law's delay,
The insolence of office, and the spurns
That patient merit of the unworthy takes,
When he himself might his quietus make
With a bare bodkin? who would fardels bear,
To grunt and sweat under a weary life,
But that the dread of something after death,
The undiscover'd country from whose bourn
No traveler returns, puzzles the will
And makes us rather bear those ills we have
Than fly to others that we know not of?
Thus conscience does make cowards of us all;
And thus the native hue of resolution
Is sicklied o'er with the pale cast of thought,
And enterprises of great pitch and moment
With this regard their current turn awry,
And lose the name of action.—Soft you now!
The fair Ophelia! Nymph, in thy orisons
Be all my sins remember'd.

Oph. Good my lord,
How does your honor for this many a day?

Ham. I humbly thank you: well, well, well.

Oph. My lord, I have remembrances of yours,
That I have longed long to re-deliver;
I pray you, now receive them.

Ham. No, not I;
I never gave you aught.

Oph. My honor'd lord, you know right well you did;
And, with them, words of so sweet breath composed
As made the things more rich: their perfume lost,
Take these again; for to the noble mind
Rich gifts wax poor when givers prove unkind.
There, my lord.

Ham. Ha, ha! are you honest?

Oph. My lord?

Ham. Are you fair?

Oph. What means your lordship?

Ham. That if you be honest and fair, your honesty should admit no discourse to your beauty.

Oph. Could beauty, my lord, have better commerce than with honesty?

Ham. Ay, truly; for the power of beauty will sooner transform honesty from what it is to a bawd than the force of honesty can translate beauty into his likeness: this was sometime a paradox, but now the time gives it proof. I did love you once.

Oph. Indeed, my lord, you made me believe so.

Ham. You should not have believed me; for virtue cannot so inoculate our old stock but we shall relish of it: I loved you not.

Oph. I was the more deceived.

Ham. Get thee to a nunnery: why wouldst thou be a breeder of sinners? I am myself indifferent honest; but yet I could accuse me of such things that it were better my mother had not borne me: I am very proud, revengeful, ambitious; with more offences at my beck than I have thoughts to put them in, imagination to give them shape, or time to act them in. What should such fellows as I do crawling between heaven and earth! We are arrant knaves all; believe none of us. Go thy ways to a nunnery. Where's your father?

Oph. At home, my lord.

Ham. Let the doors be shut upon him, that he may play the fool no where but in's own house. Farewell.

Oph. O, help him, you sweet heavens!

Ham. If thou dost marry, I'll give thee this plague for thy dowry: be thou as chaste as ice, as pure as snow, thou shalt not escape calumny. Get thee to a nunnery, go: farewell. Or, if thou wilt needs marry, marry a fool; for wise men know well enough what monsters you make of them. To a nunnery, go, and quickly too. Farewell.

Oph. O heavenly powers, restore him!

Ham. I have heard of your paintings too, well enough; God hath given you one face, and you make yourselves another: you jig, you amble, and you lisp, and nick-name God's creatures, and make your wantonness your ignorance. Go to, I'll no more on't; it hath made me mad. I say, we will have no more marriages: those that are married already, all but one, shall live; the rest shall keep as they are. To a nunnery, go. [*Exit.*

Oph. O, what a noble mind is here o'erthrown!
The courtier's, soldier's, scholar's, eye, tongue, sword:
The expectancy and rose of the fair state,
The glass of fashion and the mold of form,
The observed of all observers, quite, quite down!
And I, of ladies most deject and wretched,
That suck'd the honey of his music vows,
Now see that noble and most sovereign reason,
Like sweet bells jangled, out of tune and harsh;
That unmatch'd form and feature of blown youth
Blasted with ecstasy: O, woe is me,
To have seen what I have seen, see what I see!

Re-enter KING *and* POLONIUS.

King. Love! his affections do not that way tend;
Nor what he spake, though it lack'd form a little,
Was not like madness. There's something in his soul
O'er which his melancholy sits on brood,
And I do doubt the hatch and the disclose
Will be some danger: which for to prevent,
I have in quick determination
Thus set it down: he shall with speed to England,
For the demand of our neglected tribute:
Haply the seas and countries different
With variable objects shall expel
This something-settled matter in his heart,

Whereon his brains still beating puts him thus
From fashion of himself. What think you on't?

Pol. It shall do well: but yet do I believe
The origin and commencement of his grief
Sprung from neglected love. How now, Ophelia!
You need not tell us what Lord Hamlet said;
We heard it all. My lord, do as you please;
But, if you hold it fit, after the play,
Let his queen mother all alone entreat him
To show his grief: let her be round with him;
And I'll be placed, so please you, in the ear
Of all their conference. If she find him not,
To England send him, or confine him where
Your wisdom best shall think.

King. It shall be so:
Madness in great ones must not unwatch'd go.

[*Exeunt.*

Scene II

A hall in the castle.

Enter Hamlet *and* Players.

Ham. Speak the speech, I pray you, as I pronounced it to you, trippingly on the tongue: but if you mouth it, as many of your players do, I had as lief the town-crier spoke my lines. Nor do not saw the air too much with your hand, thus, but use all gently: for in the very torrent, tempest, and, as I may say, the whirlwind of passion, you must acquire and beget a temperance that may give it smoothness. O, it offends me to the soul to hear a robustious periwig-pated fellow tear a passion to tatters, to very rags, to split the ears of the groundlings, who for the most part are capable of nothing but inexplicable dumb-shows and noise: I would have such a fellow whipped for o'erdoing Termagant; it out-herods Herod: pray you, avoid it.

First Play. I warrant your honor.

Ham. Be not too tame neither, but let your own discretion be your tutor: suit the action to the word, the word to the action; with this special observance, that you o'erstep not the modesty of nature: for anything so overdone is from the purpose of playing, whose end, both at the first and now, was and is, to hold, as 'twere, the mirror up to nature; to show virtue her own feature, scorn her own image, and the very age and body of the time his form and pressure. Now this overdone, or come tardy off, though it make the unskilful laugh, cannot but make the judicious grieve; the censure of the which one must in your allowance o'erweigh a whole theater of others. O, there be players that I have seen play, and heard others praise, and that highly, not to speak it profanely, that, neither having the accent of Christians nor the gait of Christian, pagan, nor man, have so strutted and bellowed that I have thought some of nature's journeymen had made men and not made them well, they imitated humanity so abominably.

First Play. I hope we have reformed that indifferently with us, sir.

Ham. O, reform it altogether. And let those that play your clowns speak no more than is set down for them: for there be of them that will themselves laugh, to set on some quantity of barren spectators to laugh too, though in the mean time some necessary question of the play be then to be considered: that's villainous, and shows a most pitiful ambition in the fool that uses it. Go, make you ready. [*Exeunt Players.*

Enter Polonius, Rosencrantz, *and* Guildenstern.

How now, my lord! will the king hear this piece of work?

Pol. And the queen too, and that presently.

Ham. Bid the players make haste. [*Exit Polonius.*
Will you two help to hasten them?

Ros.
Guil. } We will, my lord.

[*Exeunt Rosencrantz and Guildenstern.*

Ham. What ho! Horatio!

Enter Horatio.

Hor. Here, sweet lord, at your service.

Ham. Horatio, thou art e'en as just a man
As e'er my conversation coped withal.
Hor. O, my dear lord,—
Ham. Nay, do not think I flatter;
For what advancement may I hope from thee
That no revenue hast but thy good spirits,
To feed and clothe thee? Why should the poor be flatter'd?
No, let the candied tongue lick absurd pomp,
And crook the pregnant hinges of the knee
Where thrift may follow fawning. Dost thou hear?
Since my dear soul was mistress of her choice
And could of men distinguish, her election
Hath seal'd thee for herself: for thou hast been
As one, in suffering all, that suffers nothing,
A man that Fortune's buffets and rewards
Hast ta'en with equal thanks: and blest are those
Whose blood and judgment are so well commingled
That they are not a pipe for Fortune's finger
To sound what stop she please. Give me that man
That is not passion's slave, and I will wear him
In my heart's core, ay, in my heart of heart,
As I do thee.—Something too much of this.—
There is a play to-night before the king;
One scene of it comes near the circumstance
Which I have told thee of my father's death:
I prithee, when thou seest that act a-foot,
Even with the very comment of thy soul
Observe my uncle: if his occulted guilt
Do not itself unkennel in one speech,

It is a damned ghost that we have seen,
And my imaginations are as foul
As Vulcan's stithy. Give him heedful note;
For I mine eyes will rivet to his face,
And after we will both our judgments join
In censure of his seeming.

Hor. Well, my lord:
If he steal aught the whilst this play is playing,
And 'scape detecting, I will pay the theft.

Ham. They are coming to the play: I must be idle:
Get you a place.

Danish march. A flourish. Enter KING, QUEEN, POLONIUS, OPHELIA, ROSENCRANTZ, GUILDENSTERN, *and other* LORDS *attendant, with the* GUARD *carrying torches.*

King. How fares our cousin Hamlet?

Ham. Excellent, i' faith; of the chameleon's dish: I eat the air, promise-crammed: you cannot feed capons so.

King. I have nothing with this answer, Hamlet; these words are not mine.

Ham. No, nor mine now. [*To Polonius*] My lord, you played once i' the university, you say?

Pol. That did I, my lord, and was accounted a good actor.

Ham. What did you enact?

Pol. I did enact Julius Cæsar: I was killed i' the Capitol; Brutus killed me.

Ham. It was a brute part of him to kill so capital a calf there. Be the players ready?

Ros. Ay, my lord; they stay upon your patience.

Queen. Come hither, my dear Hamlet, sit by me.

Ham. No, good mother, here's metal more attractive.

Pol. [*To the King*] O, ho! do you mark that?

Ham. Lady, shall I lie in your lap?

[*Lying down at Ophelia's feet.*

Oph. No, my lord.

Ham. I mean, my head upon your lap?

Oph. You are merry, my lord.

Ham. Who, I?

Oph. Ay, my lord.

Ham. O God, your only jig-maker. What should a man do but be merry? for, look you, how cheerfully my mother looks, and my father died within's two hours.

Oph. Nay, 'tis twice two months, my lord.

Ham. So long? Nay then, let the devil wear black, for I'll have a suit of sables. O heavens! die two months ago, and not forgotten yet? Then there's hope a great man's memory may outlive his life half a year: but, by'r lady, he must build churches then; or else shall he suffer not thinking on, with the hobby-horse, whose epitaph is, 'For, O, for, O, the hobby-horse is forgot.'

HAUTBOYS *play. The* DUMB-SHOW *enters.*

Enter a KING *and a* QUEEN *very lovingly; the* QUEEN *embracing him, and he her. She kneels, and makes show of protestation unto him. He takes her up, and declines his head upon her neck: lays him down upon a bank of flowers: she, seeing him asleep, leaves him. Anon comes in a fellow, takes off his crown, kisses it, and pours poison in the* KING'S *ears, and exit. The* QUEEN *returns; finds the* KING *dead, and makes passionate action. The* POISONER, *with some two or three* MUTES, *comes in again, seeming to lament with her. The dead body is carried away. The* POISONER *wooes the* QUEEN *with gifts: she seems loath and unwilling awhile, but in the end accepts his love.*

[*Exeunt.*

Oph. What means this, my lord?

Ham. Marry, this is miching mallecho; it means mischief.

Oph. Belike this show imports the argument of the play.

Enter PROLOGUE.

Ham. We shall know by this fellow: the players cannot keep counsel; they'll tell all.

Oph. You are naught, you are naught: I'll mark the play.

Pro. For us, and for our tragedy,
Here stooping to your clemency,
We beg your hearing patiently.

Ham. Is this a prologue, or the posy of a ring?
Oph. 'Tis brief, my lord.
Ham. As woman's love.

Enter two PLAYERS, KING *and* QUEEN.

P. King. Full thirty times hath Phœbus' cart gone round
Neptune's salt wash and Tellus' orbed ground,
And thirty dozen moons with borrowed sheen
About the world have times twelve thirties been,
Since love our hearts and Hymen did our hands
Unite commutual in most sacred bands.
P. Queen. So many journeys may the sun and moon
Make us again count o'er ere love be done!
But, woe is me, you are so sick of late,
So far from cheer and from your former state,
That I distrust you. Yet, though I distrust,
Discomfort you, my lord, it nothing must:
For women's fear and love holds quantity,
In neither aught, or in extremity.
Now, what my love is, proof hath made you know;
And as my love is sized, my fear is so:
Where love is great, the littlest doubts are fear;
Where little fears grow great, great love grows there.
P. King. Faith, I must leave thee, love, and shortly too;
My operant powers their functions leave to do:
And thou shalt live in this fair world behind,
Honor'd, beloved; and haply one as kind
For husband shalt thou—
P. Queen. O, confound the rest!
Such love must needs be treason in my breast;

In second husband let me be accurst!
None wed the second but who kill'd the first.

Ham. [*Aside*] Wormwood, wormwood.

P. Queen. The instances that second marriage move
Are base respects of thrift, but none of love:
A second time I kill my husband dead,
When second husband kisses me in bed.

P. King. I do believe you think what now you speak,
But what we do determine oft we break.
Purpose is but the slave to memory,
Of violent birth, but poor validity:
Which now, like fruit unripe, sticks on the tree,
But fall unshaken when they mellow be.
Most necessary 'tis that we forget
To pay ourselves what to ourselves is debt:
What to ourselves in passion we propose,
The passion ending, doth the purpose lose.
The violence of either grief or joy
Their own enactures with themselves destroy:
Where joy most revels, grief doth most lament;
Grief joys, joy grieves, on slender accident.
This world is not for aye, nor 'tis not strange
That even our loves should with our fortunes change,
For 'tis a question left us yet to prove,
Whether love lead fortune, or else fortune love.
The great man down, you mark his favorite flies;
The poor advanced makes friends of enemies.
And hitherto doth love on fortune tend;
For who not needs shall never lack a friend,
And who in want a hollow friend doth try,

Directly seasons him his enemy.
But, orderly to end where I begun,
Our wills and fates do so contrary run
That our devices still are overthrown;
Our thoughts are ours, their ends none of our own:
So think thou wilt no second husband wed;
But die thy thoughts when thy first lord is dead.

P. Queen. Nor earth to me give food, nor heaven light!
Sport and repose lock from me day and night!
To desperation turn my trust and hope!
An anchor's cheer in prison be my scope!
Each opposite, that blanks the face of joy
Meet what I would have well and it destroy!
Both here and hence pursue me lasting strife,
If, once a widow, ever I be wife!

Ham. If she should break it now!

P. King. 'Tis deeply sworn. Sweet, leave me here a while;
My spirits grow dull, and fain I would beguile
The tedious day with sleep. [*Sleeps.*

P. Queen. Sleep rock thy brain;
And never come mischance between us twain! [*Exit.*

Ham. Madam, how like you this play?

Queen. The lady doth protest too much, methinks.

Ham. O, but she'll keep her word.

King. Have you heard the argument? Is there no offence in't?

Ham. No, no, they do but jest, poison in jest; no offence i' the world.

King. What do you call the play?

Ham. The Mouse-trap. Marry, how? Tropically. This play is the image of a murder done in Vienna: Gonzago is the duke's name; his wife, Baptista: you shall see anon; 'tis a knavish piece of work; but what o' that? your majesty and we that have free souls, it touches us not: let the galled jade wince, our withers are unwrung.

Enter LUCIANUS.

This is one Lucianus, nephew to the king.

Oph. You are as good as a chorus, my lord.

Ham. I could interpret between you and your love, if I could see the puppets dallying.

Oph. You are keen, my lord, you are keen.

Ham. Begin, murderer; pox, leave thy damnable faces, and begin. Come: 'the croaking raven doth bellow for revenge.'

Luc. Thoughts black, hands apt, drugs fit, and time agreeing;
Confederate season, else no creature seeing;
Thou mixture rank, of midnight weeds collected,
With Hecate's ban thrice blasted, thrice infected,
Thy natural magic and dire property,
On wholesome life usurp immediately.

[*Pours the poison into the sleeper's ear.*

Ham. He poisons him i' the garden for his estate. His name's Gonzago: the story is extant, and written in very choice Italian: you shall see anon how the murderer gets the love of Gonzago's wife.

Oph. The king rises.

Ham. What, frighted with false fire!

Queen. How fares my lord?

Pol. Give o'er the play.

King. Give me some light. Away!

Pol. Lights, lights, lights!

[*Exeunt all but Hamlet and Horatio.*

Ham. Why, let the stricken deer go weep,
The hart ungalled play;
For some must watch, while some must sleep:
So runs the world away.

Would not this, sir, and a forest of feathers—if the rest of my fortunes turn Turk with me—with two Provincial roses on my razed shoes, get me a fellowship in a cry of players, sir?

Hor. Half a share.

Ham. A whole one, I.

For thou dost know, O Damon dear,
This realm dismantled was
Of Jove himself; and now reigns here
A very, very—pajock.

Hor. You might have rhymed.

Ham. O good Horatio, I'll take the ghost's word for a thousand pound. Didst perceive?

Hor. Very well, my lord.

Ham. Upon the talk of the poisoning?

Hor. I did very well note him.

Ham. Ah, ha! Come, some music! come, the recorders!

For if the king like not the comedy,
When then, belike, he likes it not, perdy.
Come, some music!

Re-enter ROSENCRANTZ *and* GUILDENSTERN.

Guil. Good my lord, vouchsafe me a word with you.

Ham. Sir, a whole history.

Guil. The king, sir,—

Ham. Ay, sir, what of him?

Guil. Is in his retirement marvelous distempered.

Ham. With drink, sir?

Guil. No, my lord, rather with choler.

Ham. Your wisdom should show itself more richer to signify this to his doctor; for, for me to put him to his purgation would perhaps plunge him into far more choler.

Guil. Good my lord, put your discourse into some frame, and start not so wildly from my affair.

Ham. I am tame, sir: pronounce.

Guil. The queen, your mother, in most great affliction of spirit, hath sent me to you.

Ham. You are welcome.

Guil. Nay, good my lord, this courtesy is not of the right breed. If it shall please you to make me a wholesome answer, I will do your mother's commandment: if not, your pardon and my return shall be the end of my business.

Ham. Sir, I cannot.

Guil. What, my lord?

Ham. Make you a wholesome answer; my wit's diseased: but, sir, such answer as I can make, you shall command; or rather, as you say, my mother: therefore no more, but to the matter: my mother, you say,—

Ros. Then thus she says; your behavior hath struck her into amazement and admiration.

Ham. O wonderful son, that can so astonish a mother! But is there no sequel at the heels of this mother's admiration? Impart.

Ros. She desires to speak with you in her closet, ere you go to bed.

Ham. We shall obey, were she ten times our mother. Have you any further trade with us?

Ros. My lord, you once did love me.

Ham. So I do still, by these pickers and stealers.

Ros. Good my lord, what is your cause of distemper? you do surely bar the door upon your own liberty, if you deny your griefs to your friend.

Ham. Sir, I lack advancement.

Ros. How can that be, when you have the voice of the king himself for your succession in Denmark?

Ham. Ay, sir, but 'While the grass grows,'—the proverb is something musty.

Re-enter PLAYERS *with recorders.*

O, the recorders! let me see one. To withdraw

with you:—why do you go about to recover the wind of me, as if you would drive me into a toil?

Guil. O, my lord, if my duty be too bold, my love is too unmannerly.

Ham. I do not well understand that. Will you play upon this pipe?

Guil. My lord, I cannot.

Ham. I pray you.

Guil. Believe me, I cannot.

Ham. I do beseech you.

Guil. I know no touch of it, my lord.

Ham. 'Tis as easy as lying: govern these ventages with your fingers and thumb, give it breath with your mouth, and it will discourse most eloquent music. Look you, these are the stops.

Guil. But these cannot I command to any utterance of harmony; I have not the skill.

Ham. Why, look you now, how unworthy a thing you make of me! You would play upon me; you would seem to know my stops; you would pluck out the heart of my mystery; you would sound me from my lowest note to the top of my compass: and there is much music, excellent voice, in this little organ; yet cannot you make it speak. 'Sblood, do you think I am easier to be played on than a pipe? Call me what instrument you will, though you can fret me, yet you cannot play upon me.

Re-enter POLONIUS.

God bless you, sir!

Pol. My lord, the queen would speak with you, and presently.

Ham. Do you see yonder cloud that's almost in shape of a camel?

Pol. By the mass, and 'tis like a camel, indeed.

Ham. Methinks it is like a weasel.

Pol. It is backed like a weasel.

Ham. Or like a whale?

Pol. Very like a whale.

Ham. Then I will come to my mother by and by. They fool me to the top of my bent. I will come by and by.

Pol. I will say so. [*Exit Polonius.*

Ham. 'By and by' is easily said. Leave me, friends.

[*Exeunt all but Hamlet.*

'Tis now the very witching time of night,
When churchyards yawn and hell itself breathes out
Contagion to this world: now could I drink hot blood,
And do such bitter business as the day
Would quake to look on. Soft! now to my mother.
O heart, lose not thy nature; let not ever
The soul of Nero enter this firm bosom:
Let me be cruel, not unnatural:
I will speak daggers to her, but use none;
My tongue and soul in this be hypocrites;
How in my words soever she be shent,
To give them seals never, my soul, consent! [*Exit.*

Scene III

A room in the castle.

Enter King, Rosencrantz, *and* Guildenstern.

King. I like him not, nor stands it safe with us
To let his madness range. Therefore prepare you;
I your commission will forthwith dispatch,
And he to England shall along with you:
The terms of our estate may not endure
Hazard so near us as doth hourly grow
Out of his lunacies.

Guil. We will ourselves provide:
Most holy and religious fear it is
To keep those many many bodies safe
That live and feed upon your majesty.

Ros. The single and peculiar life is bound
With all the strength and armor of the mind
To keep itself from noyance; but much more
That spirit upon whose weal depends and rests
The lives of many. The cease of majesty
Dies not alone, but, like a gulf, doth draw
What's near it with it: it is a massy wheel,
Fix'd on the summit of the highest mount,
To whose huge spokes ten thousand lesser things
Are mortised and adjoin'd; which, when it falls,
Each small annexment, petty consequence,
Attends the boisterous ruin. Never alone
Did the king sigh, but with a general groan.

King. Arm you, I pray you, to this speedy voyage,
For we will fetters put about this fear,
Which now goes too free-footed.

Ros.
Guil. } We will haste us.

[*Exeunt Rosencrantz and Guildenstern.*

Enter POLONIUS.

Pol. My lord, he's going to his mother's closet:
Behind the arras I'll convey myself,
To hear the process: I'll warrant she'll tax him home:
And, as you said, and wisely was it said,
'Tis meet that some more audience than a mother,
Since nature makes them partial, should o'erhear
The speech, of vantage. Fare you well, my liege:
I'll call upon you ere you go to bed,
And tell you what I know.

King. Thanks, dear my lord.

[*Exit Polonius.*

O, my offence is rank, it smells to heaven;
It hath the primal eldest curse upon't,
A brother's murder. Pray can I not,
Though inclination be as sharp as will:
My stronger guilt defeats my strong intent,
And like a man to double business bound,
I stand in pause where I shall first begin,
And both neglect. What if this cursed hand

Were thicker than itself with brother's blood,
Is there not rain enough in the sweet heavens
To wash it white as snow? Whereto serves mercy
But to confront the visage of offence?
And what's in prayer but this twofold force,
To be forestalled ere we come to fall,
Or pardon'd being down? Then I'll look up;
My fault is past. But O, what form of prayer
Can serve my turn? 'Forgive me my foul murder'?
That cannot be, since I am still possess'd
Of those effects for which I did the murder,
My crown, mine own ambition and my queen.
May one be pardon'd and retain the offence?
In the corrupted currents of this world
Offence's gilded hand may shove by justice,
And oft 'tis seen the wicked prize itself
Buys out the law: but 'tis not so above;
There is no shuffling, there the action lies
In his true nature; and we ourselves compell'd,
Even to the teeth and forehead of our faults,
To give in evidence. What then? what rests?
Try what repentance can: what can it not?
Yet what can it when one can not repent?
O wretched state! O bosom black as death!
O limed soul, that struggling to be free,
Art more engaged! Help, angels! Make assay!
Bow, stubborn knees, and, heart with strings of steel,

Be soft as sinews of the new-born babe!
All may be well. [*Retires and kneels.*

Enter HAMLET.

Ham. Now might I do it pat, now he is praying;
And now I'll do't. And so he goes to heaven:
And so am I revenged. That would be scann'd;
A villain kills my father; and for that,
I, his sole son, do this same villain send
To heaven.
O, this is hire and salary, not revenge.
He took my father grossly, full of bread,
With all his crimes broad blown, as flush as
May;
And how his audit stands who knows save heaven?
But in our circumstance and course of thought,
'Tis heavy with him: and am I then revenged,
To take him in the purging of his soul,
When he is fit and season'd for his passage?
No!
Up, sword, and know thou a more horrid hent:
When he is drunk asleep, or in his rage,
Or in the incestuous pleasure of his bed;
At gaming, swearing, or about some act
That has no relish of salvation in't;
Then trip him, that his heels may kick at heaven,
And that his soul may be as damn'd and black
As hell, whereto it goes. My mother stays:
This physic but prolongs thy sickly days. [*Exit.*

King. [*Rising*] My words fly up, my thoughts remain below:
Words without thoughts never to heaven go. [*Exit.*

SCENE IV

The Queen's closet.

Enter QUEEN *and* POLONIUS.

Pol. He will come straight. Look you lay home to him:
Tell him his pranks have been too broad to bear with,
And that your grace hath screen'd and stood between
Much heat and him. I'll sconce me even here.
Pray you, be round with him.
Ham. [*Within*] Mother, mother, mother!
Queen. I'll warrant you; fear me not. Withdraw, I hear him coming. [*Polonius hides behind the arras.*

Enter HAMLET.

Ham. Now, mother, what's the matter?
Queen. Hamlet, thou hast thy father much offended.
Ham. Mother, you have my father much offended.
Queen. Come, come, you answer with an idle tongue.
Ham. Go, go, you question with a wicked tongue.
Queen. Why, how now, Hamlet!
Ham. What's the matter now?
Queen. Have you forgot me?
Ham. No, by the rood, not so:
You are the queen, your husband's brother's wife;
And—would it were not so!—you are my mother.

Queen. Nay, then, I'll set those to you that can speak.

Ham. Come, come, and sit you down; you shall not budge;
You go not till I set you up a glass
Where you may see the inmost part of you.

Queen. What wilt thou do? thou wilt not murder me?
Help, help, ho!

Pol. [*Behind*] What, ho! help, help, help!

Ham. [*Drawing*] How now! a rat? Dead, for a ducat, dead! [*Makes a pass through the arras.*

Pol. [*Behind*] O, I am slain! [*Falls and dies.*

Queen. O me, what hast thou done?

Ham. Nay, I know not:
Is it the king?

Queen. O, what a rash and bloody deed is this!

Ham. A bloody deed! almost as bad, good mother,
As kill a king, and marry with his brother.

Queen. As kill a king!

Ham. Ay, lady, 'twas my word.
[*Lifts up the arras and discovers Polonius.*
Thou wretched, rash, intruding fool, farewell!
I took thee for thy better: take thy fortune;
Thou find'st to be too busy is some danger.
Leave wringing of your hands: peace! sit you down,
And let me wring your heart: for so I shall,
If it be made of penetrable stuff;
If damned custom have not brass'd it so
That it be proof and bulwark against sense.

Queen. What have I done, that thou darest wag thy tongue
In noise so rude against me?

Ham. Such an act
That blurs the grace and blush of modesty,
Calls virtue hypocrite, takes off the rose
From the fair forehead of innocent love
And sets a blister there, makes marriage vows
As false as dicers' oaths: O, such a deed
As from the body of contraction plucks
The very soul, and sweet religion makes
A rhapsody of words: heaven's face doth glow;
Yea, this solidity and compound mass,
With tristful visage, as against the doom,
Is thought-sick at the act.

Queen. Ay me, what act,
That roars so loud and thunders in the index?

Ham. Look here, upon this picture, and on this,
The counterfeit presentment of two brothers.
See, what a grace was seated on this brow;
Hyperion's curls, the front of Jove himself,
An eye like Mars, to threaten and command;
A station like the herald Mercury
New-lighted on a heaven-kissing hill;
A combination and a form indeed,
Where every god did seem to set his seal,
To give the world assurance of a man:
This was your husband. Look you now, what follows:
Here is your husband; like a mildew'd ear,
Blasting his wholesome brother. Have you eyes?
Could you on this fair mountain leave to feed,
And batten on this moor? Ha! have you eyes?

You cannot call it love, for at your age
The hey-day in the blood is tame, it's humble,
And waits upon the judgment: and what judgment
Would step from this to this? Sense sure you have,
Else could you not have motion: but sure, that sense
Is apoplex'd: for madness would not err,
Nor sense to ecstasy was ne'er so thrall'd
But it reserved some quantity of choice,
To serve in such a difference. What devil was't
That thus hath cozen'd you at hoodman-blind?
Eyes without feeling, feeling without sight,
Ears without hands or eyes, smelling sans all,
Or but a sickly part of one true sense
Could not so mope.
O shame! where is thy blush? Rebellious hell,
If thou canst mutine in a matron's bones,
To flaming youth let virtue be as wax,
And melt in her own fire: proclaim no shame
When the compulsive ardor gives the charge,
Since frost itself as actively doth burn
And reason pandars will.

Queen. O Hamlet, speak no more:
Thou turn'st mine eyes into my very soul,
And there I see such black and grained spots
As will not leave their tinct.

Ham. A murderer and a villain;
A slave that is not twentieth part the tithe
Of your precedent lord; a vice of kings;
A cutpurse of the empire and the rule,

That from a shelf the precious diadem stole
And put it in his pocket!

Queen. No more!

Ham. A king of shreds and patches—

Enter Ghost.

Save me, and hover o'er me with your wings,
You heavenly guards! What would your gracious figure?

Queen. Alas, he's mad!

Ham. Do you not come your tardy son to chide,
That, lapsed in time and passion, lets go by
The important acting of your dread command?
O, say!

Ghost. Do not forget: this visitation
Is but to whet thy almost blunted purpose.
But, look, amazement on thy mother sits:
O, step between her and her fighting soul:
Conceit in weakest bodies strongest works:
Speak to her, Hamlet.

Ham. How is it with you, lady?

Queen. Alas, how is't with you,
That you do bend your eye on vacancy
And with the incorporal air do hold discourse?
Forth at your eyes your spirits wildly peep;
And, as the sleeping soldiers in the alarm,
Your bedded hairs, like life in excrements,
Start up and stand an end. O gentle son,
Upon the heat and flame of thy distemper
Sprinkle cool patience. Whereon do you look?

Ham. On him, on him! Look you, how pale he glares!
His form and cause conjoin'd, preaching to stones,
Would make them capable. Do not look upon me,
Lest with this piteous action you convert
My stern effects: then what I have to do
Will want true color; tears perchance for blood.

Queen. To whom do you speak this?

Ham. Do you see nothing there?

Queen Nothing at all; yet all that is I see.

Ham. Nor did you nothing hear?

Queen. No, nothing but ourselves.

Ham. Why, look you there! look, how it steals away!
My father, in his habit as he lived!
Look, where he goes, even now, out at the portal!
[*Exit Ghost.*

Queen. This is the very coinage of your brain:
This bodiless creation ecstasy
Is very cunning in.

Ham. Ecstasy!
My pulse, as yours, doth temperately keep time,
And makes as healthful music: it is not madness
That I have utter'd: bring me to the test,
And I the matter will re-word, which madness
Would gambol from. Mother, for love of grace,
Lay not that flattering unction to your soul,
That not your trespass, but my madness speaks:
It will but skin and film the ulcerous place,
Whiles rank corruption, mining all within,
Infects unseen. Confess yourself to heaven;
Repent what's past, avoid what is to come,

And do not spread the compost on the weeds,
To make them ranker. Forgive me this my virtue,
For in the fatness of these pursy times
Virtue itself of vice must pardon beg,
Yea, curb and woo for leave to do him good.

Queen. O Hamlet, thou hast cleft my heart in twain.

Ham. O, throw away the worser part of it,
And live the purer with the other half.
Good night: but go not to my uncle's bed;
Assume a virtue, if you have it not.
That monster, custom, who all sense doth eat,
Of habits devil, is angel yet in this,
That to the use of actions fair and good
He likewise gives a frock or livery,
That aptly is put on. Refrain to-night,
And that shall lend a kind of easiness
To the next abstinence; the next more easy;
For use almost can change the stamp of nature,
And either . . . the devil, or throw him out
With wondrous potency. Once more, good night:
And when you are desirous to be blest,
I'll blessing beg of you. For this same lord,
[*Pointing to Polonius.*
I do repent: but heaven hath pleased it so,
To punish me with this and this with me,
That I must be their scourge and minister.
I will bestow him, and will answer well
The death I gave him. So, again, good night.
I must be cruel, only to be kind:

Thus bad begins, and worse remains behind.
One word more, good lady.
Queen. What shall I do?
Ham. Not this, by no means, that I bid you do:
Let the bloat king tempt you again to bed;
Pinch wanton on your cheek, call you his mouse;
And let him, for a pair of reechy kisses,
Or paddling in your neck with his damn'd fingers,
Make you to ravel all this matter out,
That I essentially am not in madness,
But mad in craft. 'Twere good you let him know;
For who, that's but a queen, fair, sober, wise,
Would from a paddock, from a bat, a gib,
Such dear concernings hide? who would do so?
No, in despite of sense and secrecy,
Unpeg the basket on the house's top,
Let the birds fly, and like the famous ape,
To try conclusions, in the basket creep,
And break your own neck down.
Queen. Be thou assured, if words be made of breath,
And breath of life, I have no life to breathe
What thou hast said to me.
Ham. I must to England; you know that?
Queen. Alack,
I had forgot: 'tis so concluded on.
Ham. There's letters seal'd: and my two schoolfellows,
Whom I will trust as I will adders fang'd,
They bear the mandate; they must sweep my way,
And marshal me to knavery. Let it work;
For 'tis the sport to have the enginer

Hoist with his own petar: and't shall go hard
But I will delve one yard below their mines,
And blow them at the moon: O, 'tis most sweet,
When in one line two crafts directly meet.
This man shall set me packing:
I'll lug the guts into the neighbor room.
Mother, good night. Indeed this counselor
Is now most still, most secret and most grave,
Who was in life a foolish prating knave.
Come, sir, to draw toward an end with you.
Good night, mother.
[*Exeunt severally; Hamlet dragging in Polonius.*

ACT FOURTH

Scene I

A room in the castle.

Enter King, Queen, Rosencrantz, *and* Guildenstern.

King. There's matter in these sighs, these profound heaves:
You must translate: 'tis fit we understand them.
Where is your son?
Queen. Bestow this place on us a little while.
[*Exeunt Rosencrantz and Guildenstern.*
Ah, mine own lord, what have I seen to-night!
King. What, Gertrude? How does Hamlet?
Queen. Mad as the sea and wind, when both contend

Which is the mightier: in his lawless fit,
Behind the arras hearing something stir,
Whips out his rapier, cries 'A rat, a rat!'
And, in this brainish apprehension, kills
The unseen good old man.

King. O heavy deed!
It had been so with us, had we been there:
His liberty is full of threats to all,
To you yourself, to us, to every one.
Alas, how shall this bloody deed be answer'd?
It will be laid to us, whose providence
Should have kept short, restrain'd and out of haunt,
This mad young man: but so much was our love,
We would not understand what was most fit,
But, like the owner of a foul disease,
To keep it from divulging, let it feed
Even on the pith of life. Where is he gone?

Queen. To draw apart the body he hath kill'd:
O'er whom his very madness, like some ore
Among a mineral of metals base,
Shows itself pure; he weeps for what is done.

King. O Gertrude, come away!
The sun no sooner shall the mountains touch,
But we will ship him hence: and this vile deed
We must, with all our majesty and skill,
Both countenance and excuse. Ho, Guildenstern!

Re-enter ROSENCRANTZ *and* GUILDENSTERN.

Friends both, go join you with some further aid:
Hamlet in madness hath Polonius slain,

And from his mother's closet hath he dragg'd him:
Go seek him out; speak fair, and bring the body
Into the chapel. I pray you, haste in this.

[*Exeunt Rosencrantz and Guildenstern.*

Come, Gertrude, we'll call up our wisest friends;
And let them know, both what we mean to do,
And what's untimely done. . . . .
Whose whisper o'er the world's diameter,
As level as the cannon to his blank,
Transports his poison'd shot, may miss our name
And hit the woundless air. O, come away!
My soul is full of discord and dismay. [*Exeunt.*

Scene II

Another room in the castle.

Enter Hamlet.

Ham. Safely stowed.

Ros., *Guil.* [*Within*] Hamlet! Lord Hamlet.

Ham. But soft, what noise? who calls on Hamlet?
O, here they come.

Enter Rosencrantz *and* Guildenstern.

Ros. What have you done, my lord, with the dead body?

Ham. Compounded it with dust, whereto 'tis kin.

Ros. Tell us where 'tis, that we may take it thence
And bear it to the chapel.

Ham. Do not believe it.

Ros. Believe what?

Ham. That I can keep your counsel and not mine own. Besides, to be demanded of a sponge! what replication should be made by the son of a king?

Ros. Take you me for a sponge, my lord?

Ham. Ay, sir, that soaks up the king's countenance, his rewards, his authorities. But such officers do the king best service in the end: he keeps them, like an ape, in the corner of his jaw; first mouthed, to be last swallowed: when he needs what you have gleaned, it is but squeezing you, and, sponge, you shall be dry again.

Ros. I understand you not, my lord.

Ham. I am glad of it: a knavish speech sleeps in a foolish ear.

Ros. My lord, you must tell us where the body is, and go with us to the king.

Ham. The body is with the king, but the king is not with the body. The king is a thing—

Guil. A thing, my lord?

Ham. Of nothing: bring me to him. Hide fox, and all after. [*Exeunt.*

SCENE III

Another room in the castle.

Enter KING, *attended.*

King. I have sent to seek him, and to find the body.
How dangerous is it that this man goes loose!
Yet must not we put the strong law on him:
He's loved of the distracted multitude,
Who like not in their judgment, but their eyes;
And where 'tis so, the offender's scourge is weigh'd,
But never the offence. To bear all smooth and even,
This sudden sending him away must seem
Deliberate pause: diseases desperate grown
By desperate appliance are relieved,
Or not at all.

Enter ROSENCRANTZ.

How now! what hath befall'n?

Ros. Where the dead body is bestow'd, my lord,
We cannot get from him.

King. But where is he?

Ros. Without, my lord; guarded, to know your pleasure.

King. Bring him before us.

Ros. Ho, Guildenstern! bring in my lord.

Enter HAMLET *and* GUILDENSTERN.

King. Now, Hamlet, where's Polonius?

Ham. At supper.

King. At supper! where?

Ham. Not where he eats, but where he is eaten: a certain convocation of politic worms are e'en at him. Your worm is your only emperor for diet: we fat all creatures else to fat us, and we fat ourselves for maggots: your fat king and your lean beggar is but variable service, two dishes, but to one table: that's the end.

King. Alas, alas!

Ham. A man may fish with the worm that hath eat of a king, and eat of the fish that hath fed of that worm.

King. What dost thou mean by this?

Ham. Nothing but to show you how a king may go a progress through the guts of a beggar.

King. Where is Polonius?

Ham. In heaven; send thither to see: if your messenger find him not there, seek him i' the other place yourself. But indeed, if you find him not within this month, you shall nose him as you go up the stairs into the lobby.

King. Go seek him there. [*To some Attendants.*

Ham. He will stay till you come. [*Exeunt Attendants.*

King. Hamlet, this deed, for thine especial safety,—
Which we do tender, as we dearly grieve
For that which thou hast done,—must send thee hence
With fiery quickness: therefore prepare thyself;
The bark is ready, and the wind at help,
The associates tend, and every thing is bent
For England.

Ham. For England?

King. Ay, Hamlet.

Ham. Good.

King. So is it, if thou knew'st our purposes.

Ham. I see a cherub that sees them. But, come; for England! Farewell, dear mother.

King. Thy loving father, Hamlet.

Ham. My mother: father and mother is man and wife; man and wife is one flesh, and so, my mother. Come, for England! [*Exit.*

King. Follow him at foot; tempt him with speed aboard;
Delay it not; I'll have him hence to-night:
Away! for every thing is seal'd and done
That else leans on the affair: pray you, make haste.
[*Exeunt Rosencrantz and Guildenstern.*
And, England, if my love thou hold'st at aught—
As my great power thereof may give thee sense,
Since yet thy cicatrice looks raw and red
After the Danish sword, and thy free awe
Pays homage to us—thou mayst not coldly set
Our sovereign process; which imports at full,
By letters congruing to that effect,
The present death of Hamlet. Do it, England;
For like the hectic in my blood he rages,
And thou must cure me: till I know 'tis done,
Howe'er my haps, my joys were ne'er begun.
[*Exit.*

SCENE IV

A plain in Denmark.

Enter FORTINBRAS, *a* CAPTAIN *and* SOLDIERS, *marching.*

For. Go, captain, from me greet the Danish king;
Tell him that, by his license, Fortinbras
Craves the conveyance of a promised march
Over his kingdom. You know the rendezvous.
If that his majesty would aught with us,
We shall express our duty in his eye;
And let him know so.
Cap. I will do't, my lord.
For. Go softly on.
[*Exeunt Fortinbras and Soldiers.*

Enter HAMLET, ROSENCRANTZ, GUILDENSTERN, *and others.*

Ham. Good sir, whose powers are these?
Cap. They are of Norway, sir.
Ham. How purposed, sir, I pray you?
Cap. Against some part of Poland.
Ham. Who commands them, sir?
Cap. The nephew to old Norway, Fortinbras.
Ham. Goes it against the main of Poland, sir,
Or for some frontier?
Cap. Truly to speak, and with no addition,
We go to gain a little patch of ground
That hath in it no profit but the name.

To pay five ducats, five, I would not farm it;
Nor will it yield to Norway or the Pole
A ranker rate, should it be sold in fee.

Ham. Why, then the Polack never will defend it.

Cap. Yes, it is already garrison'd.

Ham. Two thousand souls and twenty thousand ducats
Will not debate the question of this straw:
This is the imposthume of much wealth and peace,
That inward breaks, and shows no cause without
Why the man dies. I humbly thank you, sir.

Cap. God be wi' you, sir. [*Exit.*

Ros. Will't please you go, my lord?

Ham. I'll be with you straight. Go a little before.
[*Exeunt all but Hamlet.*
How all occasions do inform against me,
And spur my dull revenge! What is a man,
If his chief good and market of his time
Be but to sleep and feed? a beast, no more.
Sure, he that made us with such large discourse,
Looking before and after, gave us not
That capability and god-like reason
To fust in us unused. Now, whether it be
Bestial oblivion, or some craven scruple
Of thinking too precisely on the event,—
A thought which, quarter'd, hath but one part wisdom
And ever three parts coward,—I do not know
Why yet I live to say 'This thing's to do,'
Sith I have cause and will and strength and means
To do't. Examples gross as earth exhort me:
Witness this army of such mass and charge

Led by a delicate and tender prince,
Whose spirit with divine ambition puff'd
Makes mouths at the invisible event,
Exposing what is mortal and unsure
To all that fortune, death and danger dare,
Even for an egg-shell. Rightly to be great
Is not to stir without great argument,
But greatly to find quarrel in a straw
When honor's at the stake. How stand I then,
That have a father kill'd, a mother stain'd,
Excitements of my reason and my blood,
And let all sleep, while to my shame I see
The imminent death of twenty thousand men,
That for a fantasy and trick of fame
Go to their graves like beds, fight for a plot
Whereon the numbers cannot try the cause,
Which is not tomb enough and continent
To hide the slain? O, from this time forth,
My thoughts be bloody, or be nothing worth!
[*Exit.*

SCENE V

Elsinore. A room in the castle.

Enter QUEEN, HORATIO, *and a* GENTLEMAN.

Queen. I will not speak with her.
Gent. She is importunate, indeed distract:
Her mood will needs be pitied.
Queen. What would she have?

Gent. She speaks much of her father; says she hears
There's tricks i' the world, and hems, and beats her heart,
Spurns enviously at straws, speaks things in doubt,
That carry but half sense: her speech is nothing,
Yet the unshaped use of it doth move
The hearers to collection; they aim at it,
And botch the words up fit to their own thoughts;
Which, as her winks, and nods, and gestures yield them,
Indeed would make one think there might be thought,
Though nothing sure, yet much unhappily.

Hor. 'Twere good she were spoken with, for she may strew
Dangerous conjectures in ill-breeding minds.

Queen. Let her come in. [*Exit Gentleman.*
[*Aside*] To my sick soul, as sin's true nature is,
Each toy seems prologue to some great amiss:
So full of artless jealousy is guilt,
It spills itself in fearing to be spilt.

Re-enter HORATIO, *with* OPHELIA.

Oph. Where is the beauteous majesty of Denmark?

Queen. How now, Ophelia!

Oph. [*Sings*] How should I your true love know
From another one?
By his cockle hat and staff,
And his sandal shoon.

Queen. Alas, sweet lady, what imports this song?

Oph. Say you? nay, pray you, mark.

[*Sings*] He is dead and gone, lady,
He is dead and gone;
At his head a grass-green turf,
At his heels a stone.

Queen. Nay, but, Ophelia,—

Oph. Pray you, mark.
[*Sings*] White his shroud as the mountain snow,—

Enter KING.

Queen. Alas, look here, my lord.

Oph. [*Sings*] Larded with sweet flowers;
Which bewept to the grave did go
With true-love showers.

King. How do you, pretty lady?

Oph. Well, God 'ild you! They say the owl was a baker's daughter. Lord, we know what we are, but know not what we may be. God be at your table!

King. Conceit upon her father.

Oph. Pray you, let's have no words of this; but when they ask you what it means, say you this:
[*Sings*] To-morrow is Saint Valentine's day
All in the morning betime,
And I a maid at your window,
To be your Valentine.

King. How long hath she been thus?

Oph. I hope all will be well. We must be patient: but I cannot choose but weep, to think they should lay him i' the cold ground. My brother shall know of it: and so I thank you

for your good counsel. Come, my coach!
Good night, ladies; good night, sweet ladies;
good night, good night. [*Exit.*

King. Follow her close; give her good watch, I pray you. [*Exit Horatio.*
O, this is the poison of deep grief; it springs
All from her father's death. O Gertrude, Gertrude,
When sorrows come, they come not single spies,
But in battalions! First, her father slain:
Next, your son gone; and he most violent author
Of his own just remove: the people muddied,
Thick and unwholesome in their thoughts and whispers,
For good Polonius' death; and we have done but greenly,
In hugger-mugger to inter him: poor Ophelia
Divided from herself and her fair judgment,
Without the which we are pictures, or mere beasts:
Last, and as much containing as all these,
Her brother is in secret come from France,
Feeds on his wonder, keeps himself in clouds,
And wants not buzzers to infect his ear
With pestilent speeches of his father's death;
Wherein necessity, of matter beggar'd,
Will nothing stick our person to arraign
In ear and ear. O my dear Gertrude, this,
Like to a murdering-piece, in many places
Gives me superfluous death. [*A noise within.*

Queen. Alack, what noise is this?

King. Where are my Switzers? Let them guard the door.

Enter another GENTLEMAN.

What is the matter?
Gent. Save yourself, my lord:
The ocean, overpeering of his list,
Eats not the flats with more impetuous haste
Than young Laertes, in a riotous head,
O'erbears your officers. The rabble call him lord;
And, as the world were now but to begin,
Antiquity forgot, custom not known,
The ratifiers and props of every word,
They cry 'Choose we; Laertes shall be king!'
Caps, hands, and tongues applaud it to the clouds,
'Laertes shall be king, Laertes king!'
Queen. How cheerfully on the false trail they cry!
O, this is counter, you false Danish dogs!
[*Noise within.*
King. The doors are broke.

Enter LAERTES, *armed;* DANES *following.*

Laer. Where is this king? Sirs, stand you all without.
Danes. No, let's come in.
Laer. I pray you, give me leave.
Danes. We will, we will. [*They retire without the door.*
Laer. I thank you: keep the door. O thou vile king,
Give me my father!
Queen. Calmly, good Laertes.
Laer. That drop of blood that's calm proclaims me bastard;
Cries cuckold to my father, brands the harlot

Even here, between the chaste unsmirched brows
Of my true mother.

King. What is the cause, Laertes,
That thy rebellion looks so giant-like?
Let him go, Gertrude; do not fear our person:
There's such divinity doth hedge a king,
That treason can but peep to what it would,
Acts little of his will. Tell me, Laertes,
Why thou art thus incensed. Let him go, Gertrude.
Speak, man.

Laer. Where is my father?

King. Dead.

Queen. But not by him.

King. Let him demand his fill.

Laer. How came he dead? I'll not be juggled with:
To hell, allegiance! vows, to the blackest devil!
Conscience and grace, to the profoundest pit!
I dare damnation. To this point I stand,
That both the worlds I give to negligence,
Let come what comes; only I'll be revenged
Most throughly for my father.

King. Who shall stay you?

Laer. My will, not all the world:
And for my means, I'll husband them so well,
They shall go far with little.

King. Good Laertes,
If you desire to know the certainty
Of your dear father's death, is't writ in your revenge,
That, swoopstake, you will draw both friend and foe,
Winner and loser?

Laer. None but his enemies.
King. Will you know them then?
Laer. To his good friends thus wide I'll ope my arms;
And like the kind life-rendering pelican,
Repast them with my blood.
King. Why, now you speak
Like a good child and a true gentleman.
That I am guiltless of your father's death,
And am most sensibly in grief for it,
It shall as level to your judgment pierce
As day does to your eye.
Danes. [*Within*] Let her come in.
Laer. How now! what noise is that?

Re-enter OPHELIA.

O heat, dry up my brains! tears seven times salt,
Burn out the sense and virtue of mine eye!
By heaven, thy madness shall be paid with weight,
Till our scale turn the beam. O rose of May!
Dear maid, kind sister, sweet Ophelia!
O heavens! is't possible a young maid's wits
Should be as mortal as an old man's life?
Nature is fine in love, and where 'tis fine,
It sends some precious instance of itself
After the thing it loves.
Oph. [*Sings*] They bore him barefaced on the bier:
Hey non nonny, nonny, hey nonny:
And in his grave rain'd many a tear,—
Fare you well, my dove!

Laer. Hadst thou thy wits, and didst persuade revenge,
It could not move thus.

Oph. [*Sings*] You must sing down a-down,
An you call him a-down-a.

O, how the wheel becomes it! It is the false steward, that stole his master's daughter.

Laer. This nothing's more than matter.

Oph. There's rosemary, that's for remembrance: pray, love, remember: and there is pansies, that's for thoughts.

Laer. A document in madness, thoughts and remembrance fitted.

Oph. There's fennel for you, and columbines: there's rue for you: and here's some for me: we may call it herb of grace o' Sundays: O, you must wear your rue with a difference. There's a daisy: I would give you some violets, but they withered all when my father died: they say he made a good end,—

[*Sings*] For bonnie sweet Robin is all my joy.

Laer. Thought and affliction, passion, hell itself,
She turns to favor and to prettiness.

Oph. [*Sings*] And will he not come again?
And will he not come again?
No, no, he is dead:
Go to thy death-bed:
He never will come again.

His beard was as white as snow,
All flaxen was his poll:

He is gone, he is gone,
And we cast away moan:
God ha' mercy on his soul!
And of all Christian souls, I pray God. God be wi' ye. [*Exit.*

Laer. Do you see this, O God?

King. Laertes, I must commune with your grief,
Or you deny me right. Go but apart,
Make choice of whom your wisest friends you will,
And they shall hear and judge 'twixt you and me:
If by direct or by collateral hand
They find us touch'd, we will our kingdom give,
Our crown, our life, and all that we call ours,
To you in satisfaction; but if not,
Be you content to lend your patience to us,
And we shall jointly labor with your soul
To give it due content.

Laer. Let this be so;
His means of death, his obscure funeral—
No trophy, sword, nor hatchment o'er his bones,
No noble rite nor formal ostentation—
Cry to be heard, as 'twere from heaven to earth,
That I must call't in question.

King. So you shall;
And where the offence is let the great axe fall.
I pray you, go with me. [*Exeunt.*

Scene VI

Another room in the castle.

Enter Horatio *and a* Servant.

Hor. What are they that would speak with me?
Serv. Sailors, sir: they say they have letters for you.
Hor. Let them come in. [*Exit Servant.*
I do not know from what part of the world
I should be greeted, if not from Lord Hamlet.

Enter Sailors.

First Sail. God bless you, sir.

Hor. Let him bless thee too.

First Sail. He shall, sir, an't please him. There's a letter for you, sir; it comes from the ambassador that was bound for England; if your name be Horatio, as I am let to know it is.

Hor. [*Reads*] 'Horatio, when thou shalt have overlooked this, give these fellows some means to the king: they have letters for him. Ere we were two days old at sea, a pirate of very warlike appointment gave us chase. Finding ourselves too slow of sail, we put on a compelled valor, and in the grapple I boarded them: on the instant they got clear of our ship; so I alone became their prisoner. They have dealt with me like thieves of mercy: but they knew what they did; I am to do a good turn for them. Let the king have the letters I have sent; and repair thou to me with as much speed as thou wouldest fly death. I have words to speak in thine ear will make thee dumb; yet are they much too light for the bore of the matter. These good fellows will bring thee where I am. Rosencrantz and Guildenstern hold their course for England: of them I have much to tell thee. Farewell.

'He that thou knowest thine, HAMLET.'

Come, I will make you way for these your letters;
And do't the speedier, that you may direct me
To him from whom you brought them. [*Exeunt.*

SCENE VII

Another room in the castle.

Enter KING *and* LAERTES.

King. Now must your conscience my acquittance seal,
And you must put me in your heart for friend,
Sith you have heard, and with a knowing ear,
That he which hath your noble father slain
Pursued my life.

Laer. It well appears: but tell me
Why you proceeded not against these feats,
So crimeful and so capital in nature,
As by your safety, wisdom, all things else,
You mainly were stirr'd up.

King. O, for two special reasons,

Which may to you, perhaps, seem much unsinew'd,
But yet to me they are strong. The queen his mother
Lives almost by his looks; and for myself—
My virtue or my plague, be it either which—
She's so conjunctive to my life and soul,
That, as the star moves not but in his sphere,
I could not but by her. The other motive,
Why to a public count I might not go,
Is the great love the general gender bear him;
Who, dipping all his faults in their affection,
Would, like the spring that turneth wood to stone,
Convert his gyves to graces; so that my arrows,
Too slightly timber'd for so loud a wind,
Would have reverted to my bow again,
And not where I had aim'd them.

Laer. And so have I a noble father lost;
A sister driven into desperate terms,
Whose worth, if praises may go back again,
Stood challenger on mount of all the age
For her perfections: but my revenge will come.

King. Break not your sleeps for that: you must not think
That we are made of stuff so flat and dull
That we can let our beard be shook with danger
And think it pastime. You shortly shall hear more:
I loved your father, and we love ourself;
And that, I hope, will teach you to imagine—

Enter a Messenger, *with letters.*

How now! what news?

Mess. Letters, my lord, from Hamlet:

This to your majesty; this to the queen.
King. From Hamlet! who brought them?
Mess. Sailors, my lord, they say; I saw them not:
They were given me by Claudio; he received them
Of him that brought them.
King.. Laertes, you shall hear them.
Leave us. [*Exit Messenger.*
[*Reads*] 'High and mighty, You shall know I am set naked on your kingdom. To-morrow shall I beg leave to see your kingly eyes: when I shall, first asking your pardon thereunto, recount the occasion of my sudden and more strange return.

'HAMLET.'

What should this mean? Are all the rest come back?
Or is it some abuse, and no such thing?
Laer. Know you the hand?
King. 'Tis Hamlet's character. 'Naked'!
And in a postscript here, he says 'alone.'
Can you advise me?
Laer. I'm lost in it, my lord. But let him come;
It warms the very sickness in my heart,
That I shall live and tell him to his teeth,
'Thus didest thou.'
King. If it be so, Laertes,—
As how should it be so? how otherwise?—
Will you be ruled by me?
Laer. Ay, my lord;
So you will not o'errule me to a peace.
King. To thine own peace. If he be now return'd,

As checking at his voyage, and that he means
No more to undertake it, I will work him
To an exploit, now ripe in my device,
Under the which he shall not choose but fall:
And for his death no wind of blame shall breathe,
But even his mother shall uncharge the practice
And call it accident.

Laer. My lord, I will be ruled;
The rather, if you could devise it so
That I might be the organ.

King. It falls right.
You have been talk'd of since your travel much,
And that in Hamlet's hearing, for a quality
Wherein, they say, you shine: your sum of parts
Did not together pluck such envy from him
As did that one, and that, in my regard,
Of the unworthiest siege.

Laer. What part is that, my lord?

King. A very riband in the cap of youth,
Yet needful too; for youth no less becomes
The light and careless livery that it wears
Than settled age his sables and his weeds,
Importing health and graveness. Two months since,
Here was a gentleman of Normandy:—
I've seen myself, and served against, the French,
And they can well on horseback: but this gallant
Had witchcraft in't; he grew unto his seat,
And to such wondrous doing brought his horse,
As had he been incorpsed and demi-natured
With the brave beast: so far he topp'd my thought,

That I, in forgery of shapes and tricks,
Come short of what he did.

Laer. A Norman was't?

King. A Norman.

Laer. Upon my life, Lamond.

King. The very same.

Laer. I know him well: he is the brooch indeed
And gem of all the nation.

King. He made confession of you,
And gave you such a masterly report
For art and exercise in your defence,
And for your rapier most especial,
That he cried out, 'twould be a sight indeed
If one could match you: the scrimers of their nation,
He swore, had neither motion, guard, nor eye,
If you opposed them. Sir, this report of his
Did Hamlet so envenom with his envy
That he could nothing do but wish and beg
Your sudden coming o'er, to play with him.
Now, out of this—

Laer. What out of this, my lord?

King. Laertes, was your father dear to you?
Or are you like the painting of a sorrow,
A face without a heart?

Laer. Why ask you this?

King. Not that I think you did not love your father,
But that I know love is begun by time,
And that I see, in passages of proof,
Time qualifies the spark and fire of it.

There lives within the very flame of love
A kind of wick or snuff that will abate it;
And nothing is at a like goodness still;
For goodness, growing to a plurisy,
Dies in his own too much: that we would do,
We should do when we would; for this 'would' changes
And hath abatements and delays as many
As there are tongues, are hands, are accidents;
And then this 'should' is like a spendthrift sigh,
That hurts by easing. But, to the quick o' the ulcer:—
Hamlet comes back: what would you undertake,
To show yourself your father's son in deed
More than in words?

Laer. To cut his throat i' the church.

King. No place, indeed, should murder sanctuarize;
Revenge should have no bounds. But, good Laertes,
Will you do this, keep close within your chamber.
Hamlet return'd shall know you are come home:
We'll put on those shall praise your excellence
And set a double varnish on the fame
The Frenchman gave you, bring you in fine together
And wager on your heads: he, being remiss,
Most generous and free from all contriving,
Will not peruse the foils, so that, with ease,
Or with a little shuffling, you may choose
A sword unbated, and in a pass of practice
Requite him for your father.

Laer. I will do't;
And for that purpose I'll anoint my sword.
I bought an unction of a mountebank,
So mortal that, but dip a knife in it,
Where it draws blood no cataplasm so rare,
Collected from all simples that have virtue
Under the moon, can save the thing from death
That is but scratch'd withal: I'll touch my point
With this contagion, that, if I gall him slightly,
It may be death.

King. Let's further think of this;
Weigh what convenience both of time and means
May fit us to our shape: if this should fail,
And that our drift look through our bad performance,
'Twere better not assay'd: therefore this project
Should have a back or second, that might hold
If this did blast in proof. Soft! let me see:
We'll make a solemn wager on your cunnings:
I ha't:
When in your motion you are hot and dry—
As make your bouts more violent to that end—
And that he calls for drink, I'll have prepared him
A chalice for the nonce, whereon but sipping,
If he by chance escape your venom'd stuck,
Our purpose may hold there.

Enter QUEEN.

How now, sweet queen!

Queen. One woe doth tread upon another's heel,
So fast they follow: your sister's drown'd, Laertes.

Laer. Drown'd! O, where?

Queen. There is a willow grows aslant a brook,
That shows his hoar leaves in the glassy stream;
There with fantastic garlands did she come
Of crow-flowers, nettles, daisies, and long purples
That liberal shepherds give a grosser name,
But our cold maids do dead men's fingers call them:
There, on the pendent boughs her coronet weeds
Clambering to hang, an envious sliver broke;
When down her weedy trophies and herself
Fell in the weeping brook. Her clothes spread wide,
And, mermaid-like, a while they bore her up:
Which time she chanted snatches of old tunes,
As one incapable of her own distress,
Or like a creature native and indued
Unto that element: but long it could not be
Till that her garments, heavy with their drink,
Pull'd the poor wretch from her melodious lay
To muddy death.

Laer. Alas, then, she is drown'd?

Queen. Drown'd, drown'd.

Laer. Too much of water hast thou, poor Ophelia,
And therefore I forbid my tears: but yet
It is our trick; nature her custom holds,
Let shame say what it will: when these are gone,
The woman will be out. Adieu, my lord:
I have a speech of fire that fain would blaze,
But that this folly douts it. [*Exit.*

King. Let's follow, Gertrude:
How much I had to do to calm his rage!

Now fear I this will give it start again;
Therefore let's follow. [*Exeunt.*

ACT FIFTH

SCENE I

A churchyard.

Enter two CLOWNS, *with spades, &c.*

First Clo. Is she to be buried in Christian burial that wilfully seeks her own salvation?

Sec. Clo. I tell thee she is; and therefore make her grave straight: the crowner hath sat on her, and finds it Christian burial.

First Clo. How can that be, unless she drowned herself in her own defence?

Sec. Clo. Why, 'tis found so.

First Clo. It must be 'se offendendo'; it cannot be else. For here lies the point: if I drown myself wittingly, it argues an act: and an act hath three branches; it is, to act, to do, and to perform: argal, she drowned herself wittingly.

Sec. Clo. Nay, but hear you, goodman delver,—

First Clo. Give me leave. Here lies the water; good: here stands the man; good: if the man go to this water and drown himself, it is, will he, nill he, he goes; mark you that; but if the water come to him and drown him, he drowns not himself: argal, he that is not guilty of his own death shortens not his own life.

Sec. Clo. But is this law?

First Clo. Ay, marry, is't; crowner's quest law.

Sec. Clo. Will you ha' the truth on't? If this had not been a gentlewoman, she should have been buried out o' Christian burial.

First Clo. Why, there thou say'st: and the more pity that great folk should have countenance in this world to drown or hang themselves, more than their even Christian. Come, my spade. There is no ancient gentlemen but gardeners, ditchers, and grave-makers: they hold up Adam's profession.

Sec. Clo. Was he a gentleman?

First Clo. A' was the first that ever bore arms.

Sec. Clo. Why, he had none.

First Clo. What, art a heathen? How dost thou understand the Scripture? The Scripture says Adam digged: could he dig without arms? I'll put another question to thee: if thou answerest me not to the purpose, confess thyself—

Sec. Clo. Go to.

First Clo. What is he that builds stronger than either the mason, the shipwright, or the carpenter?

Sec. Clo. The gallows-maker; for that frame outlives a thousand tenants.

First Clo. I like thy wit well, in good faith: the gallows does well; but how does it well? it does well to those that do ill: now, thou dost ill to say the gallows is built stronger than the church: argal, the gallows may do well to thee. To't again, come.

Sec. Clo. 'Who builds stronger than a mason, a shipwright, or a carpenter?'

First Clo. Ay, tell me that, and unyoke.

Sec. Clo. Marry, now I can tell.

First Clo. To't.

Sec. Clo. Mass, I cannot tell.

Enter HAMLET *and* HORATIO, *afar off.*

First Clo. Cudgel thy brains no more about it, for your dull ass will not mend his pace with beating; and when you are asked this question next, say 'a grave-maker': the houses that he makes last till doomsday. Go, get thee to Yaughan; fetch me a stoup of liquor.

[*Exit Sec. Clown.*

[*He digs, and sings.*

In youth, when I did love, did love,
Methought it was very sweet,
To contract, O, the time, for-a my behove,
O, methought, there was nothing meet.

Ham. Has this fellow no feeling of his business, that he sings at grave-making?

Hor. Custom hath made it in him a property of easiness.

Ham. 'Tis e'en so: the hand of little employment hath the daintier sense.

First Clo. [*Sings*] But age, with his stealing steps,
Hath claw'd me in his clutch,
And hath shipped me intil the land,
As if I had never been such.
[*Throws up a skull.*

Ham. That skull had a tongue in it, and could sing once: how the knave jowls it to the ground, as if it were Cain's jaw-bone, that did the first murder! It might be the pate of a politician, which this ass now o'er-reaches; one that would circumvent God, might it not?

Hor. It might, my lord.

Ham. Or of a courtier, which could say 'Good morrow, sweet lord! How dost thou, sweet lord?' This might be my lord such-a-one, that praised my lord such-a-one's horse, when he meant to beg it; might it not?

Hor. Ay, my lord.

Ham. Why, e'en so: and now my Lady Worm's; chapless, and knocked about the mazzard with a sexton's spade: here's fine revolution, an we had the trick to see't. Did these bones cost no more the breeding, but to play at loggats with 'em? mine ache to think on't.

First Clo. [*Sings*] A pick-axe, and a spade, a spade,
For and a shrouding sheet:

O, a pit of clay for to be made
For such a guest is meet.

[*Throws up another skull.*

Ham. There's another: why may not that be the skull of a lawyer? Where be his quiddities now, his quillets, his cases, his tenures, and his tricks? why does he suffer this rude knave now to knock him about the sconce with a dirty shovel, and will not tell him of his action of battery? Hum! This fellow might be in's time a great buyer of land, with his statutes, his recognizances, his fines, his double vouchers, his recoveries: is this the fine of his fines and the recovery of his recoveries, to have his fine pate full of fine dirt? will his vouchers vouch him no more of his purchases, and double ones too, than the length and breadth of a pair of indentures? The very conveyances of his lands will hardly lie in this box; and must the inheritor himself have no more, ha?

Hor. Not a jot more, my lord.

Ham. Is not parchment made of sheep-skins?

Hor. Ay, my lord, and of calf-skins too.

Ham. They are sheep and calves which seek out assurance in that. I will speak to this fellow. Whose grave's this, sirrah?

First Clo. Mine, sir.

[*Sings*] O, a pit of clay for to be made
For such a guest is meet.

Ham. I think it be thine indeed, for thou liest in't.

First Clo. You lie out on't, sir, and therefore 'tis not yours: for my part, I do not lie in't, and yet it is mine.

Ham. Thou dost lie in't, to be in't and say it is thine: 'tis for the dead, not for the quick; therefore thou liest.

First Clo. 'Tis a quick lie, sir; 'twill away again, from me to you.

Ham. What man dost thou dig it for?

First Clo. For no man, sir.

Ham. What woman, then?

First Clo. For none, neither.

Ham. Who is to be buried in't?

First Clo. One that was a woman, sir; but, rest her soul, she's dead.

Ham. How absolute the knave is! we must speak by the card, or equivocation will undo us. By the Lord, Horatio, these three years I have taken note of it; the age is grown so picked that the toe of the peasant comes so near the heel of the courtier, he galls his kibe. How long hast thou been a grave-maker?

First Clo. Of all the days i' the year, I came to't that day that our last king Hamlet o'ercame Fortinbras.

Ham. How long is that since?

First Clo. Cannot you tell that? every fool can tell that: it was that very day that young Hamlet was born: he that is mad, and sent into England.

Ham. Ay, marry, why was he sent into England?

First Clo. Why, because he was mad; he shall recover his wits there; or, if he do not, 'tis no great matter there.

Ham. Why?

First Clo. 'Twill not be seen in him there; there the men are as mad as he.

Ham. How came he mad?

First Clo. Very strangely, they say.

Ham. How 'strangely'?

First Clo. Faith, e'en with losing his wits.

Ham. Upon what ground?

First Clo. Why, here in Denmark: I have been sexton here, man and boy, thirty years.

Ham. How long will a man lie i' the earth ere he rot?

First Clo. I' faith, if he be not rotten before he die, he will last you some eight year or nine year: a tanner will last you nine year.

Ham. Why he more than another?

First Clo. Why, sir, his hide is so tanned with his trade that he will keep out water a great while; and your water is a sore decayer of your whoreson dead body. Here's a skull now: this skull has lain in the earth three and twenty years.

Ham. Whose was it?

First Clo. A whoreson mad fellow's it was: whose do you think it was?

Ham. Nay, I know not.

First Clo. A pestilence on him for a mad rogue! he poured a flagon of Rhenish on my head once. This same skull, sir, was Yorick's skull, the king's jester.

Ham. This?

First Clo. E'en that.

Ham. Let me see. [*Takes the skull.*] Alas, poor Yorick! I knew him, Horatio: a fellow of infinite jest, of most excellent fancy: he hath borne me on his back a thousand times; and now how abhorred in my imagination it is! my gorge rises at it. Here hung those lips that I have kissed I know not how oft. Where be your gibes now? your gambols? your songs? your flashes of merriment, that were wont to set the table on a roar? Not one now, to mock your own grinning? quite chap-fallen? Now get you to my lady's chamber, and tell her, let her paint an inch thick, to this favor she must come; make her laugh at that. Prithee, Horatio, tell me one thing.

Hor. What's that, my lord?

Ham. Dost thou think Alexander looked o' this fashion i' the earth?

Hor. E'en so.

Ham. And smelt so? pah! [*Puts down the skull.*

Hor. E'en so, my lord.

Ham. To what base uses we may return, Horatio! Why may not imagination trace the noble dust of Alexander, till he find it stopping a bung-hole?

Hor. 'Twere to consider too curiously, to consider so.

Ham. No, faith, not a jot; but to follow him thither with modesty enough and likelihood to lead it: as thus: Alexander died, Alexander was buried, Alexander returneth into dust; the dust is earth; of earth we make loam; and why of that loam, whereto he was converted, might they not stop a beer-barrel?

Imperious Cæsar, dead and turn'd to clay,
Might stop a hole to keep the wind away:
O, that that earth, which kept the world in awe,
Should patch a wall to expel the winter's flaw!

But soft! but soft! aside: here comes the king.

Enter PRIESTS, *&c, in procession; the* CORPSE *of* OPHELIA, LAERTES *and* MOURNERS *following;* KING, QUEEN, *their trains, &c.*

The queen, the courtiers: who is this they follow?
And with such maimed rites? This doth betoken
The corse they follow did with desperate hand
Fordo it own life: 'twas of some estate.
Couch we awhile, and mark. [*Retiring with Horatio.*

Laer. What ceremony else?

Ham. That is Laertes, a very noble youth: mark.

Laer. What ceremony else?

First Priest. Her obsequies have been as far enlarged
As we have warranty: her death was doubtful;

And, but that great command o'ersways the order,
She should in ground unsanctified have lodged
Till the last trumpet; for charitable prayers,
Shards, flints and pebbles should be thrown on her:
Yet here she is allow'd her virgin crants,
Her maiden strewments and the bringing home
Of bell and burial.

Laer. Must there no more be done?

First Priest. No more be done:
We should profane the service of the dead
To sing a requiem and such rest to her
As to peace-parted souls.

Laer. Lay her i' the earth:
And from her fair and unpolluted flesh
May violets spring! I tell thee, churlish priest,
A ministering angel shall my sister be,
When thou liest howling.

Ham. What, the fair Ophelia!

Queen. [*Scattering flowers*] Sweets to the sweet: farewell!
I hoped thou shouldst have been my Hamlet's wife;
I thought thy bride-bed to have deck'd, sweet maid,
And not have strew'd thy grave.

Laer. O, treble woe
Fall ten times treble on that cursed head
Whose wicked deed thy most ingenious sense
Deprived thee of! Hold off the earth a while,
Till I have caught her once more in mine arms:
[*Leaps into the grave.*
Now pile your dust upon the quick and dead,

Till of this flat a mountain you have made
To o'ertop old Pelion, or the skyish head
Of blue Olympus.

Ham. [*Advancing*] What is he whose grief
Bears such an emphasis? whose phrase of sorrow
Conjures the wandering stars and makes them stand
Like wonder-wounded hearers? This is I,
Hamlet the Dane. [*Leaps into the grave.*

Laer. The devil take thy soul! [*Grappling with him.*

Ham. Thou pray'st not well.
I prithee, take thy fingers from my throat;
For, though I am not splenitive and rash,
Yet have I in me something dangerous,
Which let thy wiseness fear. Hold off thy hand.

King. Pluck them asunder.

Queen. Hamlet, Hamlet!

All. Gentlemen,—

Hor. Good my lord, be quiet.

[*The Attendants part them, and they come out of the grave.*

Ham. Why, I will fight with him upon this theme
Until my eyelids will no longer wag.

Queen. O my son, what theme?

Ham. I loved Ophelia: forty thousand brothers
Could not, with all their quantity of love,
Make up my sum. What wilt thou do for her?

King. O, he is mad, Laertes.

Queen. For love of God, forbear him.

Ham. 'Swounds, show me what thou'lt do:

Woo't weep? woo't fight? woo't fast? woo't tear thyself?
Woo't drink up eisel? eat a crocodile?
I'll do't. Dost thou come here to whine?
To outface me with leaping in her grave?
Be buried quick with her, and so will I:
And, if thou prate of mountains, let them throw
Millions of acres on us, till our ground,
Singeing his pate against the burning zone,
Make Ossa like a wart! Nay, an thou'lt mouth,
I'll rant as well as thou.

Queen. This is mere madness:
And thus a while the fit will work on him;
Anon, as patient as the female dove,
When that her golden couplets are disclosed,
His silence will sit drooping.

Ham. Hear you, sir;
What is the reason that you use me thus?
I loved you ever: but it is no matter;
Let Hercules himself do what he may,
The cat will mew, and dog will have his day. [*Exit.*

King. I pray thee, good Horatio, wait upon him.
[*Exit Horatio.*
[*To Laertes*] Strengthen your patience in our last night's speech;
We'll put the matter to the present push.
Good Gertrude, set some watch over your son.
This grave shall have a living monument:
An hour of quiet shortly shall we see;
Till then, in patience our proceeding be. [*Exeunt.*

SCENE II

A hall in the castle.

Enter HAMLET *and* HORATIO.

Ham. So much for this, sir: now shall you see the other;
You do remember all the circumstance?
Hor. Remember it, my lord!
Ham. Sir, in my heart there was a kind of fighting,
That would not let me sleep: methought I lay
Worse than the mutines in the bilboes. Rashly,—
And praised be rashness for it, let us know,
Our indiscretion sometime serves us well
When our deep plots do pall; and that should teach us
There's a divinity that shapes our ends,
Rough-hew them how we will,—
Hor. That is most certain.
Ham. Up from my cabin,
My sea-gown scarf'd about me, in the dark
Groped I to find out them; had my desire,
Finger'd their packet, and in fine withdrew
To mine own room again; making so bold,
My fears forgetting manners, to unseal
Their grand commission; where I found, Horatio,—
O royal knavery!—an exact command,
Larded with many several sorts of reasons
Importing Denmark's health and England's too,
With, ho! such bugs and goblins in my life,

That, on the supervise, no leisure bated,
No, not to stay the grinding of the axe,
My head should be struck off.
Hor. Is't possible?
Ham. Here's the commission: read it at more leisure.
But wilt thou hear me how I did proceed?
Hor. I beseech you.
Ham. Being thus be-netted round with villanies,—
Ere I could make a prologue to my brains,
They had begun the play,—I sat me down,
Devised a new commission; wrote it fair:
I once did hold it, as our statists do,
A baseness to write fair, and labor'd much
How to forget that learning; but, sir, now
It did me yeoman's service: wilt thou know
The effect of what I wrote?
Hor. Ay, good my lord.
Ham. An earnest conjuration from the king,
As England was his faithful tributary,
As love between them like the palm might flourish,
As peace should still her wheaten garland wear
And stand a comma 'tween their amities,
And many such-like 'As'es of great charge,
That, on the view and knowing of these contents,
Without debatement further, more or less,
He should the bearers put to sudden death,
Not shriving-time allow'd.
Hor. How was this seal'd?
Ham. Why, even in that was heaven ordinant.
I had my father's signet in my purse,

Which was the model of that Danish seal:
Folded the writ up in form of the other;
Subscribed it, gave't the impression, placed it safely,
The changeling never known. Now, the next day
Was our sea-fight; and what to this was sequent
Thou know'st already.

Hor. So Guildenstern and Rosencrantz go to't.

Ham. Why, man, they did make love to this employment;
They are not near my conscience; their defeat
Does by their own insinuation grow:
'Tis dangerous when the baser nature comes
Between the pass and fell incensed points
Of mighty opposites.

Hor. Why, what a king is this!

Ham. Does it not, thinks't thee, stand me now upon—
He that hath kill'd my king and whored my mother,
Popp'd in between the election and my hopes,
Thrown out his angle for my proper life,
And with such cozenage—is't not perfect conscience,
To quit him with this arm? and is't not to be damn'd,
To let this canker of our nature come
In further evil?

Hor. It must be shortly known to him from England
What is the issue of the business there.

Ham. It will be short: the interim is mine;
And a man's life's no more than to say 'One.'
But I am very sorry, good Horatio,

That to Laertes I forgot myself;
For, by the image of my cause, I see
The portraiture of his: I'll court his favors:
But, sure, the bravery of his grief did put me
Into a towering passion.

Hor. Peace! who comes here?

Enter Osric.

Osr. Your lordship is right welcome back to Denmark.

Ham. I humbly thank you, sir. Dost know this water-fly?

Hor. No, my good lord.

Ham. Thy state is the more gracious, for 'tis a vice to know him. He hath much land, and fertile: let a beast be lord of beasts, and his crib shall stand at the king's mess: 'tis a chough, but, as I say, spacious in the possession of dirt.

Osr. Sweet lord, if your lordship were at leisure, I should impart a thing to you from his majesty.

Ham. I will receive it, sir, with all diligence of spirit. Put your bonnet to his right use; 'tis for the head.

Osr. I thank your lordship, it is very hot.

Ham. No, believe me, 'tis very cold; the wind is northerly.

Osr. It is indifferent cold, my lord, indeed.

Ham. But yet methinks it is very sultry and hot for my complexion.

Osr. Exceedingly, my lord; it is very sultry,—as 'twere,—I cannot tell how. But, my lord, his majesty bade me signify to you that he has laid a great wager on your head: sir, this is the matter—

Ham. I beseech you, remember—

[*Hamlet moves him to put on his hat.*

Osr. Nay, good my lord; for mine ease, in good faith. Sir, here is newly come to court Laertes; believe me, an absolute gentleman, full of most excellent differences, of very soft society and great showing: indeed, to speak feelingly of him, he is the card or calendar of gentry, for you shall find in him the continent of what part a gentleman would see.

Ham. Sir, his definement suffers no perdition in you; though, I know, to divide him inventorially would dizzy the arithmetic of memory, and yet but yaw neither, in respect of his quick sail. But, in the verity of extolment, I take him to be a soul of great article; and his infusion of such dearth and rareness, as, to make true diction of him, his semblable is his mirror; and who else would trace him, his umbrage, nothing more.

Osr. Your lordship speaks most infallibly of him.

Ham. The concernancy, sir? why do we wrap the gentleman in our more rawer breath?

Osr. Sir?

Hor. Is't not possible to understand in another tongue? You will do't, sir, really.

Ham. What imports the nomination of this gentleman?

Osr. Of Laertes?

Hor. His purse is empty already; all's golden words are spent.

Ham. Of him, sir.

Osr. I know you are not ignorant—

Ham. I would you did, sir; yet, in faith, if you did, it would not much approve me. Well, sir?

Osr. You are not ignorant of what excellence Laertes is—

Ham. I dare not confess that, lest I should compare with him in excellence; but, to know a man well, were to know himself.

Osr. I mean, sir, for his weapon; but in the imputation laid on him by them, in his meed he's unfellowed.

Ham. What's his weapon?

Osr. Rapier and dagger.

Ham. That's two of his weapons: but, well.

Osr. The king, sir, hath wagered with him six Barbary horses: against the which he has imponed, as I take it, six French rapiers and poniards, with their assigns, as girdle, hangers, and so: three of the carriages, in faith, are very dear to fancy, very responsive to the hilts, most delicate carriages, and of very liberal conceit.

Ham. What call you the carriages?

Hor. I knew you must be edified by the margent ere you had done.

Osr. The carriages, sir, are the hangers.

Ham. The phrase would be more germane to the matter, if we could carry a cannon by our sides: I would it might be hangers till then. But, on: six Barbary horses against six French swords, their assigns, and three liberal-conceited carriages; that's the French bet against the Danish. Why is this 'imponed,' as you call it?

Osr. The king, sir, hath laid, that in a dozen passes between yourself and him, he shall not exceed you three hits: he hath laid on twelve for nine; and it would come to immediate trial, if your lordship would vouchsafe the answer.

Ham. How if I answer 'no'?

Osr. I mean, my lord, the opposition of your person in trial.

Ham. Sir, I will walk here in the hall: if it please his majesty, 'tis the breathing time of day with me; let the foils be brought, the gentleman willing, and the king hold his purpose, I will win for him an I can; if not, I will gain nothing but my shame and the odd hits.

Osr. Shall I re-deliver you e'en so?

Ham. To this effect, sir; after what flourish your nature will.

Osr. I commend my duty to your lordship.

Ham. Yours, yours. [*Exit Osric.*] He does well

to commend it himself; there are no tongues else for's turn.

Hor. This lapwing runs away with the shell on his head.

Ham. He did comply with his dug before he sucked it. Thus has he—and many more of the same breed that I know the drossy age dotes on—only got the tune of the time and outward habit of encounter; a kind of yesty collection, which carries them through and through the most fond and winnowed opinions; and do but blow them to their trial, the bubbles are out.

Enter a Lord.

Lord. My lord, his majesty commended him to you by young Osric, who brings back to him, that you attend him in the hall: he sends to know if your pleasure hold to play with Laertes, or that you will take longer time.

Ham. I am constant to my purposes; they follow the king's pleasure: if his fitness speaks, mine is ready; now or whensoever, provided I be so able as now.

Lord. The king and queen and all are coming down.

Ham. In happy time.

Lord. The queen desires you to use some gentle entertainment to Laertes before you fall to play.

Ham. She well instructs me. [*Exit Lord.*

Hor. You will lose this wager, my lord.

Ham. I do not think so; since he went into France, I have been in continual practice; I shall win at the odds. But thou wouldst not think how ill all's here about my heart: but it is no matter.

Hor. Nay, good my lord,—

Ham. It is but foolery; but it is such a kind of gain-giving, as would perhaps trouble a woman.

Hor. If your mind dislike any thing, obey it. I will forestal their repair hither, and say you are not fit.

Ham. Not a whit; we defy augury: there's a special providence in the fall of a sparrow. If it be now, 'tis not to come; if it be not to come, it will be now; if it be not now, yet it will come: the readiness is all; since no man has aught of what he leaves, what is't to leave betimes?

Enter KING, QUEEN, LAERTES, *and* LORDS, OSRIC *and other* ATTENDANTS *with foils and gauntlets; a table and flagons of wine on it.*

King. Come, Hamlet, come, and take this hand from me.
[*The King puts Laertes' hand into Hamlet's.*

Ham. Give me your pardon, sir: I've done you wrong;
But pardon't, as you are a gentleman.
This presence knows,
And you must needs have heard, how I am punish'd
With sore distraction. What I have done,

That might your nature, honor and exception
Roughly awake, I here proclaim was madness.
Was't Hamlet wrong'd Laertes? Never Hamlet:
If Hamlet from himself be ta'en away,
And when he's not himself does wrong Laertes,
Then Hamlet does it not, Hamlet denies it.
Who does it, then? His madness: if't be so,
Hamlet is of the faction that is wrong'd;
His madness is poor Hamlet's enemy.
Sir, in this audience,
Let my disclaiming from a purposed evil
Free me so far in your most generous thoughts,
That I have shot mine arrow o'er the house,
And hurt my brother.

Laer. I am satisfied in nature,
Whose motive, in this case, should stir me most
To my revenge: but in my terms of honor
I stand aloof, and will no reconcilement,
Till by some elder masters of known honor
I have a voice and precedent of peace,
To keep my name ungored. But till that time,
I do receive your offer'd love like love,
And will not wrong it.

Ham. I embrace it freely,
And will this brother's wager frankly play.
Give us the foils. Come on.

Laer. Come, one for me.

Ham. I'll be your foil, Laertes: in mine ignorance
Your skill shall, like a star i' the darkest night,
Stick fiery off indeed.

Laer. You mock me, sir.
Ham. No, by this hand.
King. Give them the foils, young Osric. Cousin Hamlet,
You know the wager?
Ham. Very well, my lord;
Your grace has laid the odds o' the weaker side.
King. I do not fear it; I have seen you both:
But since he is better'd, we have therefore odds.
Laer. This is too heavy; let me see another.
Ham. This likes me well. These foils have all a length?
[*They prepare to play.*
Osr. Ay, my good lord.
King. Set me the stoups of wine upon that table.
If Hamlet give the first or second hit,
Or quit in answer of the third exchange,
Let all the battlements their ordnance fire;
The king shall drink to Hamlet's better breath;
And in the cup an union shall he throw,
Richer than that which four successive kings
In Denmark's crown have worn. Give me the cups;
And let the kettle to the trumpet speak,
The trumpet to the cannoneer without,
The cannons to the heavens, the heaven to earth,
'Now the king drinks to Hamlet.' Come, begin;
And you, the judges, bear a wary eye.
Ham. Come on, sir.
Laer. Come, my lord. [*They play.*
Ham. One.
Laer. No.
Ham. Judgment.

Osr. A hit, a very palpable hit.

Laer. Well; again.

King. Stay; give me drink. Hamlet, this pearl is thine;
Here's to thy health.

[*Trumpets sound, and cannon shot off within.*

Give him the cup.

Ham. I'll play this bout first; set it by a while.
Come. [*They play.*] Another hit; what say you?

Laer. A touch, a touch, I do confess.

King. Our son shall win.

Queen. He's fat and scant of breath.
Here, Hamlet, take my napkin, rub thy brows:
The queen carouses to thy fortune, Hamlet.

Ham. Good madam!

King. Gertrude, do not drink.

Queen. I will, my lord; I pray you, pardon me.

King. [*Aside*] It is the poison'd cup; it is too late.

Ham. I dare not drink yet, madam; by and by.

Queen. Come, let me wipe thy face.

Laer. My lord, I'll hit him now.

King. I do not think't.

Laer. [*Aside*] And yet 'tis almost 'gainst my conscience.

Ham. Come, for the third, Laertes: you but dally;
I pray you, pass with your best violence;
I am afeard you make a wanton of me.

Laer. Say you so? come on. [*They play.*

Osr. Nothing, neither way.

Laer. Have at you now!

[*Laertes wounds Hamlet; then, in scuffling, they change rapiers, and Hamlet wounds Laertes.*

King. Part them; they are incensed.
Ham. Nay, come, again. [*The Queen falls.*
Osr. Look to the queen there, ho!
Hor. They bleed on both sides. How is it, my lord?
Osr. How is't, Laertes?
Laer. Why, as a woodcock to mine own springe, Osric;
I am justly kill'd with mine own treachery.
Ham. How does the queen?
King. She swounds to see them bleed.
Queen. No, no, the drink, the drink,—O my dear Hamlet,—
The drink, the drink! I am poison'd. [*Dies.*
Ham. O villany! Ho! let the door be lock'd:
Treachery! seek it out. [*Laertes falls.*
Laer. It is here, Hamlet: Hamlet, thou art slain;
No medicine in the world can do thee good;
In thee there is not half an hour of life;
The treacherous instrument is in thy hand,
Unbated and envenom'd: the foul practice
Hath turn'd itself on me; lo, here I lie,
Never to rise again: thy mother's poison'd:
I can no more: the king, the king's to blame.
Ham. The point envenom'd too!
Then, venom, to thy work. [*Stabs the King.*
All. Treason! treason!
King. O, yet defend me, friends; I am but hurt.
Ham. Here, thou incestuous, murderous, damned Dane,
Drink off this potion. Is thy union here?
Follow my mother. [*King dies.*
Laer. He is justly served;

It is a poison temper'd by himself.
Exchange forgiveness with me, noble Hamlet:
Mine and my father's death come not upon thee,
Nor thine on me! [*Dies.*

Ham. Heaven make thee free of it! I follow thee.
I am dead, Horatio. Wretched queen, adieu!
You that look pale and tremble at this chance,
That are but mutes or audience to this act,
Had I but time—as this fell sergeant, death,
Is strict in his arrest—O, I could tell you—
But let it be. Horatio, I am dead;
Thou livest; report me and my cause aright
To the unsatisfied.

Hor. Never believe it:
I am more an antique Roman than a Dane:
Here's yet some liquor left.

Ham. As thou'rt a man,
Give me the cup: let go; by heaven, I'll have't.
O good Horatio, what a wounded name,
Things standing thus unknown, shall live behind me!
If thou didst ever hold me in thy heart,
Absent thee from felicity a while,
And in this harsh world draw thy breath in pain,
To tell my story. [*March afar off, and shot within.*
What warlike noise is this?

Osr. Young Fortinbras, with conquest come from Poland,
To the ambassadors of England gives
This warlike volley.

Ham. O, I die, Horatio;
The potent poison quite o'er-crows my spirit:

I cannot live to hear the news from England;
But I do prophesy the election lights
On Fortinbras: he has my dying voice;
So tell him, with the occurrents, more and less,
Which have solicited.. The rest is silence. [*Dies.*

Hor. Now cracks a noble heart. Good night, sweet prince,
And flights of angels sing thee to thy rest!
Why does the drum come hither? [*March within.*

Enter FORTINBRAS, *and the* ENGLISH AMBASSADORS, *with drum, colors, and* ATTENDANTS.

Fort. Where is this sight?

Hor. What is it you would see?
If aught of woe or wonder, cease your search.

Fort. This quarry cries on havoc. O proud death,
What feast is toward in thine eternal cell,
That thou so many princes at a shot
So bloodily hast struck?

First Amb. The sight is dismal;
And our affairs from England come too late:
The ears are senseless that should give us hearing,
To tell him his commandment is fulfill'd,
That Rosencrantz and Guildenstern are dead:
Where should we have our thanks?

Hor. Not from his mouth
Had it the ability of life to thank you:
He never gave commandment for their death.
But since, so jump upon this bloody question,

You from the Polack wars, and you from England,
Are here arrived, give order that these bodies
High on a stage be placed to the view;
And let me speak to the yet unknowing world
How these things came about: so shall you hear
Of carnal, bloody, and unnatural acts,
Of accidental judgments, casual slaughters,
Of deaths put on by cunning and forced cause,
And, in this upshot, purposes mistook
Fall'n on the inventors' heads: all this can I
Truly deliver.

Fort. Let us haste to hear it,
And call the noblest to the audience.
For me, with sorrow I embrace my fortune:
I have some rights of memory in this kingdom,
Which now to claim my vantage doth invite me.

Hor. Of that I shall have also cause to speak,
And from his mouth whose voice will draw on more:
But let this same be presently perform'd,
Even while men's minds are wild; lest more mischance
On plots and errors happen.

Fort. Let four captains
Bear Hamlet, like a soldier, to the stage;
For he was likely, had he been put on,
To have proved most royally: and, for his passage,
The soldiers' music and the rites of war
Speak loudly for him.
Take up the bodies: such a sight as this

Becomes the field, but here shows much amiss.
Go, bid the soldiers shoot.

[*A dead march. Exeunt, bearing off the dead bodies: after which a peal of ordnance is shot off.*

The Swan Theater

NOTES AND COMMENT

NOTES AND COMMENT

Act I. Scene I.

The first thing which the dramatist has to do is to give the audience the facts which must be known in order to understand the play. He must make clear, to begin with, enough of what has preceded the opening of the play to enable us to grasp quickly and intelligently the significance of the situation with which the action starts; the opening scenes, that is, must look backward. We must, further, be made to feel that this situation is not put before us merely for its own sake, but because it is charged, so to speak, with latent possibilities—because it carries within it the seeds of further actions, further situations; the opening scenes, that is, must also look forward. The speakers, moreover, must be at once so presented that we shall know, without too much puzzling, who they are and where they are, with some indication of time as well; what is happening before us now, that is, must define itself without obscurity. And finally—although this last is not always attempted—the dramatist may seek to awaken in us a particular mood, to create a particular atmosphere, which shall foreshadow, in a way, the spirit of the drama. All that portion of the play (usually the first two or three scenes) which accomplishes these ends is called the Exposition.

The first scene of *Hamlet* is a very wonderful piece of exposition, and should be carefully examined in order to see just what information, of the kinds indicated, Shakespeare has actually given us, and how he has accomplished it. And this exercise will gain both interest and value, if one compare with the first scene of *Hamlet* the first scenes of *Macbeth, Romeo and Juliet,* and *Julius Cæsar*—all of them striking examples of skill in exposition—and try to discover wherein their methods are alike, and wherein different.

Moreover, all that has been indicated the dramatist must

accomplish by means of dialogue and action alone; he must do it with the extreme of brevity, because the time of performance is inexorably limited; and he must do it with the utmost freedom from obscurity or ambiguity, because the actors cannot be stopped and asked to repeat what is not clear. To the opening of a novel, however, none of these restrictions apply, and it will amply repay the time, if one compare with the first scene of *Hamlet* (and of the other plays named as well) the opening chapters of (for instance) *Ivanhoe, Silas Marner, A Tale of Two Cities, The House of the Seven Gables, The Last of the Mohicans,* and observe the totally different fashion in which the necessary information is there given. It is after four long paragraphs that Scott remarks, in *Ivanhoe:* "This state of things I have thought it necessary to premise for the information of the general reader," etc.; it is after some thirty pages of preliminary information that Hawthorne concludes: "And now . . . we proceed to open our narrative." *How does Shakespeare give us this same sort of preliminary information?*

The notes on the first three scenes are intended, in part, to emphasize their qualities as exposition, and to suggest the sort of observation that should be applied throughout the play.

2. **Nay, answer me.** Observe that *me* is emphatic. Why? Whose business is it to challenge? Notice that the first two lines of the play, with their accompanying action, disclose at once a certain nervous tension among the watchers on the platform. Shakespeare's preparation of the audience for the appearance of the Ghost begins with the first two words of the play.

8-9. **'Tis bitter cold, And I am sick at heart.** What does this add to the effect already produced?

10. **Have you had quiet guard?** Observe the implication that for some reason Bernardo thinks the watch may *not* have been quiet.

13. **Bid them make haste.** Is Bernardo unwilling to be left alone? Or is he expecting something to happen at any moment? Or is it both?

14. **Stand, ho! Who's there?** Notice that Francisco, who has been relieved, is startled into the challenge which Bernardo should now give. What impression of the state of things

on the platform has Shakespeare succeeded in producing in the first fourteen lines?

19. **What, is Horatio there?** Observe the skill with which Shakespeare leads up to Horatio's part in the scene. Has Bernardo been certain that he would come? Does the reason for his doubt appear later?

19. **A piece of him:** a playful remark, into which no deep significance is to be read.

21. **What, has this thing appear'd again to-night?** The reason for the agitation of the sentinels now begins to appear. But observe how gradually it is still led up to: "this thing"; "this dreaded sight"; "this apparition"—then the Ghost itself, and finally, "like the king that's dead." Compare the approach of the phantom ship in *The Rime of the Ancient Mariner:* "a something in the sky" (Part III, line 6); "a little speck" (line 7); "a mist" (line 8); "a certain shape" (line 10); "a sail! a sail!" (line 19)—and then the detailed description. It was Coleridge who pointed out that in Marcellus's question "even the word 'again' has its *credibilizing* effect." How?

29. **And speak to it.** Why should not the others speak to it? See note on line 42 below.

36. **Yond same star:** probably the Great Bear, or some star in it.

36. **The pole:** the pole star. Observe the heightening of Bernardo's language under the stress of his feeling, and notice, too, the naturalness of representing him as marking the time, on his lonely watch, by the position of the stars.

39. **The bell then beating one.** What time was it in line 7? What time is it now (cf. line 65)? How long does it take to speak 32 lines? The time allowed to represent the action on the stage must inevitably be very much shorter than the actual duration of the action itself, and Shakespeare's skill in making us forget that there is such a discrepancy is strikingly illustrated here.

[Enter Ghost]. The Ghost in *Hamlet* is remarkable, among other things, for the number of its appearances, and for the amazing skill with which each appearance is made to come as a surprise. We have seen how its first appearance has been led up to; the way in which the others are introduced should be carefully observed. And a comparison with the appearance of Banquo's ghost and of the ghost of Cæsar is worth making.

42. **Thou art a scholar; speak to it.** Exorcisms were usually in Latin, and frequently in the form of a palindrome (a sentence which reads the same backwards as forwards), as: *Signa te signa, temere me tangis et angis.* Moreover, it was believed that a ghost could not speak until it was spoken to.

44. **Most like,** etc. Observe the total change in Horatio's attitude, and also the "credibilizing effect" of this change upon the attitude of the *audience* towards the Ghost. What would have been the difference, in other words, if *all* the speakers had from the first believed in the Ghost?—From this time on to the end of the scene it is Horatio who holds the center of the stage.

45. **Question it:** speak to it—*not,* interrogate it. See *question* in the Glossary.

63. **The sledded Polacks:** Poles traveling in sleds or sledges. The earliest texts spell the word *pollax* (or *polax*), with or without a capital, and an alternative interpretation is that offered by the spelling of the Fourth Folio, *Poleaxe.* In this case "sledded poleaxe" is commonly explained as a pole-axe (or battle-axe) weighted with a heavy sledge or hammer. But Polacks (an emendation which is due to Pope's keenness) is probably correct. Compare the use of *Polack* elsewhere in the play (see Concordance).

68. **In the gross and scope of my opinion:** speaking generally—as contrasted with "particular thought." "Gross and scope" is probably hendiadys for "gross scope"; see Glossary under *gross.*

70. **Good now:** "an interjectional expression denoting acquiescence, entreaty, expostulation or surprise" (*Oxford Dictionary*). Observe that the four long speeches which follow (in sharp contrast with the quicker movement of the earlier dialogue) accomplish two things: they familiarize us with some of the events which have preceded the opening of the play; and they distract our attention, as we follow their rather complicated statements, from the Ghost, so that its second appearance comes, like the first, as a surprise.

84. **Our valiant Hamlet:** the elder Hamlet, not the hero of the play.

87. **Law and heraldry.** This means either common law and the regulations of heraldry, or possibly (by hendiadys; see line 68 above) the law of heraldry.

90. **A moiety competent:** a portion equivalent to that of Fortinbras. *Moiety* strictly means one-half (see, for instance, *Henry VIII,* I, ii, 12); but Shakespeare frequently uses it in the general sense of *portion.*

94. **Carriage of the article design'd:** the tenor (or import) of the stipulation just mentioned.

96. **Unimproved mettle:** probably, unimpugned courage (or spirit). But *unimproved* may possibly mean either "untutored" or "not turned to account," since *improve* has several meanings in Elizabethan English.

100. **That hath a stomach in't:** that demands stubborn courage—with a possible play on the other sense of *stomach,* namely, "appetite." Cf. *Henry V,* III, vii, 166: "they have only stomachs to eat and none to fight."

109. **Portentous:** of the nature of a portent, ominous—not merely in the sense of "prodigious, monstrous, extraordinary," as frequently in present usage. Notice especially its use in *Julius Cæsar,* I, iii, 31, when that passage is read as indicated below, under line 113.

110. **So like the king.** Turn back to lines 47-49, 58-59, 81. Why is this point so emphasized?

113 ff. Compare *Julius Cæsar,* I, iii, 1-78; II, ii, 13-31, for a fuller account. In both instances Shakespeare is recalling certain passages in Plutarch's life of Julius Cæsar, which he knew in North's translation. Compare especially the following, where Plutarch speaks of "the strange and wonderful signs that were said to be seen before Cæsar's death": "For, touching the fires in the element, and spirits running up and down in the night, and also the solitary birds to be seen at noondays sitting in the great market-place: are not all these signs perhaps worth the noting, in such a wonderful chance as happened? But Strabo the Philosopher writeth, that divers men were seen going up and down in fire. . . . Again, of signs in the element, the great comet which seven nights together was seen very bright after Cæsar's death," etc. (Temple edition, VII, pp. 202-03, 211).

117. **As stars,** etc. Either a line has dropped out before

line 117, or the passage is in some other way corrupt. Numerous emendations have been suggested.

118. **Disasters in the sun.** Cf. North's *Plutarch:* "Also the brightness of the sun was darkened, the which all that year through rose very pale, and shined not out, whereby it gave but small heat: therefore the air being very cloudy and dark, by the weakness of the heat that could not come forth, did cause the earth to bring forth but raw and unripe fruit, which rotted before it could ripe" (Temple edition, VII, pp. 211-12). Look up the etymology and first meaning of *disaster*.

118. **The moist star:** the moon. Shakespeare also calls it "the watery star" (*Winter's Tale,* I, ii, 1). Why?

119. **Upon whose influence,** etc.: to whose influence the sea is subject. The reference is, of course, to the tides. Look up the first meaning of *influence* in the dictionary, and then read over the passages under *influence* in the Shakespeare Concordance.

120. Look up *St. Matthew,* xxiv, 29.

121. **Fierce:** violent, terrible, wild. Cf. the modern slang use of the word.

122. **Harbingers.** Cf. *Macbeth,* I, iv, 45: "I'll be myself the harbinger."

123. **Omen:** here, the event which the omen portends. Notice the dramatic skill with which these lines lead up to the reappearance of the Ghost.

125. **Climatures:** regions. Compare again the parallel passage in *Julius Cæsar:* "For, I believe, they are portentous things Unto the climate that they point upon" (I, iii, 31-32).

127-39. **I'll cross it,** etc. Does Horatio need any longer to be urged to speak? Has the heightening of the rhythmic movement of the lines in his appeal to the Ghost and the refrain-like recurrence of "Speak to me," "O speak," "Speak of it," anything to do with a corresponding heightening of feeling? What superstitions are referred to in lines 127 and 136-38?

145. **As the air, invulnerable.** Cf. "the intrenchant air," *Macbeth,* V, viii, 9-10; "the invulnerable clouds," *King John,* II, i, 252. The adjectives which Shakespeare and Milton apply to the air are well worth looking up in the Concordances.

148. **Started.** The first Quarto has *faded.* Can you suggest

two possible reasons for the change? For the striking changes in lines 150-52 see the Introduction, pp. xii-xiii.

154. **The extravagant and erring spirit.** An excellent illustration of the need of care in dealing with words which, in modern English, are the same in form but different in meaning. *Extravagant* here means "straying, wandering out of bounds"; look up *Othello,* I, i, 137, and *Twelfth Night,* II, i, 11-12, for a similar use of both adjective and noun. *Erring* means simply "roaming, wandering" (as it does in *Othello,* I, iii, 362), without any hint of ethical import. Compare "we have *erred and strayed* from thy ways like lost sheep," in the Prayer Book.

162-63. **No planets strike, No fairy takes.** *Strike* is used of the malevolent influence of planets and other superhuman forces; look up *Winter's Tale,* I, ii, 201; *Coriolanus,* II, ii, 117. *Take* is similarly used; look up *Merry Wives,* IV, iv, 32; *Antony and Cleopatra,* IV, ii, 37. See the use of *both* words in *Lear,* II, iv, 165-66; compare *Lear,* III, iv, 61.

170. **Young Hamlet.** Everything that has happened, with all the interest and suspense that it has aroused, is now concentrated, at one stroke, upon Hamlet. Turn to the first scene of *Macbeth,* and see how line 8 focusses the whole effect of the witch-scene upon Macbeth. Is the same thing done in the first scene of *Julius Cæsar?* How? What difference do you notice in the first scene of *Romeo and Juliet?*

Notice the variations in style and rhythm in the scene: its beginning in a low key, almost in the tone of ordinary conversation; its passage, after the first appearance of the Ghost, into a weighty and rather involved narrative and expository style; until, after the second appearance of the Ghost, the intense feeling that has been stirred expresses itself in verse of an almost lyrical quality. Does an audience feel anything unnatural in the highly poetical quality of the closing speeches? Why not? What would have been the effect if the play had *begun* in this style? Do any of the plays you have read open in a lofty strain? Look again at the opening scenes from this point of view. *Richard III* is an exception to the general rule in this respect. In what other way does its opening differ from what you have observed? In the other scenes in *Hamlet* watch for instances of the flexibility with which the style accommodates itself to the thought.

Act I. Scene II.

The first scene dealt with a single arresting *situation;* the second, which continues the exposition, brings before us, rather, a *state of affairs*—the tense personal relations, that is, between Hamlet and the King and Queen. And this tenseness grows (we are made to feel) out of the sharply divergent attitudes of Hamlet on the one hand, and Claudius and Gertrude on the other, towards the very fact upon which our attention was concentrated in the first scene, the death of the elder Hamlet, especially as this is now linked with a new and significant fact, the precipitate marriage of the Queen with Claudius. That this new fact is of prime importance becomes clear in Hamlet's passionate soliloquy, and it is from the disclosures of this soliloquy that we are brought back again to the appearance of the Ghost. In other words, the second scene throws the appearance of the Ghost against the background of the relations of these three people—Claudius, Gertrude, and Hamlet—and it suggests to us that the clue to the mystery is to be looked for there. The scene is further linked with the previous one by the renewed emphasis upon the affair with Fortinbras. And it also looks forward, in that the prompt fixing of our attention upon Laertes, as he is singled out by the King, suggests that he is probably to play some important part in the action.

Observe the sharp and dramatic contrast between the *settings* of Scenes I and II—the bleak platform and the armed sentries: the pomp and ceremony of the court. Notice, too, the equally sharp contrast within Scene II itself, by which the somber figure of Hamlet, all in black, is set off against the brilliant court costumes of the rest, so that the central fact of the situation is presented to the *eye,* before a word is spoken.

1. Observe that the very first line takes us back, by implication, to the Ghost.

4. **Brow of woe:** an example of what is sometimes called "the 'thieves of mercy' construction." The genitive phrase is equivalent to an adjective preceding the noun which it limits: thus, "thieves of mercy" (*Hamlet,* IV, vi, 20) = merciful thieves; "a day of season" (*All's Well,* V, iii, 32) = a seasonable day; "strength of limit" (*Winter's* Tale, III, ii, 107) =

limited strength; "brow of youth" (*Lear,* I, iv, 306) = youthful brow. "Brow of woe" is equivalent to the "mourning brow" of *Love's Labour's Lost,* V, ii, 754.

5-6. **That we with wisest sorrow.** Notice that "wisest" answers to "discretion," "sorrow" to "nature," in the preceding line. See also next note for similar balanced structure. What *pronoun* does the King use in referring to himself throughout this speech? Why?

10. **A defeated joy:** joy that is marred or disfigured. Cf. *Othello,* I, iii, 346: "defeat thy favor [mar your face] with an usurped beard." Notice, too, that the antithesis involved in this phrase is worked out with threefold iteration in the next three lines.

11. **A dropping eye:** a weeping eye. The general idea of line 11 reappears in *Winter's Tale,* V, ii, 80: "She had one eye declined for the loss of her husband, another elevated that the oracle was fulfilled." Cf. "To laugh with one eye, and cry with the other."

17. **That you know, young Fortinbras:** that *which* you know—namely, that young Fortinbras, etc.

22. **He.** The pronoun is superfluous, but the usage (now incorrect) was not uncommon. Cf. II, i, 84.

25. **So much for him.** Cf. line 16: "For all, our thanks." Claudius is dispatching disagreeable matters quickly.

28. **Norway:** the King of Norway. Cf. "bloody England into England gone" (*King John,* III, iv, 8); "our brother France" (*Henry V,* V, ii, 2).

1-39. Notice the rather set rhetorical character of this first speech as contrasted with the lyrical quality of the closing speeches of the preceding scene. Is this to be interpreted merely as conventional oratorical style, or is it intended to suggest a certain embarrassment on the King's part in dealing —especially in the first sixteen lines—with a delicate subject? Observe the strong alliteration of the first twenty-five lines. In the First Quarto the scene begins at line 26. What has Shakespeare gained by inserting the first twenty-five lines? What is added, in lines 17-39, to our information regarding the affair with Fortinbras?

42-50. To whom would one expect the King to speak first? Why does he not? How many times does he *name* Laertes in this short speech? Has this any significance? Does the King use the same pronoun throughout in addressing Laertes? (Observe that in Shakespeare's English *thou* was very much like the more intimate or familiar *du* of German; *you,* like the more formal *Sie,* although the two are often rather freely interchanged.) Has the change any significance here? Does the King use the same pronoun in referring to *himself* that he has used in the preceding speech? Why *this* change?

44-45. You cannot make a reasonable request, and waste your breath. Cf. line 118.

51. **Leave and favor:** favorable leave (the First Quarto has "favorable license"). Cf. "your gracious leave and pardon" in line 56, where *pardon* = permission.

64. **My cousin Hamlet.** *Cousin* (equivalent to "kinsman") is used in Shakespeare for niece, uncle, brother-in-law, and grandchild. What is the relationship here? What of the King's tact in calling Hamlet "son"?

65. **A little more than kin, and less than kind:** that is, a little too much related (referring to "cousin" and "son") with no kinship in *nature. Kind* (pronounced in Shakespeare's time as if it rimed with "sinned") means *nature,* and Hamlet's allusion is probably to the King's marriage, which was regarded as incestuous, and so unnatural. There is also a play on the other sense of "kind"—i. e., there is no love lost between us. Notice that Hamlet's first speech is a play on words, and an aside. What light is thrown at once on Hamlet's attitude towards the King?

66. **The clouds:** an allusion to the "nighted color" of Hamlet's "inky cloak"—perhaps also to "the dejected havior of [his] visage." (Notice that the King uses *you* instead of *thou* in addressing Hamlet. What pronoun does the Queen use?)

67. **I am too much i' the sun.** Possibly (1) in direct response to the King's reference to Hamlet's garb, with ironical allusion (easily made clear by a gesture) to the bright costumes of the Court, which has put off its mourning for the wedding. Or (2) there may be an allusion to an old proverb—"out of God's blessing into the warm sun" (see *Lear,* II, ii, 168-69)—which meant to be out of house and home, so that Hamlet is referring to his loss of the throne. And there is probably in either case (3) a play upon "sun" and "son" (line 64), which

would be quite in keeping with Hamlet's fondness for verbal quibbling.

69. **Denmark:** the King; cf. *Norway,* line 28.

70. **For ever.** How long since the King's death? See line 138. What of the Queen's tact? **Vailed** is "lowered"; cf. *Venus and Adonis,* 956; *Merchant of Venice,* I, i, 28.

72. **Thou know'st 'tis common.** Remember that it is Hamlet's mother who is saying this to him of his father. Cf. *Tempest,* II, i, 3-6, and look up Tennyson's development of the idea in *In Memoriam,* VI, lines 1-8.

92. **Obsequious sorrow:** sorrow that is dutiful in showing respect to the dead. Look up *Titus Andronicus,* V, iii, 152, and especially *Sonnet XXXI,* 5-7. **Persever** in Shakespeare is always accented on the second syllable.

99. **As any the most vulgar thing to sense:** as anything which is most ordinary or commonplace to the understanding.

101-03. Observe Claudius's habit of heaping up parallel phrases; cf. lines 93-97. Can you point out instances in his first speech? Is his emphasis natural, or is he "protesting too much"?

109. Cf. III, ii, 356. The throne of Denmark was elective (see V, ii, 366-67), but royal blood was considered in determining the succession. Had Hamlet himself expected to succeed his father? See V, ii, 65; III, iv, 100. Was Claudius's remark, then, particularly consoling?

112. **Impart.** The construction is confused, for *impart* has no object. There is possibly some slight corruption of the text, but the general sense is clear.

113. See note on line 164.

114. **Retrograde:** contrary. Another astrological term; cf. notes on I, i, 118, 119, and see Greenough and Kittredge, *Words and their Ways in English Speech,* chap. IV, especially pp. 33-34.

117. **Our . . . cousin and our son.** Cf. line 64. Why does the King change the pronoun?

120. **In all my best:** to the extent of my power; cf. *Othello,* III, iv, 127. How often has Hamlet addressed *the King* in this scene? The formality of his address to his mother—"Madam," when she has said "thy mother"—is less significant, as such formality was observed in high-born families. See also lines 74-76. Juliet regularly addresses her mother as

"Madam" (except in *Romeo and Juliet,* III, v, 200, where she cries out "O, sweet my mother, cast me not away!"). Compare Hamlet's use of "mother" in Act III, Scene IV; observe, too, the way in which Laertes and Ophelia address their father in Act I, Scene III.

121-24. The King is rather making the best of a bad job.

125. Watch as you read for amplifications of this hint regarding the King's fondness for drinking.

129-59. How often has Hamlet spoken up to this point? How often more than a single line? Yet what has been in his mind all the while? Consider his restraint in the presence of others in the light of what the soliloquy discloses. What is the significance of the frequent broken constructions in the soliloquy? Is it his father's death, as the King and Queen suppose, that is uppermost in Hamlet's mind? Compare what Hamlet says in lines 137-49 with what the King says in lines 1-16. Does this make clearer Hamlet's mood in line 65? After the glimpse which the soliloquy gives into the state of Hamlet's mind are we better prepared to understand the effect upon him of Horatio's communication?

129. Too too. Emphatic reduplication, not uncommon in Elizabethan English. See *Two Gentlemen of Verona,* II, iv, 205, and cf. "most most" in *Sonnet CX,* 14. Does Hamlet's repetition in "melt, Thaw and resolve" impress you in the same way as the King's repetitions?

131-32. Cf. *Cymbeline,* III, iv, 78-80. Where is the "canon" to be found?

140. Hyperion to a satyr. Hyperion is accented on the penult in Greek and Latin; Spenser, Gray, and Keats, as well as Shakespeare, accent it on the antepenult. Hyperion was a Titan, the Sun-god dethroned by Apollo, with whom he is later identified. For a description of his beauty, see Keats's *Hyperion,* II, 371-75, and cf. *Hamlet,* III, iv, 56.

145. Within a month. Within a month of what? Is it of the elder Hamlet's death? If so, Claudius and Gertrude have been married a month (cf. line 138), yet Claudius announces the marriage as if it had just taken place. It is probable that Hamlet means within a month of the *funeral* (cf. lines 147-49), which might have been delayed two or three weeks, so that the marriage *has* just occurred. Notice Hamlet's threefold iteration (lines 145, 147, 153).

147. **Or ere.** Cf. "or ever" in line 183. The *ever* (*ere*) adds emphasis. Cf. *Psalm* xc, 2; *Ecclesiastes,* xii, 6.

149. **Niobe.** Her children were slain by the arrows of Apollo and Artemis.

150. **That wants discourse of reason:** that lacks the reasoning faculty. (The First Quarto has "devoid of reason"). Cf. particularly IV, iv, 33-39.

155. **Flushing:** probably in the sense of "reddening"—although possibly it means "flooding" (with tears).

157. **Dexterity:** celerity—possibly with the added idea of adroitness.

160. **Hail to your lordship!** How is Hamlet addressed throughout the rest of the scene? It must not be forgotten that "Lord Hamlet is a prince." Observe the pronouns used throughout this dialogue.

161. **Horatio,—or I do forget myself.** It is a question whether this is to be interpreted as implying uncertainty in Hamlet's recognition of Horatio, or merely surprise at seeing him in Elsinore. Hamlet and Horatio are friends of long standing (see III, ii, 67-79), so that the first interpretation is possible only on the assumption that Hamlet has not seen Horatio for some time—or else that he is still lost in his own thoughts. Perhaps an exclamation point after "Horatio" is best, as indicating Hamlet's surprise; then "or I do forget myself" is roughly equivalent to "surely I can't be mistaken." Notice that Hamlet has a trick of turning his mind quickly back upon his own statements; cf. lines 138, 233 (see note), 240. (The conventional greeting of line 160—with which compare II, ii, 440-41—is probably spoken before Hamlet observes that it is friends and not strangers who are approaching).

163. Read the line: "Sir, my good *friend;* I'll change *that* name with you"—i. e., I'll exchange (so that we give and take on equal terms) the name of *friend* with you. Another interpretation makes the line mean: "You are my good friend, I your poor servant." Observe throughout the rest of the scene Hamlet's exquisite courtesy.

164. **What make you from Wittenberg?** If Hamlet as well as Horatio has come from Wittenberg for the King's

funeral, why is Hamlet either uncertain in his recognition of Horatio, or surprised to see him? Do the King's words in line 113 necessarily imply that Hamlet has just come from Wittenberg? The whole matter is puzzling, but it is at least possible that Hamlet had left Wittenberg some time before the opening of the play, and was at Elsinore at the time of his father's death. With "what make you" compare the German "was machen Sie," and cf. II, ii, 278. Why is the question twice repeated (lines 168, 174)?

165. **Marcellus?** The interrogation point does not occur in either the Quartos or the Folios, which have a period. Hamlet apparently is *not* uncertain in his recognition of Marcellus, who has been at Elsinore.

170-73. Observe again the gracious courtesy of the reply. In how many lights has Shakespeare already made us see Hamlet?

175. What mood appears again in this line?

176. What reason does *Laertes* give for having come (line 53)? Why the difference?

178. What does Shakespeare mean us to see was uppermost in Hamlet's mind?

180. **Baked-meats**: pastry. Cf. *Genesis,* xl, 17. Feasts at funerals used to be customary.

182. **My dearest foe.** "'Dear' is used of whatever touches us nearly either in love or hate, joy or sorrow" (Clark and Wright). Cf. "dearest spite" (*Sonnet XXXVII,* 3); "terms so bloody and so dear" (*Twelfth Night,* V, 74).

185. What does Horatio think Hamlet means? Observe the skill with which Horatio's disclosure is led up to. In what follows, how does Shakespeare hold our interest in the account of what we have just seen for ourselves? With whose point of view do we identify ourselves? The rest of the scene is really almost equivalent to a third appearance of the Ghost.

187. **He was a man.** Edwin Booth was accustomed to pause after "man," as if contrasting it with "king." This interpretation is perhaps questionable, but cf. *Julius Cæsar,* V, v, 73-75.

190. **Saw? who?** *Who* is frequently used for *whom* in Shakespeare.—The best way to make sure that you understand a passage like this—or indeed anything in Shakespeare—is to read it aloud.

192. **Season your admiration**: temper your amazement.

198. **Vast**: vacancy, void. Cf. "that vast of night" (*Tempest*, I, ii, 327). *Dead* (cf. I, i, 65) means "still as death"; cf. "as dead midnight still" (*Henry V*, III, chor., 19); "the night's dead silence" (*Two Gentlemen of Verona*, III, ii, 85). Some of the early texts have *waste* (or *wast*) instead of *vast*.

200. **At point exactly**: equivalent to "at all points," in *Richard II*, I, iii, 2. **Cap-a-pe** is "from head to foot" (cf. line 228).

204. **Distill'd**: melted. What does the figure of jelly suggest? **Act** = agency, operation.

207. **Dreadful**: full of dread. Cf. Chaucer's "with dredeful foot" (*Knight's Tale*, 621).

214. **Did you not speak to it?** What word has the emphasis? Cf. line 206. Why "it" instead of "him," when Horatio has said "your father"? Is the use of the neuter pronoun maintained throughout the scene?

216. **It head**: an old form of the possessive which occurs sixteen times in the First Folio, as against ten occurrences of *its*. Cf. "it had it head bit off by it young" (*Lear*, I, iv, 236). *His* was the usual possessive form for both masculine and neuter.

216-20. Cf. I, i, 147. Has Shakespeare heightened the suspense by interrupting the Ghost before it has imparted its secret?

217. **Like as.** Not to be confused with the use of *like* alone as a conjunction, which is contrary to the best usage, and which has arisen from the ellipsis of *as* in the phrase that is here used.

219. Cf. I, i, 148-49.

225. What is in Hamlet's mind? Cf. line 242.

226. To what does "arm'd" refer?

229. **Then saw you not his face?** Is "his" necessarily personal here? See note on line 216. But how does Horatio understand it? The First Quarto has a period after "face." What in that case is the implication of the line?

231-32. Is this consistent with I, i, 62? How do you account for the discrepancy?

233. **Pale or red?** The First Quarto has a comma after "pale," and this is probably the better reading. The pause

gives to "or red" almost the quality of an afterthought, as if suggested by the idea (which is evidently in Hamlet's mind) that the Ghost has come in anger; and it is to "or red" that Horatio's "Nay" answers. Observe the impression of verisimilitude which Hamlet's minute questions give.

237. **Very like, very like.** Is Hamlet concerned with his own feelings, or absorbedly intent upon the Ghost?

239. **Longer, longer.** What effect does this difference of opinion have upon our impression of *reality?*

240. **His beard was grizzled,—no?** All the Folios and Quartos have a period after "no." The Quartos have a comma, the Folios an interrogation point, after "grizzled" (in the Quartos, "grizzley"). Many modern editors put an interrogation point after both words. Read the line aloud with the punctuations: . . . "grizzled? No?"; . . . "grizzled? No."; . . . "grizzled,—no?," and consider the difference in meaning. With line 242: "a sable silver'd," cf. *Sonnet XII,* 4.

242. **I will watch to-night.** Where is the emphasis? Is Hamlet lacking in decision, so far as we have yet seen?

244-46. Why such strong language on Hamlet's part?

251. **Your loves.** The plural is often used in Shakespeare (where we should use the singular) in designating attributes or qualities ascribed to more than one person; cf. I, i, 173; I, ii, 15; II, ii, 14.

254. Cf. line 163.

256. **I doubt some foul play.** Has this explanation occurred to any of the others? Cf. I, i, 68-69, 112-25, 130-39.

256. **Would the night were come!** Notice Hamlet's eagerness to have the time come round, and observe carefully, as you go on with the play, how he actually meets opportunities as they present themselves.

Summarize carefully all the additional information of which this scene has put us in possession. On whom is everything in the scene made to focus?

ACT I. SCENE III.

In Scene III our attention is, for the time being, entirely withdrawn from the Ghost; it is a new strand that is being woven.

The first scene fixed our interest, through the Ghost, upon the mystery of the elder Hamlet's death; the second joined with that the inexplicable haste of the Queen's marriage; the third adds another fact of crucial importance—Hamlet's love for Ophelia, especially as it is regarded by her father and brother. With these three people Hamlet's destiny is intimately linked, and although he does not himself appear, it is nevertheless about him that the whole scene centers. Directly or indirectly, when the first three scenes are ended, the Ghost, Horatio, the King, the Queen, Ophelia, Polonius, and Laertes have been brought into relation with Hamlet, in connection with one or the other of the three salient facts, and with the third scene the exposition proper is concluded.

The quieter setting of Scene III and the more domestic tenor of its dialogue afford a certain relief from the high tension of the preceding scenes.

1. How has this been prepared for? Watch, as you read, for other instances of Shakespeare's skill in providing beforehand the explanation (or *motivation*) of actions still to come. Would a novelist, in this case, have been under the same necessity?

2-3. **As the winds give benefit And convoy is assistant:** now that the winds are advantageous, and means of conveyance are ready.

6. **A toy in blood:** an idle fancy, due to mere impulse. For *toy* in this sense cf. "light-wing'd toys Of feather'd Cupid" (*Othello,* I, iii, 269): "no jealous toy Concerning you" (*ibid,* III, iv, 156); and cf. I, iv, 75 (with note). *Blood* is often used of passion or impulse, as opposed to reason; see especially III, ii, 74, and cf. *Merchant of Venice,* I, ii, 17: "the brain may devise laws for the blood." Notice how the idea of "toy" is carried out in "trifling" and "fashion."

7. **Primy nature:** nature in its springtime.

9. **Suppliance of a minute:** that which serves to fill up or supply the moment. Notice how the idea of transitoriness ("of a minute") is carried out in "not permanent," "not lasting," and observe the beauty of the phrasing.

10. **No more but so?** The Quartos and Folios have a period, and there is much to be said in favor of their reading. The first few words which Shakespeare puts into the mouth of

a character are often peculiarly in keeping, and Ophelia's words, so punctuated, are like those of a docile child, repeating something it knows it must learn to say. Compare especially the light thrown by lines 104-05 on Ophelia's training.

11-14. Observe how the idea of "crescent" is amplified in "grow," "waxes," "grows wide." "This temple" refers to the body (see *St. John*, ii, 21, and cf. *Macbeth*, II, iii, 73; *Rape of Lucrece*, 719, 1172), and the figure is carried out in "service." With the word-pair "mind and soul" cf. the similar pairs in lines 12, 21, 23, 26, 35, and 41.

26. **In his particular act and place:** under the limitations imposed by his rank upon his action.

14-28. Is Laertes's general position sound, from the point of view of worldly wisdom?

34. **In the rear.** Observe the military figure carried out in the next line.

40. **Buttons:** buds; cf. French *bouton*. **Disclosed** = opened.

44. Even with no tempter present, youth rebels against self-restraint. Does Laertes seem to be very sure of either Hamlet's honor or Ophelia's purity? Does this throw so much light on their character as on his?

50. **The primrose path.** Cf. "the primrose way to the everlasting bonfire" (*Macbeth*, II, iii, 21): "the flowery way that leads to the broad gate and the great fire" (*All's Well*, IV, v, 56). See also R. L. Stevenson: "Life is over, life was gay: We have come the primrose way."

51. **Recks not his own rede:** heeds not his own counsel.

51-52. **O, fear me not. I stay too long.** Is Laertes interested in hearing his "good lesson" turned against himself? *Fear me not* = have no fear about *me*.

55. Cf. I, ii, 58-60. Is there a real discrepancy?

56. **Sits.** Cf. I, ii, 124, and especially *Merchant of Venice*, I, i, 18.

57. **There.** What gesture is implied?

59. **Character:** inscribe. Accented on the second syllable.

61. **Familiar, but by no means vulgar:** unconstrainedly friendly, without making yourself cheap. The best commentary on *vulgar*, as here used, is *I Henry IV*, III, ii, 39-41.

63. What is the figure? Pope substitutes *hooks* for *hoops*. What objection to the emendation? Make clear to yourself the

figures in the next two lines. Does Shakespeare seem to think in abstract, or concrete terms? Go back over the preceding lines of this scene, and pick out the figures. Are they there for ornament, as something extraneous, or are they part of the very texture of the thought? Watch for this characteristic of Shakespeare's mode of expression as you read.

65. **Comrade.** Probably accented on the last syllable.

69. **Censure:** judgment, opinion—as constantly in Shakespeare.

71. **Rich, not gaudy.** Notice that this repeats "costly . . . not expressed in fancy" (i. e., not fantastic). Be careful to avoid the common misquotation "neat, but not gaudy."

74. This line (which appears in various forms in the Quartos and Folios) is pretty certainly corrupt, and numerous emendations have been suggested. If we read: "Are most select and generous in that," we have the gist of it. (It has been cleverly conjectured that "of" and "chief" were in the margin of the manuscript as alternatives for "in" and "best' of line 73, and that they got into line 74 by mistake).

77. **Husbandry:** thrift, economy; cf. "there's husbandry in heaven, their candles are all out" (*Macbeth,* II, i, 4).

58-81. With Polonius's advice to Laertes compare that of the Countess to Bertram in *All's Well,* I, i, 70-79, and identify the correspondences. Polonius's speech is in part suggested by a passage in Lyly's *Euphues,* in which Euphues gives to his friend Philautus (who is on his way to England, as Laertes is on his way to France) what he too calls "these few precepts." Compare the following with Shakespeare: "Be not lavish of thy tongue. . . . Every one that shaketh thee by the hand, is not joined to thee in heart. . . . Be not quarrelous for every light occasion: they are . . . ready to revenge an injury, but never wont to proffer any: they never fight without provoking, and once provoked they never cease. . . . It shall be there better to hear what they say, than to speak what thou thinkest: they have long ears and short tongues, quick to hear, and slow to utter" (*Euphues,* ed. Arber, p. 246). Look up also Lord Burleigh's "ten precepts" to his son Robert Cecil, as quoted in the *Variorum Hamlet,* Vol. II, p. 239. The gist of Polonius's sheaf of maxims seems to be the avoidance of the "unproportioned," the steering of a safe middle course.

94. **Put on**: imparted to; cf. *As You Like It,* I, ii, 99-100.

99. **Tenders**: offers; cf. "legal tender."

101. **Affection! pooh!** One object of this scene is to disclose the character of Polonius, Laertes, and Ophelia, together with their attitude towards life, as constituting an essential element in Hamlet's immediate environment. What insight into Polonius's character is given by this speech?

104. What does this tell us of Ophelia?

107. **Tender**: hold dear, take care of. Polonius—who piques himself on his powers of expression—is playing on the two senses of the word. To "crack the wind of the poor phrase" is to run it till it is out of breath.

109. **You'll tender me a fool**: either, you'll present *yourself* to me as a fool; or, you'll make *me* a public laughing-stock.

112. **Fashion you may call it.** Polonius here means what Laertes meant in line 6.

115. **Springes to catch woodcocks.** Woodcocks were proverbial for their stupidity. Cf. V, ii, 317; *Winter's Tale,* IV, iii, 36. *Springe* = snare.

122. **Entreatments**: interviews. The idea of *negotiations,* which the word has, is carried out in "command to parley."

127-30. **Brokers** are go-betweens, panders; **dye** = color; **investments** = garments (cf. "wolves in sheep's clothing"); **breathing** = whispering.

131. **For all**: once for all.

133. **Moment leisure.** *Moment* is used as an adjective. Cf. "Lethe wharf" (I, v, 33); "region kites" (II, ii, 607).

134. Cf. lines 120-23. How do you account for the change in Polonius's orders?

136. Look back over Ophelia's speeches. What tentative judgment should you form of her character? What is Polonius's reading of Hamlet's character? How does it differ from Laertes's estimate? Is it very likely that any of them will understand him?

ACT I. SCENE IV.

The first three scenes have brought before us the chief actors in the tragedy, in their relations to each other, and to certain momentous facts, but the action proper has not yet begun. The forces involved are still in equilibrium, however unstable; something must occur which shall disturb the balance, and precipitate the action. And the impulsion which releases the latent forces and sets them in motion is the revelation of the Ghost. Scene IV leads up to this; in Scene V we are put in possession of it, and Hamlet is face to face with the problem upon whose solution the rest of the tragedy depends.

The event or circumstance which initiates the action is called the Exciting Force. In *Macbeth* it is the prophecy of the witches; in *Romeo and Juliet,* the meeting between Romeo and Juliet at the Capulets' ball. What is it in *Julius Cæsar?* Can you point out the Exciting Force in any of the novels you have read or studied?

1. What connecting link in this line with Scene 1?

2. **Eager**: sharp, keen. Look up the etymology, and cf. I, v, 69.

1-4. Why does the scene open with this unimportant conversation?

10-12. Cf. V, ii, 285-89. This seems to have been actually a Danish custom.

12. **Is it a custom?** Why does Horatio not know?

15. **Manner**: custom, fashion. Be careful not to confuse with *manor.*

16. **More honor'd in the breach than the observance**: more honored by breaking than by keeping.

17. What does "east and west" modify?

19. **They clepe us drunkards.** The Danes were notorious for their prowess in drinking, but Shakespeare probably has the English in mind as well. See especially *Othello,* II, iii, 79-87.

19-20. **With swinish phrase Soil our addition**: by calling us swine they tarnish our honorable name. *Addition:* title of distinction—as constantly in Shakespeare. See II, i, 46-47, and cf. *Henry V,* V, ii, 366-69: "shall name your Highness . . . with this addition, in French, *Notre très-cher fils Henri, Roi d'Angleterre, Héritier de France*"; *Macbeth,* I, iii, 105-06: "He bade me . . . call thee thane of Cawdor; In which addition, hail!"

20. **And indeed.** Hamlet recognizes the *fact* which lies behind the reputation.

21. **Perform'd at height**: carried to the highest pitch of achievement.

22. **Our attribute**: that which is attributed to us; hence, our reputation.

23. **In particular men.** Hamlet is passing from the case of nations to that of individuals. It is characteristic of his speculative turn of mind to go off from the concrete occurrence into philosophical reflections, but the passage serves a dramatic purpose as well. For in following the rather intricate expression of Hamlet's thought, our attention is distracted, for the moment, from the expected arrival of the Ghost, and its third appearance comes, like the others, with a shock of surprise. Compare the manner in which Shakespeare led up to the first two appearances.

24. **Mole of nature**: natural blemish. For the idiom, see note on I, ii, 4.

25. With this line compare *Rape of Lucrece*, 537-39: "Worse than a . . . birth-hour's blot; For marks descried in men's nativity Are nature's faults, not their own infamy."

27. **The o'ergrowth of some complexion.** *Complexion* is here used in the sense it had in the psychology of the Middle Ages, i. e., a mingling in various proportions of the four liquid elements, blood, choler, phlegm, and black bile. There were four complexions, named according to the predominant element: the sanguine (blood), the choleric (choler or bile), the phlegmatic (phlegm), and the melancholy (black bile). Where the elements were justly mixed, health and a balanced disposition (or temperament) resulted. Cf. *Julius Cæsar*, V, v, 73-75: "His life was gentle, and the elements So mix'd in him that Nature might stand up And say to all the world, 'This was a man!'" The undue predominance of any one element disturbed the balance, and the best commentary on Hamlet's phrase is found in Ben Jonson's lines in the Induction to *Every Man out of his Humour:* "The choler, melancholy, phlegm and blood . . . Receive the name of humours. Now thus far It may, by metaphor, apply itself Unto the general disposition: *As when some one peculiar quality Doth so possess a man, that it doth draw All his affects, his spirits, and his powers, In their confluctions, all to run one way,* This may be truly said to be a humour." *Humor,* then, as Ben Jonson uses it, is almost

the exact equivalent of Hamlet's "the o'ergrowth of some complexion," with its implication of a lack of proper balance among the elements, which may even break down the strongholds of reason itself. Is Shakespeare putting into Hamlet's mouth what is in reality applicable to Hamlet himself? Keep this question in mind as you read the play.

29-30. Some habit (like that of the Danes' excessive drinking) which permeates with its corrupting influence even the pleasing forms of social intercourse.

30. **That these men.** "That" takes up the previous "that" in line 24, but the construction has changed, and it changes again within the next few lines. "The stamp of one defect" (line 31) resumes the "vicious mole of nature" (line 24). What is the cause of the broken structure of this long sentence? Is it quite the same as the cause which underlies the broken structure of the soliloquy in Scene II?

32. **Nature's livery, or fortune's star:** the mark which nature put on them (as if it were her badge or uniform) when they were born (cf. "in their birth"), or which fortune imposed through the influence of their star (see Introduction, p. xxvi).

34. **Undergo:** carry, partake of. Cf. "to undergo such ample grace and honor" (*Measure for Measure,* I, i, 24).

35. **Shall . . . take:** are sure to take.

35. **The general censure:** the opinion of everybody. This idiom is the reverse of the "thieves of mercy" construction (see note on I, ii, 4); the adjective limits the extent or sphere of the noun. Cf. "mortal preparation" (*All's Well,* III, vi, 81) = preparation for death; "the hospitable canon" (*Coriolanus,* I, x, 26) = the law of hospitality; "a Roman thought" (*Antony and Cleopatra,* I, ii, 87) = a thought of Rome.

36-38. The text of these lines is hopelessly corrupt, and not less than a hundred emendations have been suggested. The one thing that is clear is that the statement is meant to be a summary of what has preceded. "Eale" pretty certainly is "evil" (the Second and Third Quartos have "deale" for "devil" in II, ii, 628; cf. Scotch *deil*); "doubt" may be "dout," i. e., "do out," put out, banish (cf. IV, vii, 192 and note); "of a" may be a misreading of "often"; "dram" stands for a very small quantity (cf. *Merchant of Venice,* IV, i, 6: "empty From any dram of mercy"). The meaning would then be: The particle of evil often drives out in men's estimation the whole noble substance to his [i. e., the particular man's; see line 23] own scandal [i. e., he becomes traduced and taxed of other men]. Or "his" may be equivalent to "its," in which case the meaning would be: drives out the whole noble substance so that *it* becomes itself a scandal. The figure seems to be based on the "little leaven [that] leaveneth the whole lump" (*I Corinthians,* v, 6).

40. **Spirit of health:** *saved* spirit—contrasted with "goblin damned." How is the same contrast elaborated in the next two lines?

43. **Questionable:** demanding speech. Cf. "It would be spoke to" (I, i, 45, and note).

45. **King, father, royal Dane.** Many modern editors punctuate "King, father; royal Dane, O, answer me." What is gained by this reading?

47. **Canonized:** buried according to the canons or rites of the church. The accent is on the second syllable.

52. **Dead corse.** *Corpse* originally meant body in general, whether living or dead. Cf. *II Kings,* xix, 35. "Complete" is accented on the first syllable.

54. **We fools of nature:** we, the sport or playthings of nature. Strict grammatical construction would require "*us*"; and "to shake" (instead of "shakest") involves an anacoluthon.

55. **Disposition:** here equivalent to "nature, constitution."

63. **Then I will follow it.** Does Hamlet show any sign of hesitation? How often is this declaration repeated?

64. **What should be the fear:** what do you think there is to be afraid of? "Should" is used (like the German *sollen*) with reference to what some one else thinks or says.

71. **Beetles.** Apparently Shakespeare was the first to use this word as a verb. It has the general sense (probably with some reference to "beetle-browed"; see Dictionary, and quotation from *Henry V* below) of "jut, overhang." For the account of the cliff (which is here a touch of Shakespeare's imagination) see especially *Lear,* IV, vi, 1-79, and cf. *Henry V,* III, i, 11-14: "let the brow o'erwhelm it As fearfully as does a galled rock O'erhang and jutty his confounded base, Swill'd with the wild and wasteful ocean."

73. **Deprive your sovereignty of reason**: take away the control which reason exercises.

75. **Toys of desperation**: desperate fancies; cf. I, iii, 6, and note.

81. **My fate cries out.** It is not necessary, on the ground of this phrase, to make Hamlet more of a fatalist than most men are on occasion.

82. **Artery**: nerve. **Nerve**, in the next line, means sinew. The strangling of the Nemean lion (the adjective is here accented on the first syllable) was one of the twelve labors of Hercules.

85. Once more, Does Hamlet lack determination or decision? **Lets**: hinders.

91. **It**: the "issue" of line 89.

91. **Nay**: that is, instead of leaving it to Heaven, let's take a hand ourselves.

ACT I. SCENE V.

In Scene IV our interest in the Ghost was subordinated to our immediate preoccupation with Hamlet. In the first ninety lines of Scene V the subordination is reversed.

2-4. Where *is* this spirit? Cf. lines 10-13, and avoid confusing the passage with our idea of *hell.* What is "my hour"? Cf. I, i, 147-49; I, ii, 218-19, and see *Lear,* III, iv, 121.

6. **Bound.** Hamlet probably uses the word in the sense of "ready" (see III, iii, 41-42, and cf. "homeward bound"); the Ghost takes it up in the sense of "compelled."

12. **Crimes**: faults, offenses. **My days of nature**: my natural days, my life on earth.

17. **Spheres.** The stars were regarded as set in concentric spheres revolving about the earth (cf. IV, vii, 15). Look up in the Shakespeare Concordance the passages quoted under *sphere.*

19. **An end**: on end. *An* is an older form of *on.* It survives in such words as *alive, asleep* (cf. "on sleep," *Acts,* xiii, 36), *afire, a-hunting, a-fishing.*

21. **Eternal blazon**: blazon of eternity—i. e., the revelation of the secrets of his prison-house.

25. The Ghost's injunction constitutes the moving force of

the drama. It must be remembered that according to the ethics of the period to which the old story of Hamlet belongs—and indeed of Shakespeare's own time—revenge in such a case was a *duty*.

26. Does Hamlet seem to have suspected just this?

29. **Haste me to know't**: let me know it at once.

29-31. Observe the irony of the contrast between Hamlet's words and what actually happens. Is his simile characteristic? (**Meditation** here means "thought"; cf. "as quick as thought").

32-33. Cf. "a Lethe'd dullness" (*Antony and Cleopatra,* II, i, 27). Lethe is that "slow and silent stream . . . the river of oblivion" (*Paradise Lost,* II, 582-83), and the fat water-weed clinging to its crumbling wharf has absorbed its "sleepy drench." Instead of *roots* the Folio has *rots,* which may be right; cf. *Antony and Cleopatra,* I, iv, 45-47: "This common body, Like to a vagabond flag upon the stream, Goes back and back, lackeying the varying tide, To rot itself with motion." It is possible that *wharf* means here the bank of the river. For the construction of "Lethe wharf" see note on I, iii, 133.

36. **The whole ear of Denmark**: the ear of all Denmark.

37. **Process**: account, official narrative; cf. the French *procès verbal.*

40-41. Has Hamlet actually suspected his uncle of his father's murder (cf. line 26), or is it his general dislike and aversion that is referred to? Does I, ii, 256, indicate a definite suspicion, or only a general misgiving?

42. Shakespeare does not make Claudius a contemptible person, and it is a mistake so to represent him on the stage. See Introduction, pp. xviii-xix. "Wit" of course refers to intellectual power of any sort.

52. **Those of mine.** Incorrect syntax. What should it be? **To** = compared with; cf. I. ii, 140.

61. **Secure**: unsuspecting, free from anxiety or apprehension. Cf. Ben Jonson: "Man may securely sin, but safely never." Shakespeare accents *secure* sometimes on the first, sometimes on the last syllable. Which is it here?

62. Some substance having a poisonous juice, and variously interpreted as ebony, henbane, yew, hemlock,

68. **Posset:** curdle, coagulate. A posset was a hot drink composed of milk and other ingredients, curdled with wine or ale; cf. *Macbeth,* II, ii, 7.

69. **Eager:** tart, biting, acid. Cf. I, iv, 2.

71. **Bark'd about:** encrusted, as with bark.

72. **Lazar-like:** like a leper; look up the etymology of *lazar.* It must be remembered that lepers were a familiar sight in England during the Middle Ages.

77. Not having received the Eucharist, unequipped (for the last journey), without extreme unction. Compare a frequently quoted passage from Malory's *Morte Darthur:* "My fair lords, said Sir Launcelot, . . . give me my rites. So when he was houseled and aneled, and had all that a Christian man ought to have, he prayed the Bishop that his fellows might bear his body to Joyous Gard" (Book XXI, chapter xii).

80. This line should probably be assigned to Hamlet. The next line seems to be a reply to it, and we should expect some such exclamation from Hamlet anyway.

81. **If thou hast nature in thee:** if you have any natural affection.

83. **Luxury:** lust, lasciviousness. Cf. *Macbeth,* IV, iii, 58: "Luxurious, avaricious, false, deceitful." Shakespeare never uses either *luxury* or *luxurious* in their modern sense.

85. **Taint not thy mind.** The Ghost leaves entirely to Hamlet the details of his revenge ("howsoever thou pursuest this act"), but he imposes two specific injunctions. Hamlet is not to let his mind become corrupt—that is, his revenge must be sternly just, and untainted by personal feeling; and he is to spare his mother. What impression do you gain of the elder Hamlet's character?

88. **Sting:** a much stronger word in older than in modern English.

89. **Matin:** morning; used only here in this sense.

90. **Uneffectual.** Either because the glow-worm's fire is light without heat, or because its light is lost in that of the morning.

93. **Fie:** a stronger word then than now, and used with more dignified connotation. The line, however, has two extra syllables, and "O, fie!" is possibly an actor's interpolation. But see Hamlet's similar use of it in II, ii, 617.

97. **This distracted globe.** What gesture is implied?

106. **Smiling.** What hint as to the manners and bearing of the King? Cf. line 43, and recall the King's suavity in Scene II.

107. **My tables,** etc. The trick of the scholar, rather than of the man of action. Hamlet probably does almost automatically, in the terrible excitement under which he is laboring, something which he has been in the habit of doing. But see also the excellent note in Bradley, pp. 409-12. **Tables:** memorandum book.

110. **So, uncle, there you are.** Does Hamlet seem almost to feel that by putting the thing down in his little book he has really *done* something? Do you feel that his satisfaction in *formulation* promises well for *action?*

110. **Now to my word:** that is, my watchword, which perhaps he writes down too.

114. **So be it!** This probably completes "I have sworn't," rather than answers "Heaven secure him."

116. Hamlet is imitating the falconer's call to his bird.

123-24. It is entirely unnecessary to interpret Hamlet's levity as a sign of mental aberration. He is laboring under intense excitement, and his "wild and whirling words" are the expression of a nervous exaltation of a sufficiently well-known type. A tendency to half-hysterical levity on solemn occasions, when the feelings are tensely strung, is a familiar experience even with persons whose mental balance is not open to question. Add to this the fact that Hamlet cannot speak openly to Horatio in the presence of Marcellus.

125. Notice the grave dignity of Horatio's reply.

127. **Circumstance:** circumlocution. Cf. "To wind about my love with circumstance" (*Merchant of Venice,* I, i, 154).

132. **I'll go pray.** Cf. "I will go seek" (II, i, 101); "I'll go watch" (*Merry Wives,* I, iv, 7); "go sleep" (*Tempest,* II, i, 190).

134-35. Observe again Hamlet's unfeigned courtesy—and also Horatio's assurance of a friendship which cannot take offense, even where it may not understand.

136. **By Saint Patrick.** Commentators have exercised a good deal of ingenuity in explaining why Hamlet should swear

by St. Patrick. There probably *is* no special reason, except that he is using "wild and whirling words."

138. **An honest ghost.** Either an *honorable* ghost, or, a *real* ghost—i. e., not an evil spirit, as Horatio, in I, iv, 69 ff., half suspects it is. And cf. especially II, ii, 627-32.

147. **We have sworn . . . already.** "In faith" (lines 145, 146) is itself an oath.

148. **Upon my sword.** Swearing on the sword was a custom of immemorial antiquity. In Christian times the oath was taken on the hilt of the sword, so that one really swore by the cross. Cf. "swore . . . upon the cross of a Welsh hook" (*I Henry IV,* II, iv, 371-73). What significance has Hamlet's "Indeed . . . indeed"?

150. Hamlet, who has been gradually collecting himself, again shows "his recoil from horror to half-hysterical jesting" (Dowden). **Truepenny:** honest old fellow. The word was familiar to all Elizabethan theater-goers.

156. **Hic et ubique:** "here and everywhere."

163. **Pioner** (accented on first syllable). Look up *pioneer* in the dictionary. The reference here is to the Ghost's "working i' the earth."

165. **As a stranger give it welcome:** show it the hospitality accorded to a stranger—that is, receive it, take it as it is, asking no questions, not seeking to pry into its secrets.

167. **In your philosophy.** "Your" should receive the lightest possible accent. It is *not* the possessive pronoun, as if it were *Horatio's* philosophy that Hamlet meant, but it is "used indefinitely, not with reference to the person addressed, but to what is known and common" (Schmidt). Cf. IV, iii, 22, 24, and add: "there is not a more fearful wild-fowl than your lion" (*Midsummer Night's Dream,* III, i, 33); "your serpent of Egypt is bred now of your mud by the operation of your sun" (*Antony and Cleopatra,* II, vii, 29-30). "That *philosophy* we talk so much about" would be a general equivalent. The Folios have "our"—but the stress is still on "philosophy."

169 ff. Hamlet's behavior later in the play must be interpreted in the light of this definitely expressed warning of his intention. See Introduction, p. xxiii.

174. **Encumber'd:** perhaps, "folded" (cf. *Tempest,* I, ii,

224: "his arms in this sad knot"). The particular gesture is left to the actor.

182. **Rest, rest, perturbed spirit!** Hamlet's own composure has, in this last speech, returned again.

187. **Let us go in together.** Compare with the mood of lines 127-32.

189-90. These famous lines are rather an expression of Hamlet's temperamental distaste for the task which has been set him, than a passionate outcry against Fate, as they are sometimes interpreted. "Cursed spite" connotes a certain vexation at being disturbed.

191. What action is implied? Compare the Duke's "Nay, we'll go down together, sir," in Browning's *My Last Duchess.*

Try to formulate your impression of Hamlet's character, as it is disclosed in Act I. Try also to realize the practical difficulties of the situation in which he finds himself. Suppose he killed the King on sight, what motive would be urged against him (cf. I, ii, 109)? In what position would such action place his mother? What motive could he give to clear himself? Did anybody else hear the Ghost's message? Do lines 170 ff. suggest that he is planning to investigate?

Act II. Scene I.

The question that interests us, at the close of Act I, is: "What will Hamlet do?" And to that question, of course, the rest of the play is the answer. What he has done between the close of the first act and the beginning of the second we learn gradually and indirectly. That considerable time has intervened is clear. Laertes has been long enough in Paris to need more money (II, i, 1); the ambassadors have had time to go to Norway and return (II, ii, 40-41); a great change, amounting to a "transformation," in Hamlet's demeanor has been of long enough duration to permit Rosencrantz and Guildenstern to arrive (presumably from Wittenberg) in response to a message from the King (II, ii, 1-14). We can even tell pretty definitely the actual length of time that has elapsed. For in Act I the elder Hamlet had been not two months dead (I, ii, 138); in Act III he had been twice two months dead

(III, ii, 136); and between Acts II and III only one night intervenes (cf. II, ii, 565, and III, ii, 80). Two months, then, have passed, and the King is still alive. Meantime, what of Hamlet?

The first scene answers the question only indirectly. Like the third scene of Act I it centers about the household of Polonius, and it falls into two easily distinguishable parts. The first has to do ostensibly with Laertes, but it is really the disclosure of Polonius's character with which it is concerned. The second deals directly with Ophelia, but its importance lies even more in what we learn through her of Hamlet than in what she reveals about herself. And what we learn of Hamlet is significant enough.

3. **You shall do marvelous wisely.** Whom is Polonius delicately complimenting?

6. **Marry, well said,** etc. Observe again the characterising touch.

7. **Me.** The so-called "ethical dative." It is lightly accented, almost an enclitic; "for me" (which we should have to use to give its meaning) says a little too much. Cf. "Give me your present to one Master Bassanio" (*Merchant of Venice,* II, ii, 115); "hear me this" (*Twelfth Night,* V, i, 123).

10. By giving the conversation this turn in this indirect way.

11. **More nearer.** The double comparative is common in Shakespeare. Cf. (in this play) III, ii, 316; V, ii, 129; and add "more elder" (*Merchant of Venice,* IV, i, 251); "more braver" (*Tempest,* I, ii, 439); etc.

12. **Particular demands:** the questions suggested in lines 7-9. The implied contrast is not between direct questions and more general ones, but between any questions ("your" is perhaps used as in I, v, 167; see note) and the second step which Reynaldo is now to take—that of assuming a distant knowledge of Laertes.

19. **Put on him:** lay to his charge.

23. **Noted and most known.** Polonius has a trick of repeating himself; cf. lines 15, 17. Here it is mere tautology.

27. On what word (or words) is the emphasis in this line? Cf. lines 20-21. Reynaldo's and Polonius's moral standards are not quite the same.

28. **Season:** qualify, temper; cf. I, ii, 192.

29. **Another**: a further, a different. Polonius is distinguishing between the "usual slips" he has named, and *immoderate addiction* to such vices (especially the last), which he expresses by "incontinency."

31. **Breathe . . . so quaintly**: whisper his faults so delicately. For *breathe,* cf. line 44, and I, iii, 130.

34. A wildness, unruliness, in untamed blood.

35. **Of general assault**: that attack everybody.

36. **Wherefore should you do this?** Polonius evidently piques himself on his astuteness as a mind-reader.

38. **A fetch of warrant**: a warrantable stratagem.

41. **Mark you.** What action or gesture on Polonius's part may be supposed to fill up this line? Cf. also line 62, and II, ii, 105.

43-44. Having ever seen the youth of whom you whisper guilty of the aforesaid faults.

45. **Closes with you in this consequence**: agrees with you, in thus following up what you have said. *Consequence* in Shakespeare has often its general sense of "that which follows."

47. **Addition.** See note on I, iv, 20.

49-51. Polonius is not far from his dotage.

58. **A'**: a colloquialism for *he.* **O'ertook in's rouse**; overcome in his cups; or (possibly), caught or surprised as he was drinking.

63. **This carp of truth.** What does Polonius *expect* to find?

64. **We of wisdom and of reach**: we wise and far-seeing people. Cf. "we of taste and feeling" (*Love's Labour's Lost,* IV, ii, 30).

65. By circuitous ways and oblique attempts. **Assays of bias** is a metaphor from the game of bowls. The "bias" is that in the form or weighting of the bowl which gives it an oblique line of motion, so that it is aimed away from the Jack which it is to hit. Look up *King John,* II, i, 574-86, for a full working out of the figure.

66. Polonius, before his senility, was probably a practiced diplomat, and he still delights in applying to trivial affairs the elaborate machinations of statecraft.

68. **You have me**: you understand me; cf. modern slang: "You *get* me."

71. **Observe his inclination in yourself.** Either, Observe his disposition *by* yourself (as contrasted with hearsay); or, Conform yourself to his inclination; or, (less probably), Observe your own inclination, and so judge his.

73. **And let him ply his music.** It is difficult to be sure whether this is to be taken literally or figuratively. If it is literal, the upshot of all Polonius's elaborate strategy is, "Don't let him neglect his music!" If (as is more probable) it is figurative, it means: "Let him go his own gait nevertheless." In either case we learn something of Polonius. Has Shakespeare some object, related to the development of the action, in the rather terrific exposure of Polonius in this scene? Keep this in mind as you go on with the play.

79-81. Hamlet is exhibiting the conventional marks of a lover, which are described in *As You Like It,* III, ii, 391-400. But he is also showing the strain of the past two months. See further the note on II, ii, 6.

77-100. Why does Hamlet come to Ophelia as he does? Is it to see for the last time if she is the one person who can help him? Or is it a farewell? Or does he do it to heighten the impression that he is mad? In any case what has he learned about Ophelia? Is there anything in the scene which is inconsistent with the assumption that he really loved her?

102. **Ecstacy:** madness. Cf. III, i, 168; III, iv, 73-75, 138-39 (cf. 141).

103. Whose quality of violence destroys itself—i. e., love, whose very quality is violence (vehemence, lack of restraint), often undoes the lover.

107. Has Polonius forgotten what he said in I, iii, 132-35? Is there any reason for his use of "you" in this line, as compared with "thy" and "thee" in lines 85 and 113?

109-10. Observe that up to this point Hamlet has showed no sign of breaking with Ophelia. Does he know why she has repelled his letters and refused to see him? Keep this in mind for its possible bearing on the difficult question raised by his later attitude toward Ophelia.

112. **Quote:** read, observe. Cf. "I have with exact view perused thee, Hector, And quoted joint by joint" (*Troilus and Cressida,* IV, v, 232-33).

115. **Cast beyond:** overshoot. Observe the irony of the fact that Polonius is doing precisely this again.

118-19. If we keep this love secret, its concealment may work us more mischief than its declaration cause us hatred. Polonius recognizes that for Ophelia to aspire to marry into the royal family (and for him to seem to aid and abet her) would be regarded as treasonable.

ACT II. SCENE II.

This long scene is of the utmost importance. The struggle between Hamlet and the King—the two "mighty opposites" of V, ii, 62—begins to appear in clearer outline, and the coming of the players, in which Hamlet sees and seizes an opportunity, points directly toward the climax of the action. Up to the appearance of the players, however, the center of interest is Hamlet's supposed madness, which is exhibited, with amazing skill, from various angles; while at the very end of the scene, in the second of the great soliloquies, we are made to see Hamlet as he sees himself. Throughout the scene, however, Hamlet is the central figure, as he is thrown into relief against now one background, now another.

1. **Rosencrantz and Guildenstern.** These are genuine Danish names. A courtier named Rosencrantz was in England at the time of the coronation of James I, in 1603, and both names appear as those of Danish students at the University of Padua at about the same time. Curiously enough the names "Jörgen Rossenkrantz" and "P. Guldenstern" are found on the same page of a German document (dealing with Danish affairs) dated 1577.

2. **Moreover that:** over and above that. Is the King sincere, or is he merely employing the "witchcraft of his wit"?

5. **So call it.** The Folio has "so I call it"—probably the better reading. As the line stands, "transformation" must be read with five syllables.

6. **The exterior.** This hint to the actor is not always taken. Does it throw any light upon Hamlet's appearance as Ophelia described it? Is it safe, in the light of the King's words, to take for granted that Hamlet's disordered attire at that time was assumed for that particular occasion?

7-10. Does Claudius think it *is* something more than the mere fact of the elder Hamlet's death? Observe, as you go on, the difference between his attitude and that of the others toward Hamlet's "transformation."

10-18. Observe what the King is really asking Rosencrantz and Guildenstern to do, and the skill with which he disguises its rather sinister import.

30. **In the full bent:** to the limit of our power. A figure drawn from archery. *Bent* signifies the extent to which a bow may be drawn; hence, degree of endurance, limit of capacity. Cf. III, ii, 401.

33-34. Rosencrantz and Guildenstern are perhaps the only characters in Shakespeare whom it is impossible to tell apart, and the fact is scarcely accidental. Their first two speeches are almost like an antiphony, and the way in which the King and Queen thank them emphasizes their lack of individuality.

38. **Heavens.** The plural of heaven is frequently used in Shakespeare where we should use the singular. **Practices** here means simply "proceedings, actions," but the word has frequently in Shakespeare a sinister significance (cf. IV, vii, 68; V, ii, 328), and there is probably dramatic irony in its employment here.

[Stage direction]: **Enter Polonius.** Why not Ophelia too? Cf. II, i, 101, 117.

42. **Still:** always, ever—the most common sense of the word in Shakespeare.

47. **Policy:** statecraft, diplomacy.

52. **My news.** Observe Polonius's self-conceit throughout the scene.

55. **Distemper:** derangement of body or mind. The word (originally denoting a disturbance of the balance—or temper—of the elements; see note on I, iv, 27) is now applied specifically to diseases of animals.

56. **The main:** the principal point, the main cause.

57. What does the Queen add to the King's statement in line 8?

61. **Upon our first:** as soon as we presented the case.

64. **Truly.** To be taken with "was."

67. **Falsely borne in hand:** deceived by false pretences.

79. **Regards of safety and allowance**: terms that secure your safety and are subject to your approval.

80. **Likes**: pleases.

81. **More consider'd time**: time fitter for consideration.

86. **Expostulate**: discuss. Polonius is doing his worst in the next lines.

90. **Brevity is the soul of wit.** *Wit* (which must not here be given its modern meaning) is "wisdom." To state a thing briefly is the very essence of wisdom—an ironical remark in Polonius's mouth! The phrase is one which, as a proverbial expression, has come to have a quite different meaning from that which it bears in the text.

92-94. Polonius either means that if you try to define true madness, you are mad yourself; or (more probably) he has lost the thread again, and reaches the lucid conclusion that to be mad is—to be mad!

95. **More matter, with less art.** The Queen does not elsewhere say ironical or cutting things, and probably does not here. Polonius's reply shows that he takes her comment as a compliment, and we may regard it as a gentle hint to come to the point. Polonius's own idea of "art" comes out in lines 97-99.

104. Merely more "art."

105. **Perpend**: consider. "A word used only by Pistol, Polonius, and the clowns" (Schmidt). What fills out the line? Cf. note on II, i, 41.

110. **Beautified**: endowed with beauty. The word does not seem to have been uncommon. It occurs, for instance, in the dedication to Nash's *Christ's Tears over Jerusalem* (1574): "To the most beautified lady, the lady Elizabeth Carey." Shakespeare himself uses it elsewhere (*Two Gentlemen of Verona,* IV, i, 55), but with a slightly different turn.—Polonius is setting himself up as a literary connoisseur. Cf. lines 488-89, 527.

113. **These**: these *be delivered.* A common formula in superscriptions. Cf. *Two Gentlemen of Verona,* III, i, 248-50: "Thy letters . . . shall be deliver'd Even in the milk-white bosom of thy love."

114. Notice the skill with which Shakespeare keeps the audience in mind. The Queen's question anticipates

any possible misunderstanding of what it is that is being read.

116-19. Hamlet is using *doubt* in more than one sense. In the first, second, and fourth lines it probably has its ordinary meaning; in the third it means "suspect."

120. **Numbers:** metres. It has been suggested that "reckon" here means to "number metrically"—i. e., to set down in numbers.

124. **Whilst this machine is to him:** while this body is his. *Machine* was not a prosaic word in Shakespeare's time. Why has it become so now? Compare its use in Wordsworth's "She was a Phantom of delight."

109-24. Hamlet's letter is undoubtedly to be taken as genuine, and may be supposed to have been written before his letters were repelled (II, i, 109). The first part is in the artificial style that was the fashion of the day (which seems strange to us because it *was* a passing fashion), but at line 120 there is an outburst of real feeling that sweeps away the affectation, while in the closing words Hamlet reverts to his own characteristic phraseology. Its mood is complex—but Hamlet was not a simple person.

125. **In obedience.** Cf. line 107. Polonius takes no chances of any possible disregard of *his* part in the matter.

126. **More above:** moreover.

132-34. *Had* he seen it at all, till he was told? Cf. I, iii, 90 ff.

136. Probably: If I had locked it up as a secret, as in a desk or note-book.

137. **Or given my heart a winking:** or bade my heart shut its eyes. Cf. *Acts,* xvii, 30: "the times of this ignorance God winked at."

138. **With idle sight.** Either, sight that did not perceive; or, sight that did not take it seriously.

139. **Round:** roundly, directly; cf. III, i, 191; III, iv. 5.

141. **Out of thy star:** out of the sphere in which thy star moves; hence, above thy rank. Cf. *Twelfth Night,* II, v, 156; "In my stars I am above thee."

148. **Watch:** sleeplessness, insomnia.

149. **Lightness:** light-headedness. Most of what Polonius says here may have been true (although not for the reason

that he gives), but he cannot be regarded as a trustworthy witness.

159. **The center**: the earth—which, according to the Ptolemaic astronomy, was the center of the universe. Cf. *Troilus and Cressida,* I, iii, 85: "The heavens themselves, the planets, and this center."

160. **Four hours.** Four was used colloquially as an indefinite numeral. The emendation *for* is unnecessary.

162. **I'll loose my daughter to him**: i. e., I'll give her free access to him. Polonius's phrase, however, is not very happy.

169. **Presently**: immediately, on the spot—not (as in modern usage) "before long, shortly." *Soon, by and by,* and *directly* (all of which originally meant "immediately") have suffered the same change.

172. **God-a-mercy**: gramercy; i. e., thank you.

174. **A fishmonger.** Whether Hamlet is doing more than using the most incongruous word he can think of, is doubtful. *Fishmonger* seems to have had certain coarse associations in the slang of the day, and Hamlet may possibly have used it for that reason.

182. **A god kissing carrion.** The Quartos and Folios have *good; god* is Warburton's emendation, and is probably correct. Cf. *Cymbeline,* III, iv, 166: "the greedy touch of common-kissing Titan"; *I Henry IV,* II, iv, 134: "Didst thou never see Titan kiss a dish of butter?" (*Titan* in Shakespeare always refers to the sun; cf. note on I, ii, 140). The idea that the sun could produce life was prevalent in the superstitions of the time. Cf. *Antony and Cleopatra,* II, vii, 29-31: "Your serpent of Nile is bred now of your mud by the operation of your sun." "A *good* kissing carrion" would mean carrion good to kiss, and would then refer to "a dead dog."

185-86. Hamlet is intentionally obscure. And since a man who is trying to talk like a madman will talk as unlike his usual self as possible (cf. again lines 4-7), we have no right to draw any conclusions concerning Ophelia from what Hamlet says here.

188. **How say you by that?** What do you say to that? or, What have you to say *about* that?—*not,* What do you mean *by* that? *By* = concerning.

190-91. There is nothing that Polonius does not know.

196. **Between who?** Hamlet intentionally misunderstands Polonius, and takes *matter* in the sense of "difficulty, quarrel." "Who" for "whom" is frequent in Shakespeare. Cf. I, ii, 190.

204. **Honesty:** decency.

205. **Should:** would inevitably.

221. **Except my life.** Such repetition is one of Hamlet's characteristic tricks. Cf. I, ii, 132, 135, 224, 237; I, v, 93, 106, 134-35, 183; II, ii, 194; III, i, 92; III, ii, 191.

228-30. Notice the genuine cordiality of Hamlet's greeting.

258-59. **Your ambition makes it one.** Rosencrantz and Guildenstern have adopted the King's theory, and are carrying out his instructions (lines 15-16) to gather as much as they may glean. But it is worth noting who does most of the questioning!

270. **Outstretched.** Various interpretations have been suggested; as, wide-famed; glorified; a reference to the strutting stage heroes, etc. But Hamlet is intentionally riddling, and since he says he cannot reason, we need not consider too curiously his fantastic conceit.

274. **No such matter:** not at all.

277. **In the beaten way of friendship:** speaking as friend to friend.

282. **A halfpenny:** *at* a halfpenny.

283. **Were you not sent for?** etc. Hamlet's suspicions have been aroused (perhaps by Rosencrantz's quibbling answer), and his tone changes.

287. **But to the purpose.** Either, *only so that it be* to the purpose; or (if it is taken as sarcasm), *except* to the purpose.

295. **The consonancy of our youth:** our "being of so young years brought up" together. *Consonancy* = agreement.

297. **A better proposer:** a better speaker. Hamlet, in this speech, is appealing directly to Rosencrantz and Guildenstern, as (perhaps) he had appealed by his silence to Ophelia, for the support of friendship in the net of intrigue that he feels closing in on him. And the touch of self-depreciation in "a better proposer" need not be taken as assumed.

301. **Of you:** on you.

305. **Prevent your discovery:** forestall your disclosure.

318. **Express**: perfectly fitted to its function or purpose.

321. **Quintessence**: literally, fifth essence. In the old philosophies it was the subtle substance that remained after the four elements were eliminated; hence, "the most subtle component part of anything, or that which makes it what it is" (Kittredge).

332-39. Hamlet is giving a brief list of some of the stock characters in the Elizabethan drama.

335. **The humorous man**: the man who is full of humors (see note on I, iv, 27), and so is fantastic, affected, whimsical. Ben Jonson's comedies—especially *Every Man in his Humour* and *Every Man out of his Humour*—are full of such characters. The word is not to be taken in its modern sense.

337. **Tickle o' the sere**: easily moved (to laughter). The *sere* was "the balance-lever of a gun-lock"; *tickle* means "unstable, precarious" (cf. *Measure for Measure,* I, ii, 176-78: "Thy head stands so tickle on thy shoulders that a milkmaid, if she be in love, may sigh it off"). A sentence of Crockett's serves as a fair paraphrase of Hamlet's meaning: "Her laugh was hung on a hair-trigger, to go off at every jest and fancy."

338. **Or the blank verse shall halt for't.** That is, If she can't talk freely in blank verse, then let the blank verse go lame, in order that she may—for speak freely she shall.

346. **Inhibition**: hindrance, suspension (of performances). It does not necessarily refer to a formal *prohibition.* The "late innovation" (i. e., the popularity of the children's companies) had the *effect* of a prohibition.

355. **On the top of question**: at the top of their voices—above the pitch of conversation.

356. **Tyrannically**: boisterously. Thus, Bottom in the *Midsummer Night's Dream* says: "Yet my chief humor is for a tyrant: I could play Ercles rarely, or a part to tear a cat in, to make all split." And after he has recited his ranting verses (*Midsummer Night's Dream,* II, i, 33-40) he adds: "This is . . . a tyrant's vein."

357-58. **Berattle the common stages**: berate the ordinary theaters, where the men's companies played.

358. **Many wearing rapiers are afraid of goose-quills**: many fashionable gentlemen are afraid of being satirized (i. e.,

by the dramatists who write for the children's companies), if they go to the ordinary theaters.

363. **The quality**: the profession—in this case, of players. Actors to-day call themselves "the profession."

364-68. The boys in the children's companies were choristers; when their voices changed, they would themselves have to become "common players," if they went on acting at all. But (Hamlet asks) by acting in plays which satirize (and so tend to drive out) the men's companies, are they not really cutting off their own future prospects? **Succession** = that which is to come, futurity.

369. **Much to do.** The phrase as here used is on its way to the substantive form, *to-do* (cf. *ado*), in the sense of "business, fuss."

370. **Tarre them:** set them on to fight. The word is used frequently of dogs; cf. *King John,* IV, i, 116-17: "Like a dog that is compell'd to fight, Snatch at his master that doth tarre him on."

372. **Argument:** the plot of a play; cf. III, ii, 242. The general sense of the passage is: No manager would bid anything for a play unless it added its quota to this popular controversy between the poets and the players—"the war of the theaters," as it is sometimes called. *Went to cuffs* = came to blows.

377. **Carry it away:** carry things before them.

378. **Hercules and his load.** Hercules bearing the world (a reference to one of the twelve labors) was the sign of the Globe Theater, so that Shakespeare is here alluding to his own theater, which, like the rest, is suffering from the controversy.

380. **It is not very strange.** The connection lies in the idea of following the fashion. People do it in the case of the theaters; they are just as fickle in the case of kings.

384. **'Sblood:** an abbreviation of "God's blood." Cf. line 604 and note.

384. **In this:** that is, in this following of fashion.

387. **Gentlemen, you are welcome to Elsinore:** addressed to Rosencrantz and Guildenstern, not to the players.

388. **The appurtenance of:** that which belongs to.

390. **Comply with you in this garb:** observe the forms of courtesy with you in this fashion. **Extent** is "behavior, welcome." Hamlet means to welcome the players warmly, but

he does not wish to humiliate his one-time friends in the presence of others by any show of coldness.

393. **My uncle-father.** "A little more than kin"!

396-98. I am mad only when the wind's north-north-west; the rest of the time my wits are keen enough. Another of Hamlet's riddling remarks—this time suggested by the sport of falconry. **Handsaw** is probably a corruption of *hernsaw* (heron), and the phrase is proverbial in its origin.

406-07. **You say right, sir,** etc. Hamlet is addressing Rosencrantz, and intentionally misleading Polonius as to the subject of the conversation.

410. **When Roscius was an actor in Rome.** Perhaps Hamlet means to imply that Polonius's news is rather old too. And of course his mention of actors maliciously takes the wind out of Polonius's sails. Roscius was the greatest of Roman actors.

412. **Buz, buz!** Blackstone says that "*Buz* used to be an interjection at Oxford when any one began a story that was generally known before"; cf. modern slang, "chestnuts."

414. Probably a line from some old ballad.

416. The list is of course intended to raise a laugh, but it is after all merely a somewhat exaggerated classification of actual Elizabethan plays. Shakespeare's own plays were divided into tragedies, comedies, and histories; *As You Like It* might very well be called "pastoral-comical"; *Richard III* and some others of the histories, "tragical-historical"; plays like *Winter's Tale* are "tragical-comical"—and so on.

418-19. **Scene individable, or poem unlimited:** plays that observe the unity of place, or plays that are not bound down by the unities.

419-20. **Seneca . . . Plautus.** Seneca wrote tragedies, Plautus, comedies, and both powerfully influenced the Elizabethan drama.

420-21. **For the law of writ and the liberty:** for following the text and for speaking extempore.

422. **Jephthah.** For the story of Jephthah's daughter, see *Judges,* xi.

426-27. See the *Variorum* for the first stanza of the ballad from which these lines are taken. Hamlet of course means that Polonius shall tell the King of his harping on Ophelia.

432-33. **Follows.** Hamlet means "follows *logically,*" but wilfully takes Polonius's use of the word to mean "follow *in the song.*"

438. **The first row of the pious chanson.** The First Quarto has "the first verse of the godly ballet," which sufficiently explains the phrase of the text.

439. **My abridgment**: that which abridges, or cuts short, my talk—probably with a play on the other meaning of the word, i. e., an entertainment. Cf. *Midsummer Night's Dream,* V, i, 39-40: "What abridgement have you for this evening? What masque? What music?"

440 ff. Observe the charming courtesy of Hamlet's "extent to the players."

444-47. **My young lady and mistress,** etc. Women's parts were always taken by boys in Shakespeare's time, and Hamlet is addressing one of the younger actors, who has grown since he saw him last. A *chopine* was a very high-heeled shoe.

448. **Cracked within the ring.** If the crack in a coin extended within the ring that surrounded the sovereign's head, the coin ceased to be current. There is probably a play on the word *ring,* with reference to the boy's voice, which must soon change. Cf. note on lines 364-68.

450. **Like French falconers.** The French falconers were regarded as the best in the world, and the phrase "fly at any thing we see" is probably used in commendation. The suggestion that it is used contemptuously is not in harmony with Hamlet's characterization of the speech they do "fly at" as one he "chiefly loved."

451. **A taste of your quality**: a sample of your professional skill. See line 363. **Passionate** means "full of feeling."

454. **Me.** See note on II, i, 7.

457. **Caviare to the general**: not palatable to the multitude. The phrase has become proverbial. Relish for caviare (a Russian delicacy, made of sturgeon's roe) is an acquired taste.

459. **Cried in the top of mine**: were superior to mine.

461. **Modesty**: freedom from exaggeration or excess. Cf. III, ii, 21; V, i, 230.

462. **Sallet.** Our word *salad*—here used, probably, with

reference to ribald jokes. Hamlet's approbation of the absence of salaciousness may be taken as expressing Shakespeare's own judgment, for Shakespeare's plays stand out among those of his day for their comparative freedom from this sort of pandering to the taste of "the million." The whole speech, indeed, is interesting as probably an expression of Shakespeare's own views.

466. **More handsome than fine.** Cf. "rich, not gaudy" (I, iii, 71), for the same idea.

468. **Æneas' tale to Dido**: the story of the fall of Troy, which Virgil gives in the second book of the *Æneid*. **Thereabout of it** = at that part of it.

472 ff. The speech here given is in many ways puzzling. Hamlet, speaking in such a way that we seem to read Shakespeare's own judgment between the lines, praises it highly; yet to us it seems turgid, if not bombastic. One thing at least is clear: Hamlet is not speaking ironically when he commends the speech, and the assumption that in it Shakespeare is travestying the style of some rival playwright is untenable. Were that his purpose, he would be distracting attention from his own play to something wholly unrelated to it, at one of its most crucial moments. Instead of that the speech has the most direct bearing upon the action of *Hamlet* itself. The first actor is profoundly moved by his lines, and it is this emotion of his that stirs Hamlet to his depths, and brings him back to the delayed execution of his task. Shakespeare himself, then, pretty certainly thought the speech "more handsome than fine," and if one or two things are remembered, his opinion may not seem so strange. For one thing, the speech is, when well delivered, even to us a vigorous and stirring piece of declamation. Moreover, as both Coleridge and Schlegel have pointed out, the style of *Hamlet* itself is necessarily more elevated than that of ordinary speech. If this passage (which is epic rather than dramatic) is to stand out against a background already heightened, its own style must be heightened still more. And finally, an Elizabethan audience (and probably Shakespeare himself) had a certain relish for what often seems to us bombastic. It is probable that Shakespeare wrote this passage specifically for its place in *Hamlet,* and it is not impossible that he meant to challenge comparison with a similar passage

in an older play called *Dido, Queen of Carthage,* probably by Marlowe and Nash. See the *Variorum Hamlet,* Vol. I, p. 185, for the lines in question.

472. **Pyrrhus.** A son of Achilles. He was one of the Greeks who was concealed in the wooden horse; he slew Priam, king of Troy, and married Hector's wife, Andromache.

472. **The Hyrcanian beast:** the tiger. Cf. "the Hyrcan tiger" (*Macbeth,* III, iv, 101). The Hyrcanian forest, south of the Caspian Sea, was supposed to be inhabited by peculiarly fierce tigers.

479. **Gules.** An heraldic term (cf. "heraldry more dismal") for "red." Cf. *Timon of Athens,* IV, iii, 59: "with man's blood paint the ground, gules, gules." **Trick'd** (here = "adorned") is also a term of heraldry.

482. **Tyrannous:** savage. See note on line 356.

496. **Ilium:** the citadel of Troy. **Senseless** is "without feeling, insentient." That is, the very citadel itself, insentient though it is, seems to feel the blow that fells its ruler, and like him crashes to the ground.

502. **A painted tyrant:** a tyrant in a painting. Cf. IV, vii, 109-10; *Macbeth,* V, viii, 25-27; and Coleridge, *Rime of the Ancient Mariner:* "Day after day . . . We stuck, nor breath nor motion; As idle as a painted ship Upon a painted ocean."

503. **Like a neutral to his will and matter:** like one indifferent to his purpose and to the business in hand.

506. **Rack:** flying clouds in the upper air. Hudson aptly quotes Fletcher: "sailing rack that gallops upon the wings of angry winds"; Keats: "Cloudy rack slow journeying in the west"; Longfellow: "driving rack of the rain-cloud." Cf. *Tempest,* IV, i, 156; *Antony and Cleopatra,* IV, xiv, 10.

509. **Region:** sky. "Originally a division of the sky marked out by the Roman augurs" (Clarendon Press). Cf. line 607, and *Sonnet XXXIII,* 12: "the region cloud."

513. **Remorse:** pity—the most frequent meaning in Shakespeare. Cf. "the tears of soft remorse" (*King John,* IV, iii, 50), and add *Merchant of Venice,* IV, i, 20; *King John,* II, i, 478.

518-19. Bowl the broken hub of Fortune's wheel from heaven down to hell.

522. **A jig.** Here probably a comic song, accompanied by a dance.

525. **Mobled:** muffled, with wrapped-up head. Hamlet's query seems to indicate that the word was a rare one. Polonius, who had been snubbed a moment before, hastens to rehabilitate himself as a critic.

529. **Bisson rheum:** blinding tears.

537. **Mincing.** A word that did not have in Shakespeare's time the somewhat trivial associations it now has.

541. **Passion:** sorrow; cf. line 452. "Passion" is the object of "made."

550. **You were better have:** it were better you should have.

554. **Much better.** Polonius has very properly meant by "desert" the real merits of the players. But Hamlet, as usual, twists his words into another meaning.

563. **The Murder of Gonzago.** Shakespeare is leading up, as we shall see, to the climax of the play.

566-67. **A speech of some dozen or sixteen lines.** The question whether this passage can be identified or not will be taken up in connection with the play itself, in Act III.

570-71. **Look you mock him not.** Observe the dignity and consideration of Hamlet's caution. For his own ends *he* has taken liberties with Polonius, but that must not lead others to do so too.

578. **Passion:** emotion of any kind. Here used in a more general sense than in line 541 above.

579. **His own conceit:** his conception of the character he is playing.

580. **Her working:** his soul's working. *Soul* is frequently feminine in Shakespeare; cf. III, ii, 68.

582-83. **His whole function suiting,** etc.: all his faculties conspiring to give fit expression to the conception in his mind. Notice how Shakespeare has led up to all this by means of Polonius's remark in lines 542-43.

584. Compare the broken lines in this soliloquy (584, 593, 603, 610, 616) with those in II, i (see note on II, i, 41). Are Hamlet's pauses to be filled out by the actor in the same way as Polonius's?

587. **Motive:** moving cause. Notice that *cue* still keeps the idea of the stage before us.

589. **General ear:** ear of the public.

590. **Free:** here, free *from guilt.*

591. **Confound** and **amaze** are here exceedingly strong words, and should be looked up.

594. **Peak:** "to move about dejectedly or silently; to mope; 'to make a mean figure; to sneak'" (*Oxford Dictionary*—quoting Dr. Johnson). **Rascal** is probably intended to call up also the sense of "a lean and worthless deer" (cf. *I Henry VI,* IV, ii, 45-52). With *muddy-mettled* compare "high-mettled," etc.

595. **John-a-dreams:** a fellow who goes mooning about. **Unpregnant of** = unapt for, indifferent to.

597. **Property:** not quite in its modern sense, but rather "his crown, his wife, everything, in short, which he might be said to be possessed of, except his life" (Furness).

598. **Defeat:** undoing, destruction. Used here, like so many words in Shakespeare, in a sense nearer than ours to its etymological meaning.

604. **'Swounds:** an abbreviation of "God's wounds"—used also in the form *Zounds.* Cf. *'sblood,* II, ii, 384.

605. The gall was supposed to be the seat of courage; cf. *Troilus and Cressida,* I, iii, 237: "when they would seem soldiers, they have galls." The pigeon (or dove) was believed to have no gall (the bitter secretion of the liver), and this was held to account for its proverbial meekness.

607. **The region kites:** the kites of the air. See notes on I, iii, 133; II, ii, 509.

609. **Kindless:** unnatural. See note on I, ii, 65.

611. **This is most brave:** this is a fine thing.

614. **Unpack my heart with words:** relieve the oppression of my heart by words. Cf. *Macbeth,* V, iii, 44-45: "Cleanse the stuff'd bosom of that perilous stuff Which weighs upon the heart."

617. **About, my brain!** Right about face, my brain! Now that he has unpacked his heart, Hamlet begins to *think.* Compare his "Hold, hold, my heart" in I, v, 93. With the "Fie upon't!" of this line, compare the "O, fie!" of that.

620. **Presently.** See note on line 170.

631. **Such spirits**: such conditions of mind as the melancholy to which Hamlet refers.

633. **The play's the thing.** Just what is it that Hamlet means to test by the play? What has he actually done during the two months since the Ghost's injunction? What has he accomplished by his assumption of madness? Go back over this scene and try to summarize the changes of his mood. How do matters now stand between him and the King?

Act III. Scene I.

At the end of Act II Hamlet had at last made up his mind to act. The present scene gives us the state of things immediately before his plan goes into execution. But the King is on the point of action too, and even while Hamlet is preparing to put him to the test, the King is actually carrying out *his* plan, suggested by Polonius, to form his own conclusions about Hamlet. And when Hamlet appears, it is again not of his plan, or even of revenge, that he is thinking, but of death, as after all, perhaps, the best way out. The significance of the terrible interview with Ophelia may be best considered in the notes. At the close of the interview, the King is convinced that Hamlet is not really mad, but is brooding over something that bodes danger, and without hesitation he determines to act, by sending Hamlet off to England. Polonius characteristically suggests another "assay of bias," and at the end of the scene the situation stands thus: Hamlet is about to test the King's guilt by means of the play; the Queen is prepared to probe still further Hamlet's purpose, by an interview after the play; and the King is ready, if the interview warrants it, to take instant and decisive action. The opposing forces are thus arrayed against each other, and at the end of the scene the turning point of the play is at hand.

1. **Drift of circumstance**: roundabout method. Cf. "drift of question" (II, i, 10).

2. **Puts on**: clothes himself in. The phrase does not here carry any implication of *pretence*.

7. Guildenstern is putting it pretty mildly!

13-14. Rosencrantz is saving his face by misrepresenting the conversation. As a matter of fact, Hamlet has done the demanding. **Question** = talk, conversation.

14-15. **Assay him to**: try (to bring) him to. Notice the skill with which Shakespeare is leading up again to the play. Turn back to II, ii, 15, and see how he had begun the preparation for it even then. That Shakespeare was the most skillful of playwrights, as well as a supremely great dramatist, should never be forgotten.

26. **Give him a further edge**: whet him on.

31. **Affront**: confront, meet face to face. The regular meaning of the word in Shakespeare. Cf. *Winter's Tale,* V, i, 73-75: "Unless another . . . affront his eye."

43. **Gracious.** A formal epithet of courtesy, used in addressing persons of high rank.

46-49. It need not be supposed that Polonius is expressing any qualms of conscience over the trick he is playing, for he obviously has none. He is merely improving the opportunity to indulge in a pious reflection.

51-53. The harlot's painted cheek is not more ugly, compared with the paint that disguises it, than is my deed, compared with the words with which I mask it. Why does Shakespeare make Claudius disclose his guilt just at this point? What light does the disclosure throw upon the character of the man himself?

56 ff. In the First Quarto the passage corresponding to lines 56-169 (including the soliloquy and the interview with Ophelia) comes between lines 168 and 169 of what is now the second scene of Act II. That is to say, in the earlier form of the play the substance of the present scene was introduced *before* the conversation (then much shorter), with Rosencrantz and Guildenstern, the interview with the players, and Hamlet's plan to use the *Murder of Gonzago* as a test of the King's guilt. By shifting the scene from its earlier to its present position the dramatic effect of the sharp confronting of the King's and Hamlet's opposing plans, at the very moment of the climax, is greatly enhanced.

56. Is this the first time that Hamlet has dallied with the idea of suicide? Cf. I, ii, 131-37.

59. **To take arms against a sea of troubles**: to take up arms against troubles that sweep upon us like a sea. This is

sometimes criticised as a mixed metaphor. But there is all the difference in the world between the mixing of incongruous images that is due to a feeble imagination, and the swift passage of a powerful imagination (as in this case) from one idea to another related one. "Sea" is often used in the sense of host, multitude, any great quantity; cf. "a sea of care" (*Rape of Lucrece,* 1100); "this great sea of joys" (*Pericles,* V, i, 194). It is barely possible that Shakespeare may have had in mind a very old Celtic custom of actually taking arms against the sea; but it is not necessary to assume that to justify the metaphor.

65. **There's the rub.** Another figure from the game of bowls (cf. note on II, i, 65). A *rub* was an obstacle which diverted the bowl from its course. Cf. *Richard II,* III, iv, 3-5: "Madam, we'll play at bowls.—'Twill make me think the world is full of rubs, And that my fortune runs against the bias"; *Coriolanus,* III, i, 60: "this . . . rub laid . . . I' the plain way of his merit."

67. **This mortal coil:** this turmoil of mortality, the pother of this mortal life. Cf. "the wedding being there to-morrow, there is a great coil to-night" (*Much Ado,* III, iii, 100); "Yonder's old coil at home" (*ibid.,* V, ii, 98).

75. **Quietus:** the final settlement of an account. From the law-phrase: *quietus est,* it (the account) is discharged. Cf. *Sonnet CXXVI,* 11-12: "Her audit . . . answer'd must be, And her quietus is to render thee."

76. **A bare bodkin:** probably, a *mere* (not an *unsheathed*) bodkin. *Bodkin* was a name for a small dagger.

77. **Grunt:** groan. An entirely dignified word in Shakespeare's time. Cf. Fabyan's *Chronicles:* "Many knyghts . . . lay grunting upon the earth." With Hamlet's words cf. *Julius Cæsar,* IV, i, 21-22: "He shall but bear them as the ass bears gold, To groan and sweat under the business."

79-80. Avoid the common misquotation: "That bourn from which no traveler returns." **Bourn** = boundary. Hamlet is stating a general truth; he is not thinking of the entirely exceptional case of the Ghost—and even the Ghost has not returned to *stay.*

83. **Conscience:** consciousness,—i. e., knowledge that this is so. This sense of the word is very common in Shakespeare's

time (see the examples in the *Oxford Dictionary,* under I, i), and is the only one that fits the context. The fact that Shakespeare uses the word elsewhere in the more familiar sense (e. g., *Richard III,* I, iv, 124-50—especially line 138: "it [conscience] makes a man a coward") is no argument for that meaning here. Its significance must in each case be determined by its context, and the use of "thus" connects it directly with what goes before.

84-85. **The native hue of resolution . . . the pale cast of thought.** The reference is to the ruddy color associated with the sanguine temperament as contrasted with the pallor (*cast* = tinge) of melancholy (cf. *Midsummer Night's Dream,* I, i, 14-15: "melancholy . . . the pale companion"). *Thought* in Shakespeare frequently means anxious or melancholy thought.

86. **Pitch:** the summit of a falcon's flight. The Folios have *pith,* with which cf. I, iv, 22.

88. **Soft you now!** hush, be quiet. Addressed to himself.

89. **Nymph.** Frequently used as a conventional term for a young and beautiful woman. Where is the emphasis in the next line?

91. **For this many a day.** Observe the gentle reproach implied in Ophelia's words.

99-100. **Their . . . these.** *Their* refers to the "words of so sweet breath composed"; *these,* to "the things."

103. **Honest.** The word means either "chaste" or "truthful." Hamlet is possibly playing on both meanings.

109. **Commerce.** Ophelia is using a synonym for Hamlet's "discourse."

115. **Now the time gives it proof.** It should not be forgotten, in reading what follows, that what Hamlet has learned about his mother has shaken his faith in all women, Ophelia included.

119-20. **Inoculate** here means "graft"; **our old stock** (which carries out the figure) is our old evil nature; **it** refers back to *our old stock.* The sense is: You can't so graft a new nature upon the old evil one that some smack of the old will not be left.

123-31. Hamlet's self-accusation must be taken with some allowance for the highly-wrought frame of mind in which he speaks. It is rather the latent possibilities of human nature than his own actual commissions that he has in mind.

133. It is frequently said that at this point Hamlet catches sight of Polonius behind the arras, and that the terrible bitterness of the speeches that follow is due to his knowledge that Ophelia has lied in her answer, and to his intention to speak, now, for the ears of Polonius and the King. And on the stage Polonius is frequently made to peep around the curtain at this moment. But if Shakespeare had meant this, it is unlike him not to have made it clear. It is very possible—even probable—that Hamlet *suspects* the presence of Polonius, and that is sufficient to explain his attitude.

134. **At home, my lord.** Much has been made—often rather stupidly—of Ophelia's lie. There are few better comments than Professor Bradley's: "I will not discuss these casuistical problems; but, if ever an angry lunatic [and Ophelia believes Hamlet to be mad] asks me a question which I cannot answer truly without great danger to him and to one of my relations, I hope that grace may be given me to imitate Ophelia. Seriously, at such a terrible moment was it weak, was it not rather heroic, in a simple girl not to lose her presence of mind and not to flinch, but to go through her task for Hamlet's sake and her father's?" (*Shakespearean Tragedy,* p. 163).

144. **You.** Hamlet here passes from Ophelia (whom, since line 120, he has been addressing as "thou") to *all* women, and the bitterness of his next speech is not directed against Ophelia alone. See note on line 115.

151. **You amble, and you lisp:** you walk and talk affectedly.

151. **Nick-name God's creatures:** give affected names to whatever God has made.

152. **Make your wantonness your ignorance:** excuse your wantonness by pretending ignorance. *Wantonness,* in Elizabethan English, does not necessarily mean unchastity; it may simply mean affectation. Either sense fits the context here, and it is probable that Hamlet means both—i. e., immodesty veiled under the affected phraseology of the day.

153. **It hath made me mad.** Hamlet expects to be reported—even if he does not actually realize that he is overheard.

156. **All but one.** A hint let drop for the King's ear.

159. The order of the two groups of three words does not correspond, and the First Quarto reverses the order of "soldier's" and "scholar's." But Shakespeare elsewhere deals freely with similar constructions. Cf. *Merchant of Venice,* III, i, 64-65; *Rape of Lucrece,* 902.

160. The hope and the flower of this fair kingdom.

161. **The mold of form:** the model of courtly behavior.

167. **Blown youth:** youth in its full flower.

169. **What I have seen:** that is, Hamlet as he *was.*

171-72. The King is shrewder than the rest, and his diagnosis is perfectly sound.

174. **Disclose:** the breaking of the shell in hatching. Cf. V, i, 310.

175 ff. Observe the promptness with which the King acts. There is no need to suppose that, at this time, his plan included more than he here states.

182. **Puts. Brains** is treated as a singular.

193. **Find him:** detect his secret.

ACT III. SCENE II.

The rising action of the tragedy—that part of its movement in which the hero is the aggressive force—reaches its highest point in this scene and the next. By the splendidly dramatic device of the play, Hamlet has forced the King to virtual confession; in the next scene he has him for a moment absolutely in his power. He refuses the opportunity—and from this point on the King becomes the aggressor, and Hamlet is put more and more on the defensive. The turning point or climax of the play, therefore, comes in Scene II—or, better, in Scenes II and III taken together. What follows constitutes the so-called falling action, in which the hero is forced gradually to the wall.

In what scene is the climax of *Macbeth?* Of *Julius Cæsar?* Of *Romeo and Juliet?*

1. **The speech.** The "dozen or sixteen lines" referred to in II, ii, 566. Hamlet's advice to the players embodies Shakespeare's own mature opinions about the actor's art.

6. **Use all:** do everything.

12. **The groundlings**: the people who stood, literally on the ground, in the pit of the Elizabethan theater. The admission to the pit was a penny, and no seats were provided.

15. **Termagant.** An imaginary deity of the Saracens, represented, in the mediæval romances and miracle-plays, as a boisterous and overbearing figure. The word is now used as a synonym for *virago.*

16. **It out-herods Herod**: it out-rants the veriest ranter of all. The *rôle* of Herod, as the most blustering and bombastic personage in the miracle-plays, was still familiar to Shakespeare's audience.

18. **Not . . . neither.** The heaping up of negatives was perfectly good English in Shakespeare's time. Cf. *nor . . . not,* in line 4.

21. **Modesty**: moderation; cf. II, ii, 461. The gist of Hamlet's advice is the avoidance of extremes.

22. **From**: contrary to.

28. **Come tardy off**: feebly done.

30. **Censure.** See note on I, iii, 69.

30. **In your allowance**: as you must acknowledge.

34. **Not to speak it profanely.** "It" refers to what follows, and "profanely" has reference to the idea that somebody else than God had made such players.

42 ff. It was a practice of Elizabethan clowns to extemporize jests, often at inopportune moments of the play.

66. **Pregnant**: "because untold thrift is born from a cunning use of the knee" (Furness). "Candied tongue" in the preceding line stands, of course, for the flatterer himself.

68. **My dear soul.** See note on I, ii, 182.

74. **Blood and judgment**: impulse and reason. For *blood* as here used see note on I, iii, 6.

68-79. This very noble characterization of Horatio should be contrasted with Hamlet's analysis of less balanced natures in I, iv, 13-38. Observe throughout the play the manner in which Horatio's character is made to serve as a foil for Hamlet's.

82. **Which I have told thee.** Is this occurrence in the play?

84. **The very comment of thy soul**: with the concentrated attention of all your faculties.

86. **In one speech.** The reference is probably to the

"dozen or sixteen lines" (*in* = in connection with). It may, however, possibly mean some incriminating exclamation extorted from the King, as in line 280.

87. **A damned ghost.** The alternative of I, iv, 40-42 (cf. "goblin damned" there) is still in Hamlet's mind. Cf. also II, ii, 627-32.

92. **In censure of his seeming:** in reaching a conclusion from his appearance.

95. **Idle:** probably here in the sense of "mad"—i. e., "I must resume my 'antic disposition'" (Herford). Or it may simply mean: "I must seem to have nothing to do with the play."

98. **The chameleon's dish:** air. The reference is to a popular belief of the time. Cf. *Two Gentlemen of Verona,* II, i, 179: "though the chameleon Love can feed on the air."

101. **I have nothing with:** I make nothing of.

102. **Are not mine:** mean nothing to me.

109. **I' the Capitol.** A widespread error as to the place of Cæsar's assassination. Shakespeare follows it in *Julius Cæsar.*

112. **Stay upon your patience:** await your permission.

132. **Your only jig-maker:** only your jig-maker. See note on II, ii, 522.

138. **A suit of sables.** The reference is to the richest and most costly garb, as opposed to the wearing of mourning. If his father has been dead so long, Hamlet will put off mourning.

145. **The hobby-horse is forgot.** The hobby-horse was one of the figures in the May-games and morris-dances, which were rapidly going out of use, largely as a result of Puritan intervention. The line (probably from some popular song) is quoted again in *Love's Labour's Lost,* III, i, 30.

[The dumb-show]. A device of the older stage, rather than one which was common in Shakespeare's day. Its use here is puzzling. Its purpose seems to be to give to the audience the plot of the play, so that their attention may be freed to observe the King, while the play proper goes on. But the King must be supposed to see the dumb-show too, so that the trap is sprung before the play itself begins. On the modern stage the King is often represented as talking aside to the Queen, while the dumb-show is going on, and so failing to notice it. But this is quite without warrant. It seems better to suppose that the King *does* see it, and that he has strength of will enough to carry him through it without flinching. It is the *repetition* of it that is more than he can stand. Cf. the fainting of Lady Macbeth, when the story of the murder is retold.

147. **Miching mallecho:** lurking mischief. *Mich* = skulk, sneak.

162. **The posy of a ring:** the inscription engraved in a ring, hence necessarily brief. Cf. *Merchant of Venice,* V, i, 147-50: "a hoop of gold, a petty ring . . . whose posy was . . . 'Love me, and leave me not.'"

163. **'Tis brief.** Where is the emphasis?

165 ff. The "play within the play" is set off from the body of the drama by the fact that it is in rimed couplets—just as the first player's speech in II, ii, is set off by its markedly epic quality. The somewhat labored and occasionally even stilted style, too, of the *Murder of Gonzago* is different from that of the rest of the play, as if Shakespeare had intentionally used this means to throw the passage into strong relief. The attempt to determine which are the "dozen or sixteen lines" that Hamlet was to insert is probably futile, and the long discussion of the various attempts to identify them (the mere summary of which occupies over four pages of fine print in the *Variorum*) is really, as Dr. Furness remarks, "a tribute to Shakespeare's consummate art." One may be certain that "Shakespeare did not first write the *Murder of Gonzago,* and then insert in it certain lines, as though written by Hamlet." He meant to produce the illusion that Hamlet did write and insert such lines —and he succeeded in producing it. And it is a harmless amusement to attempt to pick the lines out.

165. **Phœbus' cart:** Apollo's chariot—i. e., the sun.

166. **Neptune's salt wash:** the sea.

166. **Tellus' orbed ground:** the earth. Tellus was the goddess who personified the earth.

175. **I distrust you:** I am solicitous about you.

177. **Holds quantity:** keeps proportion. "Fear and love" are taken together as the subject.

178. **In neither aught, or in extremity.** That is, there is either no fear (and hence no love), or both are extreme. The emendation "in either naught" has been suggested, but the general sense is clear.

184. **My operant powers their functions leave to do:** my active powers cease to perform their functions.

187. **O, confound the rest!** Let the rest be as if struck dumb. *Confound* is not to be given here its trivial modern sense.

193. **Respects of thrift:** considerations of profit. **Instances** (in line 192) = motives.

198. **Purpose is but the slave to memory:** we keep our purpose only so long as we remember it.

201. **Fall.** A false construction, probably due to "fruit," which has suggested the plural. Somewhat similarly *destroy,* in line 207, is attracted to the number of *enactures.*

202-03. **Necessary:** inevitable. **What to ourselves is debt** refers to our resolves, the keeping of which we owe ourselves.

207. **Enactures:** the carrying out into action of either grief or joy.

219. **Seasons him:** ripens him as, turns him into.

229. **An anchor's cheer:** an anchorite's fare. **Scope** = range. The sense is: "May I know no luxury or liberty if I do so."

230. **Each opposite, that blanks the face of joy. Opposite** = adversary, here used abstractly of "all that is at enmity with joy." **Blanks** = blanches, makes pale.

247. **Tropically:** figuratively. The First Quarto has *trapically*—doubtless for the pun.

255. **As good as a chorus.** Shakespeare's audience was familiar with many plays—especially those which were influenced by Seneca—in which the chorus interpreted the action. Among Shakespeare's own, see *Romeo and Juliet, Henry V, Winter's Tale.*

263. **Pox:** an imprecation, equivalent to "the pox take you!"

264-65. **The croaking raven doth bellow for revenge.** Hamlet is parodying two lines of a well-known old play, *The True Tragedie of Richard the Third:*

> "The screeking raven sits croaking for revenge,
> Whole herds of beasts comes bellowing for revenge."

267. The time conspiring, and no spectator but the time.

269. **Hecate's ban.** Hecate, in the Middle Ages, was regarded as the goddess of witchcraft (cf. *Macbeth*). In classical

mythology the same goddess was Luna in Heaven, Diana on earth, and Hecate (or Proserpine) in hell.

273-74. **The story is extant,** etc. Shakespeare is merely heightening the impression of verisimilitude, and search for the story is probably as useless as that for the "dozen or sixteen lines."

282. See the idea of this line elaborated in *As You Like It,* II, i, 33-40.

286. **This:** this playwriting of mine. The rest of the speech is an exaggerated description of an actor's costume. There are many contemporary allusions to the wearing of feathers on the stage; **Provincial roses** were probably rosettes of ribbon, shaped like the roses either of Provins or Provence; **razed shoes** is a reference to the fashion of wearing shoes extravagantly slashed in patterns. All the allusions are to well-known vogues of the day, and would be perfectly intelligible to the audience. To **turn Turk** was to change completely; cf. *Much Ado,* III, iv, 57: "An you be not turned Turk, there's no more sailing by the star." **A fellowship in a cry of players** was a share in a theatrical company—*cry* being humorously transferred from a pack of hounds. Throughout this part of the scene Hamlet's pent-up feelings are finding relief (as they did after the appearance of the Ghost in I, v) in almost hysterical abandon.

292. **O Damon dear.** Damon and Pythias (look up their story) were proverbial for their friendship. Hamlet is either quoting from some lost ballad, or making up the lines as he goes.

295. **Pajock:** a word found only here. Probably a dialect form for "peacock"; possibly another spelling of *patchock,* a clown or ragamuffin. The riming word which Hamlet does not use is obvious.

312. **Distempered.** See note on II, ii, 55.

318. **Purgation.** Hamlet is playing on the two senses—purging the body, and clearing from the imputation of guilt.

339. **Admiration:** wonder. Cf. I, ii, 192.

349. **These pickers and stealers:** my hands. The church catechism has the phrase: "to keep my hands from picking and stealing." Cf. *II Henry VI,* I, iii, 193: "by these ten bones."

354. **Sir, I lack advancement.** Hamlet is giving Rosen-

crantz the answer he expects, rather than the real one. Cf. II, ii, 258-59.

358-59. "While the grass grows the horse starves" is the proverb in full.

360. **To withdraw with you**: probably, to speak in private with you.

361-62. The figure is from hunting. To recover the wind of an animal was to get to the windward of it, so as to drive it into the snare.

363-64. Since Hamlet did not understand this, we are perhaps absolved from the attempt. Guildenstern seems to mean that his love is unmannerly because his sense of duty is strong —but his expression is anything but lucid.

386. **'Sblood.** See note on II, ii, 384.

388. **Fret.** The *fret,* in certain musical instruments, is the device to regulate the fingering. Hamlet is playing on the two senses of the word.

392. **Presently.** See note on II, ii, 170, and cf. lines 53, 400, 402.

401. **To the top of my bent**: as far as I could wish, to the utmost degree. See note on II, ii, 30. **Fool me** = treat me like a fool.

412. **Nero**: the Roman emperor, who murdered his mother. Cf. *King John,* V, ii, 152-53: "You bloody Neroes, ripping up the womb Of your dear mother England."

417. **Give them seals**: confirm by action.

ACT III. SCENE III.

In this scene Hamlet has reached the point at which he has supposedly been aiming. He has the evidence which he has sought of the King's guilt; he has the King himself completely in his power. He deliberately lets the opportunity slip, and spares the King. But the King—although Hamlet does not know it—has already assumed the offensive, and in this scene (the only one in which the two protagonists are alone together) the control of the situation passes from Hamlet's hands into those of his opponent.

1. I like him not: not an expression of personal aversion, but rather: I don't like the turn things have taken.

5. The terms of our estate: the conditions on which our kingship rests.

11. The single and peculiar life: the private individual. Observe in these two speeches that Rosencrantz and Guildenstern are antiphonal again.

15. The cease of majesty: the death of the King. **Dies** is used as if Rosencrantz had said "majesty ceasing."

16. A gulf: a whirlpool. Cf. *Henry V,* II, iv, 10: "as waters to the sucking of a gulf."

24. Arm you: provide yourselves, get ready. Has the King paid much attention to the courtiers' fine phrases?

25. This fear: this object of fear.

29. Tax him home: rate him roundly.

30. And wisely was it said. Who said it? See III, i, 188 ff., and cf. note on II, i, 3.

33. Of vantage: from a point of vantage.

37. The primal eldest curse: the curse of Cain.

46. To wash it white as snow. Probably a reminiscence of *Psalm* li, 7: "Wash me, and I shall be whiter than snow." Cf. also *Macbeth,* V, i, 31 ff., and II, ii, 60-61.

49-50. Cf. the Lord's Prayer: "Lead us not into temptation, but deliver us from evil." **Forestalled** = prevented.

56. The offence: the benefits accruing from the offence. In what senses is the word used in lines 36, 47, 58?

61. Lies: is sustainable—i. e., is *not* shoved by, bought out, or shuffled.

64. What rests? What remains?

68. Limed: caught, as a bird in bird-lime. **Engaged** = entangled, hampered.

69. Assay: probably, trial; possibly, onset.

36-72. This soliloquy of the King's is a marvelous piece of psychological analysis, and its truth to certain inexorable facts makes it well worth careful study. What light does it throw on the character of the King?

73-75. Are the three *now's* in these lines quite the same? Are the two *so's?*

75. That would be scann'd: that demands scrutiny. And for Hamlet, that means the end of *action.*

78. What fills out the line?

80-82. Compare these lines with I, v, 76-79.

80. **Full of bread.** Look up *Ezekiel,* xvi, 49.

81. **With all his crimes broad blown.** Cf. I, v, 76: "cut off even in the blossoms of my sin." *Blown* is used as in III, i, 167. **Flush** = lusty, full of vigor.

83. **In our circumstance and course of thought:** as *we* (opposed to *heaven*) think. *Circumstance* seems to suggest the ranging abroad, *course,* the more direct movement, of thought.

85. **Purging.** See note on III, ii, 318.

96. **This physic:** this delay in execution. Make clear to yourself just what the reason is that now leads Hamlet to delay. Is it so much a reason as an excuse?

ACT III. SCENE IV.

In this scene Hamlet, being caught without a chance to think, acts. But by a stroke of tragic irony he kills Polonius, supposing him to be the King. And in killing Polonius he sets in motion the forces that are to lead to his own doom. The interview with his mother gives him an opportunity again to unpack his heart with words, and in the midst of it—at the beginning of the falling, as at the beginning of the rising action—the Ghost appears again. And the scene ends with Hamlet's determination to act—only this time it is *defensive* action, made necessary by the King's initiative, that he is forced to undertake.

1. **Lay home.** Cf. III, iii, 29.

4. **Much heat:** the King's anger. *Sconce* is Hanmer's emendation (perhaps unnecessary) for *silence* of the Quartos and Folios.

6. **Fear me not.** Cf. note on I, iii, 51.

26. **Is it the king?** That Hamlet thought it *was* the King is clear from line 32. Why does he no longer feel the scruple of the preceding scene?

29, 30. **As kill a king.** Does Hamlet think that his mother was privy to his father's murder? Is there any evidence that she *was?*

38. **Proof and bulwark:** like tested armor and a rampart. **Sense** = feeling.

44. **Sets a blister there.** Harlots were branded in the forehead. Cf. *Comedy of Errors,* II, ii, 138.

46. **Contraction:** the marriage contract (see "marriage-vows" above).

48. **Glow:** burn with shame.

49. The earth, as the center of the universe.

50. **The doom:** the last judgment. Cf. "the great doom's image" (*Macbeth,* II, iii, 83); "the crack of doom" (*ibid.,* IV, i, 117).

52. **In the index:** in the prologue or prelude. *Index* is here the table of contents *prefixed* to a book; cf. *Othello,* II, i, 263: "an index and obscure prologue to the history"; and especially *Troilus and Cressida,* I, iii, 343-46.

53. Stage tradition has varied greatly in the translation of this line into stage business. Some of the devices have been: two miniatures produced by Hamlet; two full-length portraits on the wall; a miniature of his father drawn from Hamlet's bosom, and either a miniature of Claudius worn by the Queen, or a full-length picture of him on the wall. Many later actors represent both pictures as imagined by Hamlet. The justification of the miniatures is found, of course, in the "pictures in little" of II, ii, 383.

54. **Counterfeit presentment:** portrayed representation. *Counterfeit* did not necessarily have its modern connotation. Cf. *Merchant of Venice,* III, ii, 116: "Fair Portia's counterfeit."

56. **Hyperion's curls.** See note on I, ii, 140.

58. **Station:** attitude in standing. Cf. *Antony and Cleopatra,* III, iii, 22: "her motion and her station are as one." Mercury was the messenger of the gods. Note the vividness of Hamlet's description.

64-65. The reference is to the thin and blasted ears that devoured the full ears in Pharaoh's dream. See *Genesis,* xli, 5-7.

69. **Hey-day:** a state of exaltation or excitement. Notice again the contrast (in this line and the next) between "blood" and "judgment," and cf. note on III, ii, 74.

71. **Sense:** feeling, sensation. In line 74 its meaning is rather reason, common sense; in line 72 there is a mingling of both. **Motion** (line 72) = impulse, desire.

73. **Apoplex'd:** paralyzed. Hamlet means that his mother's

faculties must be completely benumbed or stupefied, for even madness would have left her some power of choice. The *so* of line 74 is understood before *err* in the preceding line.

80. **Sense.** The reference here is to one of the "five senses."

91. **Leave their tinct**: part with their hue.

98. **A vice of kings.** The Vice was the buffoon in the old morality plays. Cf. *Twelfth Night,* IV, ii, 134-39. The phrase here means "a buffoon of a king."

99-101. The King is not even a robber—merely a sneak-thief.

102. **A king of shreds and patches**: a king in motley. The phrase carries out the idea of "a vice of kings."

[Enter Ghost]. What marked difference between this and the preceding appearances of the Ghost is brought out by the ensuing dialogue? What parallel is there in *Macbeth?*

107. **Lapsed in time and passion**: having allowed time to slip by and feeling to grow dull. **Important** (line 108) = urgent.

110. **Do not forget.** What was Hamlet's "word"? Cf. I, v, 91-112.

112. **Amazement**: utter bewilderment. Cf. III, ii, 339.

114. **Conceit**: mental impression, imagination. Cf. II, ii, 579, 583.

121. **Excrements**: that which grows out of the body; here, hairs (used also of nails, feathers). **Bedded** carries out the idea of *sleeping.* For *an end* cf. note on I, v, 19. With the description in lines 119-22 cf. that in I, v, 17-20.

123. **Distemper.** See note on II, ii, 55, and cf. III, ii, 351.

128-29. **Convert my stern effects**: transform the stern deeds I have to do.

135. **In his habit as he lived.** Since *habit* could scarcely apply to armor, it is probable that the Ghost appears this time in ordinary garb. In the First Quarto the stage direction before line 102 reads: *Enter the Ghost in his night gowne*—i. e., in his dressing gown.

143. I will repeat in the same words what I have said; madness would keep leaping aside in the attempt.

152. **Forgive me this my virtue**: forgive this virtue of mine. Hamlet is still addressing his mother—not, as is sometimes said, apostrophizing his virtue. Lines 154-55 are an elaboration of the idea in line 152. **Curb** = bow, bend the knee.

161 ff. That monster, custom, who devours all sensibility (i. e., sensitiveness to moral distinctions), devil though he be with reference to bad habits, is yet an angel in this, that, etc. That is, custom makes habits automatic (a very modern way of saying "all sense doth eat"), but the same power of custom that fixes evil habits may fix good ones too.

169. **And either . . . the devil.** The verb has dropped out in the early texts. The *master* of the Fourth Quarto is perhaps as good a word as any of those that have been suggested.

171-72. When the Queen is penitent enough to pray for blessing, she will then be fit to grant to Hamlet the blessing which he cannot now ask.

183. **Mouse:** a pet name. Cf. *Love's Labour's Lost,* V, ii, 19: "What's your dark meaning, mouse?"; *Twelfth Night,* I, v, 69: "Good my mouse of virtue, answer me."

188 ff. Hamlet cannot repress his bitter irony.

190. **Paddock . . . gib:** toad . . . tom-cat. The three animals named were the familiars of witches, which gives a sinister turn to Hamlet's taunt.

194. **The famous ape.** The allusion is to a story that is lost. **Conclusions** = experiments.

197. **If words be made of breath.** Cf. III, i, 98.

200. **I must to England.** How had Hamlet learned this? Cf. III, i, 177; III, iii, 4, for the other references to the plan.

206. **To have the enginer Hoist with his own petar:** to have the one who lays the mine blown up with his own bomb.

210. **Two crafts.** There is probably a play on the two meanings of the word—ship, and cunning.

206-10. Has Hamlet a definite plan laid, or is he merely counting on his own skill in a contest of wits?

211. **This man:** Polonius. **Set me packing:** set me lugging him away; probably with the added idea: send me off in a hurry (i. e., cause my flight).

212. **Guts.** This word was less offensive in Shakespeare's time than now.

213-16. Is there any indication that Hamlet thinks of Polonius as Ophelia's father?

ACT IV. SCENE I.

The first three scenes of Act IV immediately follow the last scene of Act III, and form with it a single group. There seems to be no good reason why the division between the two acts should come just where it does, and it has been frequently suggested that Act IV should really begin with what is now its fourth scene—an arrangement which has much to be said in its favor (see also introductory note to Scene IV). At all events, the first three scenes still have to do directly with the death of Polonius, and lead up to the full disclosure (at the end of Scene III) of the King's plan.

9. **Hearing something stir.** Why does Gertrude thus garble her account?

11. **Brainish:** a rare word, variously defined as brainsick; headstrong, passionate; imaginary, unfounded on fact.

16. Hamlet, of course, has played directly into the King's hands.

19-23. If Gertrude had known that Claudius had murdered her husband, is it likely that he would have found it necessary to dissemble as he does here?

25. **Ore:** a precious metal (used chiefly of gold). **Mineral** (line 26) is a mine.

27. **He weeps for what is done.** Is Gertrude telling the truth? What motive underlies her statement?

31. **All our majesty:** all the weight and authority of our office.

40. Some words have dropped out at the end of the line. Capell, following a suggestion of Theobald, read: "So, haply, slander," and this reading has been adopted by many modern editors. Lines 41-44 ("whose . . . air") are not in the Folios.

42. **Blank:** the white spot in the center of a target, the bull's-eye.

44. **Woundless:** invulnerable. Cf. "the viewless winds" (*Measure for Measure,* III, i, 124); "the sightless couriers of the air" (*Macbeth,* I, vii, 23).

Act IV. Scene II.

12. **To be demanded of:** to be questioned by.

19. **Like an ape.** The reading of the Folio. The First Quarto (in which the speech immediately follows the present III, ii, 389) has "as an ape doth nuts," which makes the meaning of the Folio reading clear. The Second Quarto has "like an apple."

29-32. Hamlet is deliberately talking nonsense. For the interpretations offered by those who think it sense, see the *Variorum.*

32-33. **Hide fox, and all after.** Probably a phrase from a children's game, like hide-and-seek. If so, Polonius is the fox.

Act IV. Scene III.

4. This is unprejudiced testimony to a fact of great importance. What qualities has Hamlet shown in the play that would win him the affection of the people? **Distracted** = crazy.

5. Whose liking is determined by appearances, instead of being a matter of judgment.

6. **The offender's scourge:** the punishment the offender receives.

9. **Deliberate pause:** the result of deliberate consideration. For *pause,* cf. III, iii, 42.

21. **Convocation of politic worms.** Hamlet's phraseology is punctiliously chosen to fit the body of a statesman. The use of the words "convocation," "politic," "worms," "diet" (perhaps also "emperor") makes it highly probable that Shakespeare had the Diet of Worms in mind. For the use of "your" (lines 22-25) see note on I, v, 167. Hamlet is still feigning madness, but it is difficult to doubt that he has also a certain intellectual pleasure in what he is saying.

33. **Go a progress.** *Progress* was the regular word for a royal journey of state. Cf. *II Henry VI,* I, iv, 76: "the king is now in progress towards Saint Albans."

43. **Tender:** regard, hold dear. Cf. I, iii, 107.

45. **Fiery quickness.** Cf. "hot haste."

46. **The wind at help.** Cf. I, iii, 2-3.

47. **Tend:** wait. Cf. I, iii, 83.

56. **At foot:** at his heels.

61. **Thereof may give thee sense:** may make thee cognizant of it.

63. **Free awe.** Opposed to awe that is the result of compulsion.

64. **Set:** value, esteem. Cf. I, iv, 65.

66. **Congruing:** agreeing. This is the reading of the Quartos. The Folios have *conjuring.* Cf. Hamlet's description of the letter in V, ii, 38.

ACT IV. SCENE IV.

Scene IV is transitional between the death of Polonius and the working out of its results in the plot against Hamlet's life, in the madness and death of Ophelia, and in the return of Laertes to avenge his father's murder. From this point on it is Hamlet's life rather than the King's that is under direct and constant menace. But just as the sight of the player enacting Hecuba stirred Hamlet to fresh resolution when aggressive action was still possible, so now, after command of the situation has slipped through his hands, the sight of the army of Fortinbras kindles a new resolve to act.

Sufficient time must have elapsed between Scenes III and IV for Claudius's permission to Fortinbras to pass through Danish territory (see line 2, and cf. II, ii, 76-82) to reach him. And the request for this license was presented to Claudius only the day before the death of Polonius (see introductory note to Act II, Scene I). Some days, at least, must accordingly have intervened. This is (strictly speaking) inconsistent with the fact that Hamlet leaves for England the very night of Polonius's murder (IV, i, 29-30; IV, iii, 46-48, 55-57), and there is nothing to indicate that the port was distant from Elsinore (cf. I, iii, 1, 55-57). But it must be remembered that Shakespeare is writing a drama (with the attendant necessity of producing certain illusions as to time in the mind of his audience), not presenting a statement of *facts*. See, for a somewhat similar instance, the note on I, i, 39.

6. **In his eye**: in his presence, face to face.

8. **Softly**: slowly, leisurely. Cf. *Julius Cæsar,* V, i, 16: "lead your battle softly on."

9. **Good sir.** Cf. lines 11, 13, 15, 29, and observe again Hamlet's fine courtesy in dealing with his inferiors in rank. Lines 9-66 are omitted in the Folio, probably for the same reason that dictates the omission of the entire scene on the modern stage—namely, the necessity for a shorter acting version. For the light which it throws on Hamlet's character, however, as well as for its noble poetry, the scene is of the utmost importance.

20. To pay a rent of five ducats, only five, I would not take a lease of it. **Farm** (= lease) is contrasted with **sold in fee** (i. e., fee simple, absolute possession) in line 22. **Ranker** = greater, higher.

26. **Will not debate**: will not be sufficient to fight out.

34. **Market of his time**: either, "that for which he sells his time" (Johnson); or, "the business in which he employs his time" (Clarendon Press).

36. **Discourse**: range of thought. Cf. I, ii, 150.

40. **Bestial oblivion**: such oblivion as characterizes the beasts that sleep and feed (cf. line 35).

40-41. **Scruple Of**: scruple that consists in. **Event** = outcome (as also in line 50). Cf. especially, for the idea expressed, III, i, 84-85.

50. **Makes mouths at**: mocks at. Cf. II, ii, 381-82.

53-56. To stir without great matter for dispute (*argument*) is not rightly to be great; but it *is* rightly to be great to find quarrel, etc. For *argument* in this sense cf. *Troilus and Cressida,* I, i, 95-96: "I cannot fight upon this argument; It is too starv'd a subject for my sword." How does Hamlet's statement differ from that of Polonius in I, iii, 65-67?

58. **My reason and my blood.** Cf. notes on III, ii, 74, and III, iv, 69-70.

61. **Trick of fame**: trifle that promises fame.

62. **Plot**: plot of ground.

65-66. Since Hamlet is on his way to England, just what does he mean?

ACT IV. SCENE V.

Scene V reverts to Ophelia and Laertes (compare Act I, Scene III, for contrast)—to Ophelia mad in reality, as Hamlet is mad in seeming; to Laertes rushing headlong to the same revenge (for "a father kill'd") with which Hamlet has been dallying. And it looks directly back to the murder of Polonius —itself the result of Hamlet's fatal delay,—and forward to the catastrophe. For the gentle and innocent Ophelia is caught in the net which Hamlet's failure to act at the crucial moment has woven, and her madness becomes a new and potent factor in Laertes's already fixed determination to be revenged. That determination is at first directed against the King. But before the scene is ended, its transfer from the King—through "the witchcraft of his wit"—to Hamlet is foreshadowed.

6. **Spurns enviously:** kicks spitefully. Cf. *Antony and Cleopatra,* III, v, 17: "[He] spurns the rush that lies before him." For *envious* in the sense of "malicious," cf. IV, vii, 174. In her madness Ophelia wreaks pitiful vengeance on whatever trifling objects come in her way.

6-13. Observe, as you read on in the scene, how aptly the Gentleman has characterized Ophelia's broken speeches.

9. **To collection:** to an attempt to gather her meaning. **Aim** = guess, conjecture.

15. **Ill-breeding minds:** minds that hatch mischief.

19. **Artless jealousy:** suspicion that knows no art to conceal itself. Guilt is so full of such suspicion, that it betrays itself by its very fear that it *will* betray itself. The Queen's speech reveals to us, for the first time in the play, something of her inner thoughts.

25. **Cockle-hat:** a hat with a scallop-shell in it—one of the insignia of a pilgrim. A pilgrim's garb was a conventional disguise for a lover; Romeo, for example, went so disguised to the Capulets' ball (cf. especially *Romeo and Juliet,* I, v, 95 ff.).

26. **Shoon:** an archaic plural of *shoe.* Ophelia is singing snatches of old ballads that deal with the two themes uppermost in her distracted mind—love and death.

38. Both Quartos and Folios read: "did *not* go." If this is the true reading—and it is difficult not to take it so—

Ophelia probably has dimly in mind her father's "obscure funeral" (line 213; cf. line 84), and so inserts the "not."

41. **God 'ild you:** God yield you—i. e., I thank you.

41. **They say, etc.** The reference is to an old legend of a baker's daughter who reproved her mother for putting too large a piece of dough in the oven to bake a loaf for Christ, and who was transformed into an owl. Ophelia's next words perhaps indicate a pathetic half-consciousness of some change that *she* has undergone.

45. **Conceit upon:** fancies about.

70. **My brother shall know of it.** Observe the hint here given of Laertes's return, as another example of Shakespeare's craftsmanship.

84. **In hugger-mugger:** secretly, clandestinely—with the added idea of haste.

89. Broods over the strange thing that has happened, keeps his thoughts to himself.

94. **In ear and ear:** either, in each other's ears; or, in everybody's ears.

95. **A murdering-piece:** a cannon loaded with case-shot, that scatter, when fired.

96. **Superfluous death:** more deaths than one.

97. **Switzers:** Swiss guards—employed by the King of France in Shakespeare's day, and still by the Pope in ours.

99. **Overpeering of his list:** rising above its boundaries.

105. The line refers to "antiquity" and "custom."

110. **Counter.** "To run counter" is to follow the trail in the wrong direction. Cf. the preceding line.

118-20. Cf. III, iv, 42-44.

122, 126. **Let him go, Gertrude.** Whatever else Claudius may be, this scene shows that he is no coward. And Gertrude's devotion to him is here unmistakable.

124. **Peep:** look—used with a touch of contempt. Treason can only get a peep at what it wants; it cannot act out its will.

133-36. One function of Laertes in the play is to stand in sharpest contrast to Hamlet. Each has a father's death to avenge; and Laertes's swift recourse to action throws into the strongest possible relief Hamlet's procrastination. With Laertes's curt dismissal of this world and the next in line 134 compare especially Hamlet's broodings in III, i, 76-82.

142. **Swoopstake:** indiscriminately. The figure is from a game of cards, where the winner draws the stakes of both sides.

146-47. The pelican was fabled to pierce its breast with its bill, and feed its young with its blood.

[Re-enter Ophelia]. Why does Shakespeare bring Ophelia back at this point? Cf. lines 168-69.

161-63. The general idea of these lines is clear, but the expression is somewhat obscure. *Fine* seems to mean "delicate, sensitive"; *instance* is "proof, token." The "precious instance" is Ophelia's sanity, which has followed Polonius ("the thing it loves") to his grave.

172. **The wheel.** This reference is also obscure, but it is probable that Ophelia imagines that she is singing at the spinning-wheel. Compare the reference to the "old and plain" song that "the spinsters [i. e., spinners] and the knitters in the sun . . . Do use to chant" (*Twelfth Night,* II, iv, 43-47).

172. **It is the false steward,** etc. This allusion has never been identified.

174. **This nothing's more than matter:** these unintelligible words move more than if they had meaning.

175-86. Flowers have been regarded from time immemorial as having a symbolic language, and Ophelia is using it here, as Perdita uses it in *Winter's Tale,* IV, iv, 73 ff.

175-77. **Rosemary . . . pansies.** Rosemary was supposed to strengthen the memory; the reference to *pansies* is a play on the word (from French *pensée,* thought). Ophelia probably gives these to Laertes—possibly taking him for Hamlet. If so, the "pray, love, remember" is a pathetic counterpart of the injunction of the Ghost.

178. **Document:** lesson, instruction.

180. **Fennel . . . columbine:** symbolic of flattery and unchastity, and probably given to the King.

181. **There's rue for you:** i. e., for the Queen. For the significance of rue, cf. *Richard II,* III, iv, 105-06: "I'll set a bank of rue, sour herb o' grace: Rue, even for ruth, here shortly shall be seen."

182. **We may call it,** etc. That is, its *religious* name is the proper one for Sundays.

183. **With a difference.** A difference, in heraldry, was some mark by which the arms of one branch of a family were

distinguished from those of another. What Ophelia means is that the Queen will wear hers for repentance, Ophelia hers for regret.

184. **A daisy . . . violets.** The daisy often (not always) symbolized dissembling; violets stood for faithfulness. It is not clear to whom those flowers are given—the daisy possibly to the Queen, the violets perhaps to Horatio.

188. **Thought:** here in its sense of *anxious* thought, melancholy.

199. **And of all Christian souls:** a common ending of epitaphs.

Act IV. Scene VI.

This scene serves to introduce the element of suspense, just as the King seems to have gained his point. His plan has miscarried; Hamlet is back on Danish soil; the opportunity that he seemed to have lost is in his hands again. And the question is, How will he use it?

20. **Thieves of mercy:** merciful thieves. See note on I, ii, 4.

21. **They knew what they did:** they knew what they were about. That is (probably), they had promise of reward. The phrase is sometimes taken to mean that the encounter with the pirates was prearranged by Hamlet, and that it was to this that he had referred in III, iv, 205-10. But this seems very unlikely. If Hamlet had any definite plan in his mind in the lines referred to (instead of merely the confidence that his wits would serve him at the critical moment), it was probably that of the exchange of the letters (see V, ii, 12-55). The fight with the pirates is rather to be thought of as a happy accident. Accident, to be sure, may not play too large a part in a tragedy, where the movement of events is chiefly determined by the inexorable working out of what is latent in *character*. But accident plays a vital part in life, and the dramatist may legitimately use it as it seems to be used here. What part is played by accident, for instance, in *Macbeth?*

26-27. **Too light for the bore of the matter:** the charge is too light, considering the caliber of the gun. That is, weighty as the words are, they are yet inadequate for the matter they have to express.

ACT IV. SCENE VII.

At the very moment when the King is about to disclose to Laertes the plan by which he thinks he has rid himself of Hamlet, word is brought that Hamlet has returned. Without a moment's hesitation Claudius seizes on the opportunity to turn Laertes to his purpose, and before Hamlet has a chance to act, a new and sinister plot is under way against him. And before the plot is fairly formed, Laertes's ardor for revenge is fanned to fierce flame by the account of Ophelia's death, and the act ends with a sense of crowding events moving swiftly to the catastrophe.

1. **Conscience:** consciousness (that all this is so), knowledge. See note on III, i, 83.

3-5. Can you make out what it is that the King has told Laertes? Notice Laertes's characterization of "these feats" in the next speech.

13. **Be it either which:** whichever of these it be.

15. See note on I, v, 17.

19-21. Springs which have the property referred to here are known in many localities. **Gyves** = fetters, and the literal meaning gives perfectly good sense: the people will regard as ornaments the fetters I impose upon him.

27. **If praises may go back again:** i. e., to what she *was*.

28. Stood on an eminence as challenger of all the age.

33. **You shortly shall hear more.** What the King *expects* that Laertes shall hear is the news of Hamlet's death. What he *does* hear is the news of his escape. Observe the dramatic irony of the situation.

34. **I . . . we.** In the first half of the line Claudius is speaking as a man; in the second, as a king.

37. **This to the queen.** We hear no more of this letter; why is it mentioned here?

40. Who is Claudio?

63. **Checking at.** A technical term from falconry. A hawk "checks," when it abandons its proper prey to fly after another.

68. **Uncharge the practice**: make no charge against the stratagem. *Practice* is here used in its frequent sinister sense.

74. **Your sum of parts . . . together**: all your other qualities combined. **Siege** (line 77) = rank.

82. **Importing health and graveness.** Either, *health and graveness* refer together to *his sables and his weeds* (in which case *health* means either "attention to health" or "prosperity"); or, *health* refers back to *light and careless living*, and *graveness* to *his sables and his weeds.*

85. **Can well**: have great skill. *Can* is frequently used absolutely in Elizabethan (and earlier) English, in the sense of knowing how, being able. Cf. German *können.*

89. **So far he topp'd my thought**: so far he outdid what I could imagine.

90. **In forgery of**: in imagining, contriving.

94. **Brooch**: here, ornament in general.

96. **Confession.** Lamond would reluctantly acknowledge the superiority of a fencer of another nation.

97. **A masterly report**: a report describing Laertes as a master.

107. **Now, out of this.** Why does the King pause here?

113. **Passages of proof**: proved instances.

117. Nothing remains constantly in the same state of excellence. **Plurisy** = plethora, excess.

123-24. Sighs were supposed to draw blood from the heart. The sense of the lines is that the recognition of a duty gives but fallacious relief, when the will to perform it is gone. Shakespeare is giving—this time altogether incidentally—another keen analysis of Hamlet's own malady.

127. **To cut his throat i' the church.** Laertes has no such scruples as stayed Hamlet's hand when the King was praying. Observe the sharpness of the contrast.

128. **Sanctuarize**: serve as sanctuary to protect from punishment. *Murder* refers to Hamlet's killing of Polonius.

132. **Put on those shall**: instigate those who shall.

136. This tribute to Hamlet's nobility of character serves to emphasize the King's baseness. **Remiss** (line 135) = careless, indifferent.

139. **A pass of practice**: a treacherous thrust. For *practice,* cf. line 68, and note.

146. **Under the moon**: i. e., collected by moonlight, in order to enhance their virtue.

151. **Fit us to our shape**: "enable us to assume proper characters" (Johnson).

152. If our intention should be disclosed through our unskilful acting.

155. **Blast in proof**: miscarry when put to the test.

157. Why the pause in this line?

161. **For the nonce**: for the purpose.

170. **Crow-flowers**: either the buttercup, or the Ragged Robin; **long purples**: a variety of orchid.

173-74. Ophelia chooses a willow, because it is the symbol of forsaken love.

180-81. **Indued Unto**: suited to live in.

189-90. **When these . . . be out**: when my tears are all shed, the woman in me will be gone.

ACT V. SCENE I.

This scene is almost of the nature of an interlude. The swift movement of the action is suspended, and the dialogue between the clowns, into which Hamlet's philosophizing merges, serves momentarily to break the tension. But the subtle and ineffective musings upon death are sharply interrupted by the intrusion of reality, and the scene ends with a clash between Hamlet and Laertes which foreshadows the catastrophe.

2. **Salvation.** Shakespeare's clowns, like many persons not in Shakespeare, have the foible of using words which convey a different meaning from that intended.

9. **Se offendendo.** The clown means *se defendendo,* in self-defence.

11. **An act hath three branches.** Shakespeare is putting into the clown's mouth a parody on legal phraseology. And it seems highly probable that he has an actual case in mind. See the abstract of the argument in the *Variorum* note on this line.

13. **Argal**: the clown's attempt at *Ergo,* i. e., "therefore, consequently."

24. **Crowner's quest**: coroner's inquest.

29. **There thou say'st.** Cf. modern slang, "Now you're talking."

32. **Even Christian:** fellow Christian.

44. **Confess thyself—.** The first gravedigger was going on with the rest of the proverb, "and be hanged."

59. **Unyoke:** that is: after such an effort, you may rest.

68. **Yaughan:** probably the name of an ale-house. Various words of which it may be a corruption have been suggested.

69 ff. The clown is singing a humorously garbled version of an actual song, attributed to Lord Vaux, and printed in *Tottel's Miscellany.* See the *Variorum* for the real text, which is worth looking up and comparing. The "O's" and "Ah's" merely represent the exertion of digging.

75-76. **A property of easiness:** a characteristic that now is easy.

85. **Cain's jaw-bone, that:** the jaw-bone of Cain, who. According to an old tradition Cain slew Abel with the jaw-bone of an ass, and the reference may be to that. Cain's own jaw-bone, however, may, of course, be meant.

86. **Politician:** plotter, schemer. The word has usually a bad sense in Shakespeare.

100. **Loggats:** a game in which little logs (loggats) of apple-wood are thrown at the jack, a wooden wheel placed on an ash-strewn floor.

111-121. The legal terms which Hamlet uses scarcely need exact definition here. It is worth noting that, according to good authorities, they are used with a clear sense of their meaning.

115. **The fine of his fines.** The first *fine* is "end"; the second is a technical legal term. No two of the four *fine's* have the same meaning.

119. **A pair of indentures.** "Indentures were agreements made out in duplicate, of which each party kept one. Both were written on the same sheet of paper, or parchment, which was cut in two in a crooked or indented line (whence the name), in order that the fitting of the two parts might prove the genuineness of both in case of dispute" (*Clarendon Press*).

126. **In that:** i. e., in such parchments.

131-33. **Thine . . . you.** Observe the use of pronouns throughout this dialogue between Hamlet and the clown.

149. **By the card**: by the chart; hence, with precision.

176-77. This statement, taken in connection with lines 155-62, gives Hamlet's age explicitly as thirty years. Many—perhaps most—commentators have felt that the Hamlet of the play is younger. For a full discussion of the question see the note on line 153 in the *Variorum,* and cf. Bradley, pp. 407-09.

182. **You.** See note on II, i, 7.

188. **Your.** See note on I, v, 167.

189, 193. **Whoreson**: "a term of coarse familiarity . . . reproach or ludicrous dislike" (Schmidt).

190-91. **Three and twenty years.** That is, Yorick died when Hamlet was seven years old—a statement which fits perfectly with the implications of lines 176-77.

206. **My gorge rises at it.** A reference to the heaving sensation of nausea.

212. **Chap-fallen.** Hamlet is playing on the literal and figurative senses of the word—i. e., "with shrunken, hanging jaw," and "dejected, crest-fallen."

218. **Alexander**: Alexander the Great.

227-28. Observe Horatio's sane common sense, set once more as a foil over against Hamlet's subtle imaginings. In these imaginings there is no trace of *madness;* they show, rather, the workings of a keen and acute intellect which is seeking some outlet under conditions of abnormal strain.

230. **Modesty.** See note on III, ii, 21.

240. **Aside**: step aside.

241. **Who is this they follow?** Observe the dramatic effectiveness of the way in which Hamlet learns of Ophelia's death, and note, too, how the highly wrought mood in which we have just seen him prepares us for the outburst that follows.

242. **Maimed**: curtailed, imperfect. This, and the words of the priest which follow, refer to the fact that suicides were not granted the full burial rites of the church.

244. **It.** See note on I, ii, 216.

251. Compare the Second Clown's words in lines 26-28.

262-63. Cf. Fitzgerald's *Rubáiyát:*

> And this reviving Herb whose tender Green
> Fledges the River-lip on which we lean—

Ah, lean upon it lightly! for who knows
From what once lovely Lip it springs unseen!

And cf. Tennyson's *In Memoriam,* xviii.

276. **Pelion.** Pelion and Ossa were two famous mountains in Thessaly. According to Greek mythology, when the Titans tried to dethrone the gods, they piled Ossa (see line 306) on Pelion, in order to scale the sky. Olympus (line 277) was another mountain, between Thessaly and Macedonia, which was regarded as the home of the gods.

279. **The wandering stars:** the planets (look up the etymology of *planet*).

287. Contrast the implications of the King's and the Queen's outcries.

290. **Wag:** move. The word had not in Shakespeare's day its present rather undignified associations.

292-94. There is no reason to doubt the immediate sincerity of Hamlet's words. He had, we may believe, loved Ophelia, but the bitterness and suspicion awakened by his mother's sin, and his own intense preoccupation with the revelation of the Ghost seem to have dulled, if not quite deadened it. The powerful revulsion of feeling caused by the sudden disclosure of Ophelia's tragic death brings back, with overwhelming force, the realization of his love—and of his loss.

298-99. **Woo't:** wilt thou—a colloquial form.

299. **Eisel.** The Folios have *Esile;* the First Quarto, *vessels;* the Second, *Esill,* and only the "dram of eale" passage (I, iv, 36) has occasioned more discussion. The mass of interpretations may be reduced to two: (1) that the word is a misprint for the name of some river; or, (2) that it stands for the word in the present text, meaning vinegar. The latter is on the whole the more probable explanation; cf. *Sonnet CXI,* 9-10: "I will drink Potions of eisel 'gainst my strong infection," and note that *eisel* is used a number of times (see *Oxford Dictionary*) as one of the constituents of the bitter drink offered to Christ on the cross. To "drink up" did not necessarily mean to exhaust by drinking, but to *quaff*. For a summary of the numerous and interesting suggestions that have been made, see the *Variorum* note. It must be remembered that Hamlet is naming (and adding to) the extravagant feats demanded by convention of

mediæval lovers to attest their love; cf. his "Show me what thou'lt do."

305. **The burning zone**: the sphere in which the sun moves. Cf. *Antony and Cleopatra,* IV, xv, 9-10: "O sun, Burn the great sphere thou mov'st in."

307. **This is mere madness.** The Queen is mistaken. A wild outbreak of pent-up feeling it certainly is, but it shows no signs of mental aberration. Hamlet has lost for the moment his self-control (cf. V, ii, 75-79), under the shock of Ophelia's tragedy and of Laertes's unexpected and (to him) astounding attack (cf. line 247), and he utters "wild and whirling words," as he did at the time of the Ghost's disclosure. Does he assume madness again in the play?

310. **Golden couplets.** The young of the dove (which lays but two eggs) are covered with yellow down when hatched (*disclosed:* see note on III, i, 174).

318. **Present push**: instant test.

320. A sinister reference, understood only by Laertes, to the plot against Hamlet.

Act V. Scene II.

The last scene of the play is devoted to the execution—not of any plan of Hamlet's for revenge, but of the King's plot against Hamlet. But the return of Hamlet, regarding which we have been left in suspense, is first accounted for, and both in Hamlet's recital of his escape and in his dialogue with Osric (which throws a gleam of grim humor on the somber background), we are made to see him restored to self-control. And it is by no preconceived plan, but by as sudden an impulse as that which caused Polonius's death, that at last he reaches his revenge—at the cost (through his delay) of the lives of Polonius, Ophelia, Rosencrantz and Guildenstern, Laertes, the Queen, and himself. Only Horatio, of the major characters, remains, and it is on Horatio and Fortinbras—the man of balanced blood and judgment, and the man of action—that the curtain falls.

1. **This . . . the other.** What *this* refers to, it is impossible to say—perhaps to Ophelia's death. *The other* is of course Hamlet's own escape.

6. **The mutines in the bilboes**: mutineers in shackles.

6. **Rashly**. This modifies "up from my cabin . . . groped I," in lines 12-14; what comes between is parenthetical. And in the parenthesis Hamlet is again acutely interpreting his own case. For *his* deep plots have come to nothing; when he has acted, it has been on impulse. Cf. below, lines 30-31.

13. **Scarf'd**: hastily thrown about the shoulders, like a scarf.

22. **Such bugs and goblins in my life**: such bugbears and mischiefs, if I am allowed to live.

23. **On the supervise**: immediately upon perusal; at sight.

33-34. You can verify Hamlet's statement by looking at any collection of facsimiles of the signatures of Elizabethan worthies. **Statist** = statesman.

36. **Yeoman's service**. The English yeomen (small freeholders) composed the bulk of the English infantry in war, and were famed for their valor.

42. **Stand a comma 'tween their amities**. An obscure and puzzling line. *Comma* is frequently interpreted as a mark of connection and continuity, which distinguishes, rather than divides, the parts of a sentence. *Comma* also meant, in Shakespeare's day, "a short member of a sentence or period" (*Oxford Dictionary*), and Professor Dowden interprets: "Here amity begins and amity ends the period, and peace stands between like a dependent clause." But no explanation is very satisfactory, and the line may be corrupt.

43. **'As'es of great charge**. Hamlet is punning upon *as* (still pronounced *ass* in some of the midland dialects) and *ass*. *Charge* means both "weight, importance," and "load, burden."

58. **They are not near my conscience**. How far is Hamlet's justification of his action adequate?

63. **Does it not . . . stand me now upon**: is it not incumbent upon me? **Thinks't thee**: seems it to thee. *Think* is here the old verb meaning to seem, and *thee* is dative; cf. *methinks*.

70. **In**: into.

84. **Water-fly**. "A water-fly skips up and down upon the surface of the water, without any apparent purpose, and is thence the proper emblem of a busy trifler" (Johnson).

89. **Chough:** either, a chattering jackdaw; or, a *chuff* or churl.

97-104. Cf. III, ii, 393-99.

108. Cf. *Love's Labour's Lost,* V, i, 103-04: "I do beseech thee, remember thy courtesy; I beseech thee, apparel thy head."

109-16. Osric is speaking an extremely affected court jargon.

112. **Excellent differences:** various excellences.

117-20. Hamlet is outdoing Osric at his own game, and intentionally speaking so as to perplex him. *But neither* = for all that; a boat *yaws,* when it sheers from its course, or steers wildly. The general sense of the opening lines is: His description suffers no loss in your account, though, I know, to enumerate his qualities after the manner of an inventory would be to make memory dizzy in the effort to compute them, and (for all that) stagger in its attempt to overtake him.

122. **Of great article:** "of great moment, importance" (*Oxford Dictionary*).

123-25. The only thing that resembles him is his own reflection in his mirror, and whoever would follow him must emulate his shadow.

128. **The concernancy:** come to what concerns us. A coined word.

129. **More rawer.** See note on II, i, 11.

131-32. Can you not understand your own jargon when another uses it? Surely you can, if you try. This seems, at least, to be the sense of Horatio's words.

133. **What imports the nomination:** what does the naming signify, lead up to?

141. **Would not much approve me:** would not be much to my credit.

149-50. **In his meed he's unfellowed:** in his merit he has no equal.

155. **Imponed:** staked, laid as a wager. It is clear from line 171 that Osric is employing the word in a sense of his own. No other use of it in this sense is known.

157. **Hanger:** the strap by which the rapier was suspended from the girdle.

160. **Liberal conceit:** elaborate design.

162. **Must be edified by the margent:** would need the instruction of a marginal commentary.

174. **Twelve for nine.** The statement of the wager is somewhat obscure. For various interpretations see the *Variorum*. As Dr. Johnson remarked: "The passage is of no importance; it is sufficient that there was a wager."

193-94. "It was believed that the young lapwings were in such haste to be hatched, that they ran off with the shell upon their heads. The bird was therefore the symbol of a forward fellow" (*Clarendon Press*).

195. **He did comply with his dug:** he paid compliments to his mother's breast.

197. **Drossy:** mixed with impurities. Variously interpreted here as "frivolous," or, "pinchbeck, imitation."

198. **Outward habit of encounter:** external forms that belong to conversation.

199. **Yesty collection:** frothy mass (of words).

200. **Fond and winnowed:** foolish and well-sifted (or, perhaps, over-refined)—the reading of the Folios. *Fann'd, profound,* and *sound* have all been suggested for *fond,* which does not seem to fit here. The general sense is apparently that the frothy verbiage of such affected persons as Osric either (1) gives them the appearance of expressing well-sifted opinions; or, (2) leads them into the most absurd and fantastic opinions. The passage is obscure.

214. **In happy time:** a mere phrase of courtesy; cf. *à la bonne heure.*

220-21. Why has Hamlet kept himself in practice?

222-35. Compare this sense of foreboding on Hamlet's part with the opposite presentiment in Romeo's case, just before the catastrophe (*Romeo and Juliet,* V, i, 1-11). What dramatic reason for the difference?

237-55. It is difficult not to wish, with Dr. Johnson, that Hamlet had made some other apology to Laertes than the false excuse of madness. Yet a moment's thought is sufficient to show that there was no other reason that he could give. He still meant to carry out his purpose (see line 73); to tell the truth now would be to defeat that design at the crucial moment. And his disclaimer of a purposed evil (lines 251-55) is absolutely sincere.

257-61. The *elder masters of known honor* are authorities in the code of honor; when they give their opinion, fortified by precedent, that Laertes may accept Hamlet's reparation without injury to his own name, he will be reconciled. Laertes's speech, of course, is basely treacherous.

266. **Foils.** Hamlet is playing on the two meanings of *foil:* a background which sets off a jewel; and a blunted rapier for fencing.

268. **Stick fiery off:** stand out in its brilliancy.

283. **Union:** a fine pearl. The mention of the pearl is merely a pretext for putting poison in the cup at the proper moment.

298. **He's fat and scant of breath.** Tradition has it that this line was written to meet the needs of Richard Burbadge, the great actor, who *was* fat, and required a moment's relief in the fencing. But *fat* may simply mean "out of training, 'soft.'"

310. **Make a wanton of me:** trifle with me, as if I were a spoiled child. For *wanton,* cf. *King John,* V, i, 70: "a beardless boy, A cocker'd silken wanton"; *Richard II,* V, iii, 10: "Young wanton and effeminate boy."

328. **Practice.** See notes on II, ii, 38; IV, vii, 68, 139.

333. **Then, venom, to thy work.** And so, at last, Hamlet attains his revenge—too late.

347. **Sergeant:** "an officer whose duty it is to enforce the judgment of a tribunal or the commands of a person in authority" (*Oxford Dictionary*). The figure is *not* that of a sheriff's officer who arrests for debt, as is frequently stated.

352. Cf. *Antony and Cleopatra,* IV, xv, 86-88: "What's brave, what's noble, Let's do it after the high Roman fashion, And make Death proud to take us." Cf. also *Julius Cæsar,* V, iii, 89; *Macbeth,* V, viii, 1-2.

355. **A wounded name.** Cf. line 261.

361-63. What structural part has the expedition of Fortinbras played in the drama? Why is it introduced here?

364. **O'er-crows:** triumphs over—a figure drawn from the cock-pit.

367. **Voice:** here equivalent to "vote," as also in line 403.

368-69. **The occurrents . . . Which have solicited:** the occurrences which have prompted my action.

370. **Cracks:** breaks. Another word of more dignified connotation then than now.

375. **Cries on:** either, proclaims; or, incites to. Probably the first.

400. **Rights of memory:** rights that are remembered.

403. **His mouth:** i. e., Hamlet's. In line 383 the same phrase refers to the King. **Draw on more** = lead more to speak.

408. **Put on:** put to the test. In line 394 *put on* = instigated.

409. **Proved most royally:** showed himself most royal.

It is often said that the play should have ended with Hamlet's "The rest is silence" (line 369), or at least with the two lines that immediately follow. Justify the close of the play as Shakespeare gives it.

QUESTIONS ON THE PLAY

What are some of the most marked differences that you observe between a tragedy like *Hamlet* and one like *Macbeth?* With which of the two is *Julius Cæsar* the more closely related? Why? What have Hamlet and Brutus in common? What have Hamlet and Macbeth in common? When Macbeth hesitates to act, what are his grounds? Compare them with Hamlet's reasons.

Collect all the occasions in the play when Hamlet really *acts.* In how many cases is his action planned by him? In how many is it on the spur of the moment? Turn back to the Introduction, pages xx-xxii, and consider carefully the analyses there given of Hamlet's character. With which do you most nearly agree?

What differences can you point out between Ophelia's real and Hamlet's assumed madness? If you have read *King Lear,* consider also the real and assumed madness in that play.

Summarize the characteristics of Claudius as they are shown in what he says and does. In what sense is it true that he and Hamlet are "mighty opposites"? If you have seen *Hamlet* on the stage, criticise the usual interpretation of Claudius's part.

Contrast Gertrude and Lady Macbeth in their relation to their husbands. Compare both with Brutus's Portia. Contrast Laertes and Horatio with Hamlet. Could any of the characters be spared from the play?

Study the soliloquies in the play. For what purpose does Shakespeare use them? Compare the number in *Hamlet* with the number in *Macbeth* and *Julius Cæsar*. Can you account for the difference? Why is the soliloquy rarely used in modern plays?

Why is *Hamlet,* in spite of all its problems, still one of the most popular of all plays, old or new? What elements of melodrama are in the play? What is it that keeps it from being melodrama?

Collect the passages in *Hamlet* that have become proverbial. What has given them their hold on everybody's mind? What passages in the play seem to you to be the greatest poetry?

GLOSSARY

Absolute, literal, exact to the point of hair-splitting; V, i, 148; consummate, perfect; V, ii, 111.

Abstract, epitome, summary; II, ii, 548.

Abuse, deceive; I, v, 38; II, ii, 632.

Abuse, deception, hoax; IV, vii, 51.

Adulterate, adulterous; I, v, 41.

Aery, brood (in a nest); II, ii, 354.

Affection, inclination, tendency; III, i, 170.

Amiss, mischief, disaster; IV, v, 18.

An, if—frequently used together with *if;* I, v, 176, 177.

Angle, fishing-hook and line; V, ii, 66.

Antic, odd, fantastic; I, v, 172.

Appointment, equipment; IV, vi, 16.

Approve, corroborate, justify; I, i, 29.

Argument, plot; III, ii, 149, 242.

Arras, hangings of tapestry; II, ii, 163.

Assign, appurtenance; V, ii, 157.

Avouch, avowal; I, i, 57.

Bate, except, deduct; V, ii, 23.

Batten, glut oneself; III, iv, 67.

Beaver, the lower part of the face-guard of a helmet; I, ii, 230.

Beshrew, a mild imprecation, not so strong as *curse;* II, i, 113.

Bespeak, speak to; II, ii, 140.

Bestow, stow, place; III, iv, 176.

Beteem, permit, allow; I, ii, 141.

Blazon, publication, proclamation; I, v, 21.

Blench, flinch; II, ii, 626.

Bloat, bloated; III, iv, 182.

Board, accost; II, ii, 169.

Bodykins, a diminutive (expressing affection) of *body;* II, ii, 554.

Bravery, ostentation, display; V, ii, 79.

Broad, free, unrestrained; III, iv, 2.

Bruit, noise abroad; I, ii, 127.

Bulk, frame, especially the breast; II, i, 95.

Candied, sugared, honeyed; III, ii, 65.

Canon, rule, law; I, ii, 132.

Capable, susceptible of impression; III, iv, 127.

Carouse, drink a toast; V, ii, 300.

Cast, casting; I, i, 73.

Cataplasm, salve; IV, vii, 144.

Cautel, deceit, duplicity; I, iii, 15.

Cerements, waxed linen, used as a shroud; I, iv, 48.

Chapless, without the lower jaw; V, i, 97.

Character, handwriting; IV, vii, 52.

Charge, expense; IV, iv, 47.

Cicatrice, scar; IV, iii, 62.

Clepe, call; I, iv, 19.

Closely, secretly; III, i, 29.

Closet, a private room; II, i, 77.

Coagulate, clotted; II, ii, 484.

Color, give a pretext for, make seem more natural; III, i, 45.

Commutual, mutual; III, ii, 170.

Compost, manure; III, iv, 151.

Compulsive, compelling; III, iv, 86.

Condolements, sorrow, mourning; I, ii, 93.

Confine, appointed limits; I, i, 155; place of confinement; II, ii, 251.

Conjunctive, closely joined; IV, vii, 14.

Constantly, firmly, fixedly; I, ii, 235.

Continent, receptacle; IV, iv, 64; summary, abstract; V, ii, 115.

Cope, encounter, have to do with; III, ii, 60.

Cote, pass by, leave behind; II, ii, 330.

Countenance, favor; IV, ii, 16; encouragement, authority; V, i, 30.

Cozen, cheat, delude; III, iv, 77.

Cozenage, cheating, deceit; V, ii, 67.

Crants, wreaths; V, i, 255.

Credent, credulous; I, iii, 30.

Crowner, coroner; V, i, 4.

Cunning, skilful contrivance; II, ii, 619.

Dalliance, trifling, wanton play; I, iii, 50.
Dansker, Dane; II, i, 7.
Dearth, dearness, value; V, ii, 123.
Delate, convey; I, ii, 38.
Denote, indicate, mark; I, ii, 83.
Dispatch, deprive by death; I, v, 75.
Disposition, nature, constitution; I, iv, 55; mood; III, i, 12.
Doubt, fear; II, ii, 56; III, i, 174; hesitate to believe; II, ii, 116, 117, 119; suspect; I, ii, 256; II, ii, 118.
Dout, extinguish; IV, vii, 192.
Down-gyved, hanging like gyves, or fetters; II, i, 80.
Drab, a lewd woman; II, ii, 615.
Drabbing, following loose women; II, i, 26.
Drift, tendency, turn; II, i, 10.

Ecstasy, madness; III, i, 168; III, iv, 74.
Emulate, emulous; I, i, 83.
Enact, act; III, ii, 108.
Encompassment, circuitous course; II, i, 10.
Escot, to pay a reckoning (or scot) for, to maintain; II, ii, 262.
Espial, spy; III, i, 32.
Even, fair, honest; II, ii, 298.
Exception, disapprobation; V, ii, 342.
Eyas, a young unfledged hawk; II, ii, 355.

Faculty, power, ability; II, ii, 317.
Fantasy, imagination; I, i, 23, 54.
Fardel, burden, pack; III, i, 76.
Favor, aspect, features, face; V, i, 214.
Fay, faith; II, ii, 271.
Feature, shape; III, ii, 25.
Fee, value; I, iv, 65.
Fell, fierce, cruel; V, ii, 61, 347.
Felly, the wooden rim of a wheel, into which the spokes fit; II, ii, 517.
Fierce, violent, terrible; I, i, 121.
Flaw, a blast of wind; V, i, 239.
Fond, foolish; I, v, 99.
Fordo, destroy; V, i, 244.
Forgery, lie, false attribution; II, i, 20.
Frame, shape, form; I, ii, 20; order; III, ii, 321.
Fretted, adorned; II, ii, 313.
Front, brow, forehead; III, iv, 56.

Fust, grow mouldy; IV, iv, 39.

Gage, pledge; I, i, 91.
Gaingiving, misgiving; V, ii, 225.
Gender, kind, sort; IV, vii, 18.
Gentry, gentility, courtesy; II, ii, 22; V, ii, 114.
Germane, related, akin; V, ii, 165.
Gib, tom-cat; III, iv, 190.
Grained, ingrained, indelible; III, iv, 90.
Greenly, foolishly; IV, v, 83.
Gross, sum, entirety; I, i, 68; palpable, obvious; IV, iv, 46.

Hap, fortune; IV, iii, 70.
Happily, haply, perhaps; I, i, 134; II, ii, 402.
Happiness, felicity (of speech); II, ii, 212.
Hatchment, escutcheon; IV, v, 214.
Haunt, resort; IV, i, 18.
Hautboy, oboe; [stage direction, after] III, ii, 145.
Havoc, indiscriminate slaughter; V, ii, 375.
Head, armed force; IV, v, 101.
Hearsed, coffined; I, iv, 47.
Hectic, a fever; IV, iii, 68.
Hem, to cry "hem"; IV, v, 5.
Hent, grip, seizure; III, iii, 88.
Hold up, maintain; V, i, 34.
Hoodman-blind, blind-man's buff; III, iv, 77.

Impasted, made into paste; II, ii, 481.
Imperious, imperial; V, i, 236.
Importing, concerning; V, ii, 21.
Imposthume, abscess; IV, iv, 27.
Incapable, unable to feel; IV, vii, 179.
Incorpsed, of one body with; IV, vii, 88.
Incorrect, unsubdued, unchastened; I, ii, 95.
Indifferent, average, neither good nor bad, high nor low; II, ii, 231.
Indirections, indirect means; II, i, 66.
Infusion, endowments; V, ii, 122.
Ingenious, keen, quick; V, i, 271.
Inheritor, possessor; V, i, 121.
Inquire, inquiry; II, i, 4.
Insinuation, meddling; V, ii, 59.

Instant, instantaneous; I, v, 71.

Instrumental, helpful, serviceable; I, ii, 48.

Jointress, dowager; I, ii, 9.

Jowl, knock, dash; V, i, 84.

Jump, just, exactly; I, i, 65; V, ii, 386.

Keep, resort; II, i, 8.

Kettle, kettle-drum; V, ii, 286.

Kibe, chilblain; V, i, 153.

Lard, garnish; IV, v, 37; V, ii, 20.

Lenten, meager, like the fare in Lent; II, ii, 329.

Liberal, free-spoken, licentious; IV, vii, 171.

List, muster-roll, number; I, i, 98; I, ii, 32.

Marry, an exclamation—originally the name of the Virgin Mary; I, iii, 90.

Mart, traffic; I, i, 74.

Mazzard, head (a term of contempt); V, i, 97.

Merely, completely, absolutely; I, ii, 137.

Milch, moist (lit., milk-giving); II, ii, 540.

Mope, to be stupid, or incapable of reason; III, iv, 81.

Mortal, deadly, fatal; IV, vii, 143.

Mortised, joined by . mortise; III, iii, 20.

Mountebank, quack, impostor; IV, vii, 142.

Mow, grimace; II, ii, 282.

Mutine, mutiny; III, iv, 83; mutineer; V, ii, 6.

Naked, destitute, stripped of one's belongings; IV, vii, 44.

Napkin, handkerchief; V, ii, 299.

Native, cognate, kindred; I, ii, 47.

Note, denote, show; I, v, 178.

Note, attention; III, ii, 89.

Noyance, injury; III, iii, 13.

Occulted, hidden; III, ii, 85.

O'erreach, overtake; III, i, 17.

O'ersized, smeared; II, ii, 484.

O'erteemed, worn out with child-bearing; II, ii, 531.

Ominous, fatal; II, ii, 476.

Opposite, opponent; V, ii, 62.

Orchard, garden; I, v, 35.

Ordinant, ordaining, ruling; V, ii, 48.

Organ, instrument; IV, vii, 71.

Orisons, prayers; III, i, 89.

Outrageous, violent, extreme; III, i, 58.

Overlook, peruse; IV, vi, 13.

Paddock, toad; III, iv, 190.

Pall, become vain, decay; V, ii, 9.

Pandar, play the go-between for; III, iv, 88.

Pardon, leave, permission; III, ii, 329; IV, vii, 46.

Parle, parley; I, i, 62.

Partisan, a kind of halberd; I, i, 140.

Pass, thrust; V, ii, 61.

Pat, in the nick of time, exactly, aptly; III, iii, 73.

Perdy, a corruption of *par Dieu;* III, ii, 305.

Perusal, study, examination; II, i, 90.

Peruse, examine; IV, vii, 137.

Picked, refined, choice; V, i, 151.

Plausive, pleasing; I, iv, 30.

Porch, vestibule, entrance (fig.); I, v, 63.

Porpentine, porcupine; I, v, 20.

Powers, forces; IV, iv, 9.

Precurse, forerunning, heralding; I, i, 121.

Pregnant, ready - witted, clever; II, ii, 212.

Pressure, impress, stamp; I, v, 100; III, ii, 27.

Probation, proof; I, i, 156.

Proof, resisting power, impenetrability; II, ii, 512.

Proper, peculiar, belonging to, own; II, i, 114; V, ii, 66.

Proposer, speaker, talker; II, ii, 297.

Providence, foresight; IV, i, 17.

Pursy, short-winded; hence, fat, pampered; III, iv, 153.

Quarry, a heap of slaughtered game; V, ii, 375.

Question, talk, converse, (trans.) speak to; I, i, 45.

Question, conversation; II, i, 10.

Quick, living; V, i, 137.

Quiddits, subtleties, fine distinctions; V, i, 107.

Quillets, quibbles; V, i, 108.

Quit, requite, pay off scores; V, ii, 68, 280.

Recorder, a kind of flageolet; III, ii, 303.

Reechy, filthy, stinking; III, iv, 184.

Relative, closely related, to the purpose; II, ii, 633.

Repast, feed, IV, v, 147.
Replication, reply; IV, ii, 13.
Resolve, dissolve; I, ii, 130.
Resort, visit; II, ii, 143.
Respect, consideration; III, i, 68.
Rivals, partners; I, i, 13.
Robustious, boisterous, noisy; III, ii, 10.
Romage, bustle, turmoil, I, i, 107.
Rood, cross, crucifix; III, iv, 14.
Round, direct, straightforward, plain-spoken; III, i, 191; III, iv, 5.
Rouse, a deep draught, a bumper; I, ii, 127; I, iv, 8.

Sans, without; III, iv, 79.
Saw, saying, maxim; I, v, 100.
Sconce, head (a term of contempt); V, i, 110.
Scrimer, fencer; IV, vii, 101.
Secure, keep from danger or harm; I, v, 112.
Seized of, possessed of (legal term); I, i, 89.
Sense, understanding, reason; I, ii, 99.
Sensible, perceiving, feeling; I, i, 57.
Shard, fragment of pottery; V, i, 254.
Shark up, gather up eagerly and indiscriminately; I, i, 98.
Shent, reproved, rebuked; III, ii, 416.
Shrewdly, sharply, keenly; I, iv, 1.
Simple, medicinal herb; IV, vii, 145.
Sith, since; II, ii, 6, 12.
Skyish, reaching the sky; V, i, 276.
Slander, disgrace; I, iii, 133.
Sliver, a branch; IV, vii, 174.
Sometime, one-time, former; I, ii, 8.
Sometimes, sometime, formerly; I, i, 49.
Sort, harmonize, be fitting; I, i, 109; class, associate; II, ii, 274.
Spies, scouts; IV, v, 78.
Splenitive, passionate, impetuous; V, i, 284.
Springe, snare; V, ii, 317.
Stithy, smithy, forge; III, ii, 89.
Stoup, a drinking vessel; V, i, 68.
Straight, immediately; III, iv, 1.
Strumpet, prostitute; II, ii, 515.
Stuck, thrust; IV, vii, 162.
Subject, the people, subjects; I, i, 72; I, ii, 33.
Supposal, opinion; I, ii, 18.

Table, tablet; I, v, 98.

Tax, censure, reproach; I, iv, 18.

Tell, count; I, ii, 238.

Tempered, mixed, compounded; V, ii, 339.

Tenable, kept back, retained; I, ii, 248.

Tent, probe; II, ii, 626.

Tetter, a skin disease; I, v, 71.

Thereon, on that account; II, ii, 165.

Thews, sinews; I, iii, 12.

Throughly, thoroughly; IV, v, 136.

Toil, cause to toil; I, i, 72.

Touched, implicated; IV, v, 207.

Toward, near at hand, imminent, in preparation; I, i, 77; V, ii, 376.

Toy, trifle; IV, v, 18.

Trace, follow; V, ii, 125.

Tristful, sad; III, iv, 50.

Trumpet, trumpeter; I, i, 150.

Unbated, unblunted; IV, vii, 139; V, ii, 328.

Unbraced, unfastened; II, i, 78.

Unction, salve, ointment; III, iv, 145; IV, vii, 142.

Ungored, unwounded, unhurt; V, ii, 261.

Ungracious, graceless; I, iii, 47.

Unkennel, disclose, reveal; III, ii, 86.

Unprevailing, unavailing; I, ii, 107.

Upspring, the name of a dance; I, iv, 9.

Valanced, fringed (with a beard); II, ii, 442.

Variable, various; III, i, 180.

Ventages, orifices for the passage of air; III, ii, 372.

Videlicet, that is to say; II, i, 61.

Virtue, power, efficacy; IV, v, 155; IV, vii, 145.

Vulgar, ordinary, commonplace; I, ii, 99.

Wake, to hold nightly revel; I, iv, 8.

Wassail, a drinking bowl, carousal; I, iv, 9.

Whiles, while; III, iv, 148.

Wholesome, sane, sensible; III, ii, 328.

Windlass, winding turn, circuitous path; II, i, 65.